SPECIAL MESSAGE TO READERS

THE ULVERSCROFT FOUNDATION
(registered charity number 264873)
was established in 1972 to provide funds for
research, diagnosis and treatment of eye diseases.
Examples of major projects funded by
the Ulverscroft Foundation are:-

- The Children's Eye Unit at Moorfields Eye Hospital, London
- The Ulverscroft Children's Eye Unit at Great Ormond Street Hospital for Sick Children
- Funding research into eye diseases and treatment at the Department of Ophthalmology, University of Leicester
- The Ulverscroft Vision Research Group, Institute of Child Health
- Twin operating theatres at the Western Ophthalmic Hospital, London
- The Chair of Ophthalmology at the Royal Australian College of Ophthalmologists

You can help further the work of the Foundation by making a donation or leaving a legacy. Every contribution is gratefully received. If you would like to help support the Foundation or require further information, please contact:

**THE ULVERSCROFT FOUNDATION
The Green, Bradgate Road, Anstey
Leicester LE7 7FU, England
Tel: (0116) 236 4325**

website: www.foundation.ulverscroft.com

Sonja Price was born in Bristol and now lives in Germany, where she teaches English and writes fiction. When in England, Sonja loves staying on Dartmoor, which gives her the perfect conditions to let her imagination take flight: peace, quiet, and spectacular surroundings.

You can discover more about the author at www.sonja-price.com

THE GIANTS LOOK DOWN

Ten-year-old Jaya Vaidya decides she wants to follow in the footsteps of her beloved father and become a doctor — much to the chagrin of her mother and her local community. It is the late 1960s and the family enjoy an idyllic life in the Vale of Kashmir, despite the area being riddled with conflict and poverty. But after a devastating earthquake wipes out her entire family, Jaya is taken into the care of relatives in Delhi — who attempt to marry her off and keep secret from her the possibility that Tahir, her younger brother, has survived the disaster . . .

SONJA PRICE

THE GIANTS LOOK DOWN

Complete and Unabridged

ULVERSCROFT
Leicester

First published in Great Britain in 2016 by
Robert Hale
London

First Large Print Edition
published 2017
by arrangement with
Robert Hale
an imprint of The Crowood Press Ltd
Wiltshire

The moral right of the author has been asserted

A catalogue record for this book is available
from the British Library.

ISBN 978–1–4448–3301–0

Published by
F. A. Thorpe (Publishing)
Anstey, Leicestershire

Set by Words & Graphics Ltd.
Anstey, Leicestershire
Printed and bound in Great Britain by
T. J. International Ltd., Padstow, Cornwall

This book is printed on acid-free paper

PART 1

1

Kashmir, 1967

When I was ten, I found out what I wanted to be. In fact, I can remember the very day I decided to become a healer. On that late summer's morning, I could still see my breath when I climbed up into our battered old Land Rover. You know what those kinds of vehicles are like. I was up high and I felt so much bigger anyway, because I was in the front next to Pa. If I shut my eyes and concentrate, I can still smell his pipe smoke lingering on the leather seats. The radio was on that morning because Pa, being such a huge cricket fan, had started listening to the Ashes long before the sun cut the peaks of the Nun Kun. In India you hear talk of three things on every village corner: cricket, movies and politics and the Vale of Kashmir was no exception.

The tiny red figure of Lord Vishnu, the protector, bobbed about under the rear view mirror as I scanned the skies for golden eagles. We had a good chance of seeing them at that time of the year when they had hungry chicks to feed. I spotted one, riding the winds, soaring and circling before dropping hundreds of feet to pluck a groundhog from the mountain slopes. All around us, tiny mauve and yellow flowers danced in the breeze as the snowy summits of Pir Panjal meditated in the early morning sun. Beneath them, rocks gave way to forests, emerald green valleys and the glint of the Jhelum River. In the far distance Wular Lake slumbered peacefully under its blanket of mist. Above us the Thajiwas Glacier sparkled ice blue beside the conelike peak of Gwash Brari where settlements hugged its foothills. All Pa's territory, because he was the only doctor for miles.

The crowd roared and the man on the radio was getting terribly excited when a posh voice cut in:

News has just reached us that a suicide attack in Indian-administered Kashmir has killed three people, including the bomber, and injured more than seventeen. The explosion occurred in the Nowgam area on the outskirts of Srinagar, the region's summer capital. A Pakistan-based Islamic militant group has claimed responsibility for the explosion in a telephone call to local news

4

agency Current News Service.

Pa switched off the radio. 'Madmen! Outsiders! Trying to turn us against each other! Sufi, Hindu, Sikh, what does it matter? We've been smoking *beedi* together in the teahouses of Dal Lake for centuries. Long before the British came. Long before Partition. Now they make us play the Great Game and fight like cockerels. Should I not attend to Mrs Durrani simply because she is a Muslim? And what about Kaliq? Should we throw our beloved servant out? How could the gods tolerate bloodshed in our beautiful Vale?'

I certainly didn't understand. How could grown-ups fight and kill each other when we children were always being told to be nice to each other? Diwali, our festival of light, includes their Muslim god Ali and Ramadan includes our Lord Ram, so how were we so different? It didn't make any sense.

Still, I decided nothing was going to spoil my day now that I was here. Ma was so strict with me. Rajan and Tahir could do what they wanted and get away with almost anything because they were boys. They didn't have to lay the table for dinner or clear up afterwards. Boys got up and played. Mothers coddled them until their wives took over. But I smiled to myself because I had stood up for myself yesterday.

'Mamiji, why can't I go with Pa? If I don't get out I shall go mad!' I hadn't been out for a fortnight because of chicken pox. Even so, I wouldn't have got my way if Pa hadn't overheard us from his study.

He came in, gold spectacles in hand. 'What's all this about?'

I ran over and pulled at his sleeve. 'Pa, you want me to come along with you, don't you?'

He sighed. 'Palomi,' he said to my mother. 'I don't see what harm it will do to let Jaya see what I get up to when I leave this house.'

'Babee. She's much too young to witness sickness and pain!' She stamped her foot. Ma always called him Babee even though he was Darshan to everyone else.

'My dear, it is only childbirth. I promise I will keep her outside until the mess is over. After all, she will have to learn about it someday. If I let her come along this once, that will be the end of it. You'll see. What possible interest could my work be to her in the long run?'

Ma could fight like a Bengal tigress but at that moment she was in a fix. The boys were covered in spots themselves. Of course I felt sorry for them, the scabs itched like mad and made you feel rotten yet I couldn't help feeling a little pleased, too. I had Pa all to myself for a change and wouldn't have to pander to Ma's little princes.

The bumpy road threw us this way and that on our climb up the steep winding track. It fell away right next to my window and I thought of how every day on the school run we passed a burnt-out lorry sprawled upside down like a giant metal beetle on a crevice far below. Pa had to drive fast that day, though. I didn't know much about having babies, only that you had to get there in a hurry.

I wasn't scared because I knew the gods were watching over us. We lived in the valley of the gods. In summer I would climb the mulberry tree outside my bedroom window to watch the long line of people trekking up to the Cave of Amaranth through Pa's binoculars. They came from all over India and beyond just to see Lord Shiva, who lived there as a stalagmite. Further up the mountains, Nag, Lord of the Serpents, made the water in Lake Sheshnag turn the same colour as Ma's turquoise earrings.

Pa pointed to an arrow of geese clearing the gleaming summit of Gwash Brari. He kept a little notebook under the wooden dashboard to write the names of the birds in and every so often, he would ring up a man in Bombay. The man was a birdwatcher, an

7

ornithologist, Pa told me. I made a note of it, because it was a brilliant word to know for Scrabble. Pa must have been a falconer in one of his previous lives, when there was no such thing as ornithologists or binoculars, because he could spot a pariah kite by its forked tail when it was little more than a dot in the sky. He noticed everything, even the budding heads of mountain primroses before they broke through the snow and being a doctor, he knew their Latin names too. You needed Latin as a doctor, he told me, but we often spoke English together, because it reminded him of his time studying in Scotland. He said it would prepare us for secondary school where everything would be in English.

He cranked the car back into first gear as we approached the final bend that brought us level with the moss-covered roof of a tiny stone building perched on a narrow ledge. A great shaggy dog, straining on a short rusty chain, sounded our arrival. A man with a long grey beard rushed out. He was wearing a loose-fitting *kurta* tunic and a purple *doshalla* around his head.

'My son, you must save my son!'

Pa bowed and said, 'Namaste,' before calling over his shoulder to me, 'Jaya, you stay in the car, do you hear? Don't come in until I call for you.'

I opened my red silk bag and took out the book about a girl called Heidi who went to live in the mountains with her grumpy grandpa. I could read English, something Rajan and Tahir could not yet do. We spoke Koshur — the ancient language of Kashmir — at home and Urdu at school and I could also understand Hindi. Rajan had mastered Urdu, which was a big step for him, but he didn't read much anyway, and poor Tahir, who was struggling terribly, had developed a stutter. He hated being away from home, even for a few hours. I liked school not only because I could play marbles with the other children or jump rope, but because I loved finding out new things. Now that Pa had taught me the English alphabet, I could read the books in his study; the ones with stories in them, not the medical ones with disgusting pictures. This book *Heidi* was my very own, a birthday present sent all the way from Scotland, wrapped in strong brown paper. It had a musty smell about it, which I couldn't place. Someone's name had been rubbed out just inside the cover. I had traced it with my pencil and it said Lily and I wrote my own name above hers. I hoped Lily didn't mind me having it now.

Once Heidi settled in, she grew to love the mountains and her grandpa and he came to love her, too. Living together changed their whole lives and made them so much happier. She made a friend called Peter. Just when everything began to fall into place, she had to leave. I looked at the mountains in front of me and knew how Heidi must have felt. I would never go away. Of that I was quite sure.

Heidi was very sad; she got ill because she couldn't see the mountains. She began sleepwalking and not eating properly. My stomach rumbled so I reached for the naan Sabri had slipped into the pocket of my *kameez* before we left. Sabri used to be our amah but now we were older she was more of a cook. I read until the words started to swim before my eyes. How long did babies take?

I clambered down from the car. The dog cocked its head and started to wag its tail.

Its ribs stuck out like fish bones. I gave it a bit of bread and talked to it softly. When I stroked its matted fur, it closed its eyes as if it had been waiting for me for weeks.

Soft moaning sounds, like the ones my granny made in her sleep, issued from the house. The moans turned into cries of pain and the dog pulled away. Why wasn't Pa doing anything about it? That was why we were here. Even with my hands over my ears I could still hear the woman. On and on it went. The man started shouting and the dog collapsed on the ground with a sigh. The woman's cries reminded me of a Tibetan fox caught in a trap up in the forests around Gangabal Lake. Kaliq had to shoot it as the iron teeth had bitten clean through its back leg.

Silence. Even worse! Only swallows swooping overhead as the entire valley held its breath, shattered by the cries of a baby and a jubilant, 'A boy!'

Brahma be praised, it was over. We could finally go home.

But the dreadful screaming recommenced. Perhaps Pa had done something to her. I had to see what was going on. Like a snow leopard stalking a deer, I crept into the house, which was only slightly larger than our woodshed. It reeked of animal hide and smoke. My eyes took a moment to get used to the gloom. I could make out two rooms: a kitchen and another one where the woman lay. Our house was all sunny rooms and places where I could play. I edged my way towards the grown-ups, towards the man with the bundle in his arms and Pa tending the woman, still writhing in agony.

She screamed and screamed. She was ever so young. She could have been his granddaughter. I wasn't going to have a baby, ever. Then I caught a glimpse of something round between her blood-smeared legs. Not another one! Pa eased out a head, then a shoulder and then the rest before the woman fell back onto the messy covers.

'A girl!' he said.

Limp, lifeless and smeary-white, the baby looked more like a skinned rabbit. Pa tried to rub it to life but the woman was not moving, either. He looked to the man for help but he merely shrugged his shoulders as if to say why bother with a girl? Pa laid the baby carefully in the cot by the fire, turned to the woman and drew up a syringe.

I ran around the bed and picked the baby up. I couldn't believe how small she was. Tiny hands and feet just like my dolly. Only she was warm. The boy was crying for all he was worth; loud screeches that you'd never believe could come from anyone that little. He was rosy and angry, and his sister was pale, almost white. 'Shiva!' I wanted to shout. She was slipping away before she had even arrived. Pa was doing everything he could for the woman and there was no point in talking to the man if he wouldn't even listen to Pa. I rubbed her like Pa had done before he put her down but she was growing colder and colder.

I stared into the flames and then my eyes rested on the one set of baby's clothes laid out in front of the fireplace. It wasn't fair! Why should she have to die? A ragdoll nobody wanted to play with. No! I wouldn't allow this to happen. What had the herdsman done to the newborn yak? I bent and blew into her tiny mouth. Her cheeks soft and cool like goat's cheese. No reaction. I blew more strongly into her. Nothing.

Tears pricked my eyes. There was absolutely nothing I could do. Stupid of me to think I could make a difference. All I wanted to do was run outside. I went to kiss her goodbye but instead found myself trying one last time. The baby's lips puckered; her face screwed up. She turned a deep red before letting out the most wonderful cry I had ever heard. The woman opened her eyes. Tears ran down her face as she reached out for her little girl. Pa looked from the baby to me and smiled.

Half an hour later we climbed back into the car.

'When I'm big, Pa, I want to be a healer just like you!' He stroked my head and switched the radio back on.

2

Bang, bang, bang. I sat bolt upright in bed. Men shouting. My heart raced and my mouth went dry. I pulled the cover up over my head, then peeped back out as I heard my door open. First Tahir, then Rajan ran over to my bed and scrambled under the covers.

'Shhhh!' I said.

Something was being dragged around downstairs. Low hushed voices and the sound of a door shutting. No more sounds. We waited for ages.

'Stay here,' I said and crept down the stairs, avoiding the ones that creaked. I tiptoed across the hall and gently pushed down the door handle of Pa's study. A man lay on the floor; a huge soggy patch of blood covering one of his thighs and staining our beautifully patterned carpet. Another man with all but his eyes covered by a scarf was pointing a gun at Pa! I gasped and he swung round and pulled me in by my hair.

'Ow!' I was looking down the barrel of a gun.

'Stop. My daughter!' Pa shouted. 'She can help,' he added. 'Jaya, come here.'

The gunman eyed me suspiciously.

My whole body was shaking as Pa started to cut away the man's trouser leg with some scissors. I passed him the long pointed tweezers from the instruments spread out on the white cloth next to him. He eased the bullet out and the man screamed as blood spurted out like a fountain. Pa stopped the flow, disinfected and dressed the wound and our visitors were gone as quickly as they appeared.

'Who were they?' I asked.

'Freedom fighters,' Pa replied. 'No one must hear of this, do you understand? No one!'

★　★　★

I had learned all about Partition from Pa when we were last snowed in. About Hari Ahmed having to choose between India and Pakistan, and Kashmiris becoming Indians overnight. No one seemed happy about this because soon war broke out and afterwards everything was in such a mess that Pa had to go to Scotland to study. That was all long before I was born but when I was about four there was another war. Pa had to leave to treat the wounded and I can remember crying with Ma when he left. It seemed to me

15

that he was gone for an eternity. Granny cooked the most massive meal when he came back again after a few weeks.

Even after that the call for *Azadi*, which meant freedom, could be heard throughout Kashmir. Gunshots often woke me and flashes lit the high ground in the dark near the Pakistani border. Ma once suggested moving south like Uncle Desh who lived in Delhi but Pa would have none of it: 'Never! Kashmir is our home!'

After the outbursts of violence there were regular curfews and the passes to and from the valley were often closed because the army was looking for 'terrorists'. The dispute was making our Vale poor and draining its lifeblood. In Srinagar, the buildings on the river front were crumbling, their windows boarded up or gaping, their rusty roofs ready to cave in under the next heavy snowfall. Rubbish lay on the slopes of the Jhelum River in which people bathed and washed their clothes. When I crossed the footbridge that straddled the swollen torrent, I held Ma's hand tightly and prayed that we would make it to the other side. The dusty side alleys in the shadow of the pristine white Hazratbal Mosque were little more than overcrowded slums. Whole families were crammed into one room amongst pots and pans and the occasional chicken, whilst children played on the dirty floor or warmed their hands over wicker baskets of hot coals in winter. Outside, soldiers patrolled the alleys with machine guns strapped to their shoulders, keeping the peace, or, as some said, keeping it at bay.

Higher up in the foothills there was little chance of the wounded or ill reaching a clinic when it mattered. People bled to death from bullet wounds and illness claimed lives far too easily. Children often saw people die so nobody questioned the slip of a girl struggling with the black leather case on her father's coat-tails. Slowly, Pa began to discuss the cases with me in terms I could understand, making me want to leaf through the medical journals in his study. Looking back, it sounds strange to say that I tried to help him as much as I could. On one particular visit with Pa, an old man with two broken ribs called me 'little Miss Doctor'. I walked out at least two inches taller.

* * *

We lived in one of the finest houses in the foothills, built of stone with a sweeping view of the valley from the veranda. From my bed I could see the Gilgul Pass and the rock face that looked like a woman's face with snow-white hair. She used to smile at me when the moonlight fell on the stone. In early spring, the scent of mulberry blossoms filled my room so that in summer I would climb and harvest basketfuls of berries from the tree outside my window for Sabri, who made delicious chutney from them. With plenty of food in store winter never posed a problem. We always had a taste of summer in the house even when we were snowed in for days. I loved those days, when even Pa couldn't get away. A blizzard would be raging outside as we gathered around the fire to listen to stories of what Pa got up to as a boy.

From our terrace, I could marvel at the Sind River winding its way down the valley through a patchwork of emerald-green fields, pale pink almond orchards and dashes of yellow mustard flowers as it passed the occasional poplar tree. Amongst the splurges of purple girls my age collected petals to make saffron. In the background, the jagged white peaks stabbed the sky and formed a wall that protected us from the harsh winters of the north and the scorching summers of the south, bestowing on us the most splendid of climates and fertile land. Although our homeland was a Muslim stronghold, it had always been a home to us Hindus, too. In the past numbers didn't matter much. We were neighbours who went to school, played cricket, got the harvest in together and often intermarried. Kashmir was home, sweet home to us all. Yet we were the envy of our neighbours, who wanted to slice our Vale up like a wedding cake, with religion as their knife.

All troubles were forgotten when I chased butterflies across the wildflower meadows near Sonamarg, or dipped my toes in Krishnasar Lake on hot days as my brothers bathed amongst the brown trout darting around in its clear water. And we used to fly kites in the wide open spaces above the sycamore forests that clothed the mountain slopes.

⋆　⋆　⋆

Ma liked having visitors, whether they were Avani's family, friends from the valley, relatives from Delhi or old friends from my father's student days. Then she would draw up lists with Sabri to cook huge meals together and sit back and smile as Pa presided over a dining room table laden with dishes fit for royalty. She was truly in her element as she urged her guests to have another helping while Pa led discussions on anything from the future of our Vale to some

19

mild gossip. We children enjoyed both the food and the talk.

Once a couple of yetis came to visit. Well, of course they weren't real yetis but they might as well have been. Such light skin, such a weird way of talking! The man was big and strong with blond, coarse curly hair and his wife tall and willowy with wonderful freckles and a bun of bright red hair. They were Mr and Mrs Hamilton, the people who had sent me my book about Heidi. Although I spoke English I couldn't understand them at first. Even Ma kept saying 'pardon' and 'excuse me' when the lady chatted to her. I kept quiet and snuck sidelong glances at this strange beautiful creature.

I wanted to see if the lady's hair was real. She didn't seem to mind when I touched it and I couldn't resist playing with her hair until to my horror the bun came undone in my hands. The long ginger mass fell through my fingers like wild silk. With a sharp intake of breath, Ma went to pull me away.

'No, no, let her!' The lady beamed at me. 'I'm enjoying the attention. Alastair's away at boarding school, you know.'

When the men went out to smoke cigars, which was not like Pa at all, their voices got louder and I heard the man say, 'Running backwards, you were. And then you fell to the ground. Durham thought they'd clinched it. Hit right in the face! But you had the ball in your hands. What a dream finish! Put an end to their innings and us back in the driving seat just like that. Shame about your nose, though!'

Pa did have a slightly crooked nose. I peered round the front door to see Pa doubled up with laughter and the Scotsman slapping him on the back. 'It's my trophy, dear Stuart, my trophy!' Pa straightened up, tears of laughter in his eyes.

When Pa went out on his rounds with Mr Hamilton the next day, I showed Mrs Hamilton all around our place.

'Is that Pakistan over there?' she asked, pointing to the mountains in the far distance as if I was grown up.

I was sad when she left. She seemed like some kind of goddess I'd dreamt up.

★   ★   ★

Kaliq, grey-haired and hunchbacked, more family member than servant, drove us down to the village school every morning and picked us up when the final bell rang. I attended a girls' school where we wore a navy-blue uniform complete with *hijab*. Schoolwork wasn't a problem for me as I was eager to learn.

My brothers, however, were more interested in life outside the heavy gates of the school which our father and his father before him had attended. Rajan, a year younger than me and stocky like Ma, was strong and agile, and spent all his free time playing cricket, fishing or climbing with his friends. You could hear Rajan thundering through the house no matter where you were. He used to hide my schoolbooks and I once found a dead rat in my satchel. While he had loads of friends, I liked the background din, the feeling of being in the midst of everything even when I was studying. I once sat in my room with the door open when his best friend Ali asked, 'What are you up to, Jaya?'

'Learning.'

'But you're a girl!'

* * *

There were only ten months between Rajan and Tahir so that Ma often called them her 'twins'. They couldn't have been more different, though. Tahir was slightly built and had the brightest blue eyes in a caramel face. We were very close. So close that I often guessed what he would say before he actually said it. We shared a love of the outdoors and when I was allowed, he would take me to all

22

his secret places and dens. Garuda, his falcon, meant more to him than any friends, because strangers triggered his stutter so that sometimes he wouldn't talk to them at all. But when it was just the two of us, he was the funniest boy ever.

3

'A doctor! Beti Jaya, look in the mirror. You're a girl, my dear, and very pretty, too. On top of that there are dangers out there you cannot even imagine.' Ma was brushing my hair in preparation for Avani's wedding. Avani was my friend and our neighbour's daughter.

'Ouch!' I cried.

'Don't pull away then.'

My frustrated reflection, fair-skinned and green-eyed like so many fellow Kashmiris stared back at me. I wished I hadn't told her. I had kept my secret from her like some precious jewel in my pocket until it sparkled so brightly that I simply had to show it to her. And here she was telling me it was nothing more than a dirty stone.

'Ma, I come from a long line of doctors. Even our name Vaidya means physician!'

'What are you thinking? They're all men. Rajan or Tahir may follow in Pa's footsteps if they want but you . . . '

Neither of them show the slightest interest in medicine, I wanted to say but I knew it was pointless.

'What would your husband say to all this

nonsense? A family, respectability. What more could a girl possibly want? I want you to make us proud like Avani. You will see the folly of such thoughts all too sure, believe me. The world is going mad and it is my duty to protect you and the good name of our family. Why, your dear father told me only last night that they've made a pill so women can sleep with whoever they want. They don't even need to get married! How do their families live with the shame of it? What happens to these daughters afterwards?'

There was no stopping her now but what did this all have to do with me becoming a doctor?

'Love rides on reason, not romance. Why don't these girls trust their families to choose a compatible partner?'

I suppose she was speaking from experience. *Her* experience. She had fallen for the quiet, bespectacled young medic she first clapped eyes on a week before their wedding, long after the respective families had settled the matter. Ma and Pa were so different; she, forthright and talkative, and he pensive with a love of books. Yet it worked. I would often hear them whispering on the veranda late at night as they sat holding hands, catching up on the day's events. They hardly ever argued but when

25

they did, I hate to say it was usually over me.

So Ma wanted the best for me, which in her eyes meant finding me a suitable husband. 'We won't just pick anyone. No, it will be most delicately planned so that you and the groom, and more importantly our families, will be compatible. We might even go to the local pandit. He knows which astrological constellations go together best. A veritable science — one he spends his entire life studying.'

Was that all there was to life? To stand by and watch my husband leaving the house and going about his business while I stayed behind? What about joining in and changing things, healing people and saving lives? There was one little girl in our Vale who wouldn't be alive if not for me. Could there be a better feeling?

* * *

Avani didn't seem unhappy at all as I watched the married women in her family paint *mehendi* patterns in henna on her hands, before plaiting and treating her hair with oil.

'You will have six sons,' said an elderly aunt, draping her in gold and jewels as the others giggled loudly.

Avani looked regal in her embroidered *lehenga* wedding dress and when Madhav, the bridegroom, arrived at the head of the wedding procession on a white mare, wearing a sky-blue silk suit, golden turban, orange waistband and sword, he looked every inch her prince. They had been promised to each other as children but she kept her eyes steadfastly fixed on the ground as rose petals showered down on the two of them at the wedding feast.

The air was heavy with the delicious aroma of eggplant *brinjal*, spinach and cheese, potato stew, *pulao*, green beans with coconut, *dum aloo*, *paneer* in lemon and honey sauce, fluffy white or saffron-coloured rice and mouth-watering sauces and chutneys so that my stomach was already rumbling when a gong announced the feast. I queued with Ma at the huge metal container for a plate of steaming *biryani* before taking my place at the long table reserved for us women. I had never been to such an event before.

'Now don't show us up, Jaya,' said Ma as I drank my second glass of lassi. I loved the feel of the thick goat's yoghurt slithering down my throat but Ma soon got distracted by all the commotion and was smiling and enjoying herself like all the rest of us.

Only I couldn't completely forget poor Tahir who was sitting with the men on the other side of the tent. He wasn't like other boys; he hated crowds and strangers and simply stared blankly in front of him or played with the rice on his plate. How I would have loved to run over and lead him to us but it wouldn't do, I knew.

Avani's father clapped his hands and the *rabab* and *sarangi* players started to sing. My feet couldn't help tapping to the age-old melodies that touched my heart. Someone tugged my arm as all the women on my table got up and we danced the *Hafiza* until we nearly dropped.

I stayed long enough to watch money shower down on the newlyweds before Kaliq came to take us children and Granny home. Much too soon. After all, I was already twelve.

The evenings were cold once the sun sank behind the ridges. Much too excited to sleep, I sat outside on our porch wrapped in Granny's shawl. Made from the down of the *chiru*, the dainty Tibetan antelope, the shatush shawl was so soft and incredibly warm even though it had faded over time. It was so fine that Granny could even pull it through her wedding ring.

Down in the valley, the lights of the

28

wedding tent glittered in the darkness while faint chords of music drifted up through the stillness. The wolves didn't howl in summer when they had so much to prey on higher up.

The gigantic orb of a Kashmiri moon doused the rocky slopes in its silvery light and the wedding made me briefly want to become the figure who began to exchange stolen looks with her handsome young husband. I wasn't keen on the *being* married bit, but the *getting* married bit seemed perfectly splendid. I could faintly hear Granny snoring through the shutters. She had written poems when she was young, but she raised Pa. Ma did the same for us and my life was as predictable as the sun rising up over the Zolija Pass next morning. I was more likely to marry a Maharajah than become a doctor.

★ ★ ★

A shooting star burst overhead. I made my wish.

4

One sweltering day in July, I was sitting out on the porch with Pa as plume-like clouds gathered over Mount Kunyirhayan. We had been allowed home early before the storm and I was labouring over my sums as Pa puffed in silence on his pipe. He had spoken only a couple of words since coming back from a call far up in the hills. I could hear the boys playing in the bathroom and looked up in exasperation. It was no good. I simply could not concentrate on my equations. In the distance Avani's brother was herding a flock of geese to safety. Bats darted between the trees at the side of our house as the sky darkened under an advancing armada of clouds. A crack of lightning resounded around the valley.

'Appendicitis — no reason to die!'

I looked at Pa.

'The boy I went to see today. He was only five!' he added.

I put my book aside.

'We must build a clinic. It's the only solution. With no operating theatre up here, we might as well leave them to die.'

My excitement was ignited by more than lightning. Pa's vision would crown my own aspirations. The only problem being money.

★　★　★

'Don't encourage her, Babee.' Ma handed Pa another helping of *dal*. 'This talk about a clinic. All good and well but nothing that should concern Jaya. She should be thinking about other things. Jaya, you've got a lot to learn right here.' She tapped on the dining table.

'But, Ma!'

She put her hand up to silence me. I knew better than to argue. Outside, the rain hammered relentlessly on the rooftop. Out of the corner of my eye I could see Pa nod almost imperceptibly in my direction.

★　★　★

And learn I did. I learned how to cook simple dishes, wash and repair clothes and balance the household budget. Ma told me that I had to be able to do all these things before I could instruct the servants. Apart from Kaliq and Sabri, we also had a girl to do the cleaning. Ranjana was only slightly older than me and had joined us after Mara, our former help,

31

moved to her husband's family in Patan.

Although the three of them worked for us, we were not separated by castes as in other parts of India where some people were even classed as untouchables.

'We are all masters or *batta* in Kashmir,' Ma pointed out proudly. 'You must be both firm and considerate and then you will have no problem with them.'

I found it awkward telling someone the same age as me what to do. Ranjana, however, did not seem to find this strange. She carried out my wishes with a constant smile on her face and an air of absent-mindedness, even calling me *memsahib*. Occasionally, her youngest sister Adhita, who must have been only about seven or eight, would come along when her mother went to visit her father. He was a labourer in Rajasthan and away for months on end. Adhita used to watch me with big brown eyes and kept very quiet, but sometimes I let her come into my room. She would climb up onto my bed and sit there whilst I did my schoolwork. Ma thought there was something the matter with her but I managed to teach her how to write her name.

Fridays were a real highlight for me, when Dal Lake turned into a huge floating market. Fruit and vegetable sellers would gather in the morning mist, their gondola-like *shikaras* full of lotus stems, roots and fresh vegetables to jostle for best position with their heart-shaped paddles. The air carried the scent of their produce as they discussed the prices loudly above the sound of birdsong and the morning prayers that drifted across the water like a hypnotic wave.

Kaliq once told me to watch him as he found the one soggy turnip in an otherwise splendid display of spinach, lotus roots, tomatoes, pumpkins, cabbages and cauliflower. He showed the root to the vendor.

'Twenty rupees a pound! A goat would spit these out.' In this way he got what we needed at half the price. I quickly learned this trick and became so good that Kaliq would bow out of most of the haggling.

My brothers didn't do much about the house apart from chopping firewood or repairing things under Kaliq's watchful eyes but even then not that often. Ma nagged them about school but they knew how to get round her. I had a plan, though: to get my chores out of the way as quickly as possible so that I would have time for myself. When Ma was quite satisfied I would read a book or, as I got older, go out by myself which wasn't always easy.

'How come Rajan and Tahir can go out

whenever and wherever they please? You never think anything will happen to them.'

'Don't be cheeky, young lady!' Ma replied. 'You are safe here!'

I looked out and all I could see was our beloved mountains and the Vale, so rich, so inviting that my heart refused to see the slightest point in her argument. She might be scared of the world, I was not.

'She is now of an age where people *will* get ideas,' she argued with Pa.

'Ideas? Come now, my dear, we cannot influence what goes on in people's minds. My daughter shall not be imprisoned by moral hypocrisy. She shall go where she pleases as long as she does her duty,' he replied.

These last words silenced my mother and became a catchphrase. Pa's studies accounted for his more relaxed, less traditional attitude; he had known women in Scotland who became GPs and even specialists. They lived a different kind of life. They walked about quite freely, he once told me.

'Cover your head when you go out, though. You don't want to draw undue attention to yourself.'

From our house you could hear the thunder of ice cold water rushing down from the melting glaciers to the lakes below. Almost a third of our Vale was covered by water. Once I lay down in one of the hillside meadows, enjoying the warmth of the sunshine on my bare arms and tried to imagine life elsewhere. Where did the migrating flocks of bar-headed geese come from? The birds that flew clean over the Giants on their way down to the Bay of Bengal.

'What was Scotland like, Pa?' I asked one day.

'The sea, it's the sea I remember most. I've never known anything like it here. Nothing compares with it, not even Wular Lake. I could actually hear the sound of the waves crashing on the beach like some monster outside my window taking great bites of sand! Other days I would walk along the beach with a glistening mirror of water at my side.'

I knew that Wular Lake was a hundred miles across. The sea was even greater. It would have been easier to picture the moon.

5

Ma burst into my room waving a letter in her hand. 'Uncle Desh has invited you to Delhi!'

Uncle Desh wasn't really my uncle; he was much too old for that, but we called all kinds of people auntie and uncle. It just meant they were close to the family. I put my pen down.

'Why me?' I asked.

'Don't be so ungrateful. It's a tradition in our family for a girl of a certain age. I went there at that time myself. I even saw the Taj Mahal with them — the most beautiful building in the world.'

The prospect was beginning to shine for me.

'The second time I went, it was to meet your father! Uncle Desh arranged it all. You and your brothers wouldn't be here if not for your uncle.'

I smiled at the thought of Ma and Pa finding each other.

'You are old enough to go alone now and you will be in such good hands. Auntie Samvitra is not getting any younger, you know. You could help out and cheer them both up. They don't have any children, all very sad. What do you say?'

She looked at me impatiently. When Uncle Desh was here last he had told us so many tales of Delhi. I would at last be able to witness the buzz of the city with my own eyes and become the envy of my friends. Exams were looming but surely I could take my books with me over the break and see the world at the same time? After all, it would only be for a month or so.

'It'll be fun, but how will I get there?'

'By train, my dear. We'll put you on it ourselves and you'll be collected on the other side. I shall call Uncle Desh immediately.'

Too distracted now to carry on reading, I went to find Tahir and Rajan. A sharp smell of glue hit me in Rajan's room.

'You'll miss the puppy!' he said. He was sticking together some kind of model aeroplane.

In my excitement I had completely forgotten about the much longed for new family member, the newborn puppy Tahir and Rajan had been talking about for days.

'No, I won't,' I replied. 'I'll be back before we get it. I'm only going for a month or so. Where's Tahir?' I asked.

'Oh no!' he said as a wing dropped on the floor. I quickly shut the door.

I dipped under the washing line that waved in the wind like a string of colourful flags against a bright blue sky, only to find Tahir huddled on the ground behind the woodshed, his left eye so swollen that he could barely open it. The piercing blue eye stared at me from his blood-smeared face.

'What happened? Let me get you to the house!'

He shook his head violently.

'Did someone do this to you?'

He looked away and wiped his nose on his sleeve. I offered him my handkerchief.

'Wait here. I'll get something to clean you up.'

I returned with some water and a towel but he still wouldn't talk to me.

'Do you want me to make something up for Mamiji?'

He nodded. I told Ma that he had been running through a wood and hadn't seen the branch that hit him in the eye. She believed me, and she and Granny made a terrible fuss of him.

I got it out of him eventually, though. Some boys from the village had been picking on him because of his stutter. He didn't want Ma or Pa to know. There was enough trouble between Hindus and Muslims as it was, he said.

I hardly slept the night before I left. Pa said goodbye at bedtime. 'Have a wonderful time with Desh and Vitra but don't forget your schoolwork.' He kissed me on the top of my head.

By the time I got up he was out on a call. I was just putting my books into my suitcase when Granny pressed her shawl onto me.

'But it's hot in Delhi.'

'You never know, Jaya, and you might forget us!'

Granny hadn't been well those past months, sitting for hours at a time in the wicker chair in the shade of the mulberry tree. She was usually so busy helping Ma, but now she seemed to have shrunk, her eyes clouded grey, her skin a yellowish hue. It wouldn't hurt to pack the shawl if it made her happy, I told myself. Rajan was still asleep in the early morning but Tahir came out of his room, sleepy-eyed and warm from his bed, and put his arms around me.

'Come back soon. You wouldn't want to miss the puppy, would you?'

'Course not. Wait a moment!' I wanted to give him something. Something that would make him think of me. I went into my room and grabbed the first thing that fitted the bill.

'Look, here's my precious copy of *Heidi*. I want you to take care of it until I get back.' He nodded. 'You can read it if you want. Say goodbye to Rajan from me. I'll write soon.'

Tahir waved at me in his dark green pyjamas as I got into the car. It was a long trip to the station because a landslide caused a detour. That kind of thing happened all the time but Kaliq drove like the wind so we arrived just as the white and blue striped train was pulling into Jammu Tawi. Bars covered the open windows of the carriages that were already bursting at the seams. There were people clinging to its side and sitting on the roof, as it was going all the way to Jaipur. I looked at Ma.

'Don't worry. You have a reservation. Otherwise you wouldn't need to get on that train. Go on in now and see you soon.' Her eyes were moist after she gave me a kiss. I followed Kaliq, who pushed his way through the people in the gangway until he found my seat. He heaved my case up onto the rack and I touched his legs, as is our way with our elders, and said goodbye. Then he turned and left. The beloved faces outside smiled and nodded in the uncomfortable minutes before the sharp whistle of departure. Smoothing down my yellow sari, I felt incredibly grown up. The train finally shunted forward and gathered speed until I could no longer see the two lonely figures on the platform. Thank Shiva that was over. I hated goodbyes.

As the train snaked slowly south, the mountains lined our path until we entered the mouth of a long dark tunnel. When it spat us out on the other side, they were behind us and the landscape opened up like the petals of a lotus blossom.

6

The heat was trapped in the brightly lit streets of the capital where many of the shops were still open at midnight. Next to stands selling delicacies or household wares, people slept out on the pavements. The air was heavy with exhaust fumes, smoke, dust and the spicy smell of cooking. Children cried, people shouted, lorries thundered by and horns hooted continuously. How could anyone get a wink of sleep in Delhi? The rickshaw-wallah seemed oblivious to the danger as he forged his way on through the maze of streets which got progressively narrower until he finally dropped us off at an ancient block of flats in the centre of Old Delhi. A number of faded posters decorated the facade and the interior badly needed a coat of paint. I had never seen such a large building before, where people actually lived. On the ground floor two giant fans revolved over the space between a hairdresser, a temple and a post office but it was almost as baking hot as in the streets outside.

I carried my suitcase into the building behind a tottering Uncle Desh. He was much older than I could remember. A liftboy in a tattered maroon uniform with gold tassels on his shoulders pressed the button for the eighth floor. Uncle Desh nodded ever so slightly to him as the elevator shuddered into motion. Giddiness overcame me. I had never been in a lift before, although Rajan had used one, when he needed an X-ray in Srinagar. I braced myself for the moment when the steel cables would snap and send us plunging to our deaths. We reached the eighth floor to my relief and my uncle stepped out over a young boy who was sleeping in the corridor.

'The neighbour's servant,' he explained.

It was past midnight when we finally entered the apartment, which was only slightly cooler than outside. Auntie Vitra, as slight as my uncle was rotund, smiled and pressed her hands together in front of her and bowed. I bowed back.

'Welcome to our home. You look so much like Darshan.' She took my hands and examined them gently. 'Even his hands. Come; let me show you your room. You must be exhausted.'

There was a fan in the hallway and one in every room. I remember little else that evening beyond spreading Granny's shawl on the bed and crawling in underneath it.

In the morning I explored my temporary

home. The rooms were full of dark heavy furniture which must have been standing there for decades. There were a couple of plants, which badly needed repotting and fresh soil as their withered tentacles drooped despondently from the shelves. Every corner was crammed with paraphernalia: model trains, a mini Buddha, souvenirs from our homeland, old magazines and books. The carpets, once colourful, had faded over time and the stale smell of my uncle's cigar smoke lingered in the air despite all the cleaning and polishing Auntie Vitra did when she wasn't cooking. She had a permanent frown and grey hair, which made her look older than I knew her to be.

Although retired, Uncle Desh still did the accounts for a local pest-control company. 'I don't want to stay at home like a woman,' he reasoned.

When he came home in the afternoon of my first day, he lay down on the divan where he spent the rest of the day reading and being served by Auntie. I wondered what I should do with myself, for it was obvious that he didn't want to be disturbed.

'Auntie, can I help you?'

'Not today, my dear, you have only just arrived. You enjoy yourself.'

Enjoy myself? Doing what? I went to my

room and read a little. But soon I became restless. At home I could have just walked outside but here ... I was way up in some kind of a museum where no friends came to visit, where nothing moved or made a noise apart from the distant drone of traffic from the busy pulsating street below.

'Can I go down to the street?' I asked.

'No!' Auntie looked shocked. 'That is totally out of the question.' She did not explain why but instead added, 'But you can go out on the roof if you can stand the heat.'

I slipped my feet into my leather *chappals* and climbed the four floors (I didn't want to take the lift by myself) where people hung their washing and grew tomatoes and beans. Auntie was right; it was like a frying pan up there as I squinted through the haze over the sprawling housing, mosques, temples and trees as far as the park, lining the river Yamuna. Pigeons dotted the roof of the temple nearest to us but there were no hawks or buzzards in the skies, no flocks of geese migrating overhead. You couldn't see the sky properly at all — it was like wearing dirty sunglasses. I walked tentatively to the very edge of the roof and looked down at the street. Crowds of people were milling about on the streets in amongst yellow buses like ants on a mission and I was up here all by myself. I resolved to return at dusk and watch the sun dip beneath the skyline. Later, though, the orange dusk brought little relief from the oppressive heat and the crowds below were undiminished.

That evening I asked Uncle whether I could venture out the following day.

'Much too dangerous! All those pickpockets. You might get abducted or just plain lost,' warned Uncle Desh. 'You may, however, accompany Vitra when she goes out.'

The rest of our meal was taken in relative silence until Uncle put down his napkin and asked, 'How are Rajan and Tanay? What do they want to be when they grow up? Will they follow in their father's footsteps and become doctors, too?'

'You mean Rajan and Tahir.'

He frowned.

'I don't know,' I continued, 'Rajan says he wants to captain India at Lords and Tahir loves animals. He wants to be a herdsman but Ma doesn't think much of any of that. You are right; she wants them both to become doctors or lawyers.' Ma had some strange ideas. I didn't tell him the truth about my littlest brother, that he could barely string two words together in the presence of strangers, let alone talk in a courtroom. I suddenly missed them all terribly but especially Tahir.

'And yourself?'

Pa had told him! I was surprised that he had shared our secret with anyone else, especially with Uncle Desh. I didn't know they were that close. I was about to elaborate when my uncle added, 'Have your parents chosen a husband for you? Surely it is high time.'

I was dumbstruck as the reasons behind my visit and why Ma had actually suggested me coming here by myself slowly dawned on me. My voice came out strange and croaky, 'I don't think they're considering that yet.'

'Well, I suppose your dear parents know what is best for you, but if you were my daughter . . . ' The sentence hung in the air like a sabre. Then he slashed me with it. 'I shall have a word with Palomi. I know some good families. She can trust me.'

After helping Auntie with the dishes I sought the sanctuary of my room. That night I dreamed about being dressed in a rust-red *lehenga*, my hands exquisitely painted not with henna but with blood.

* * *

Finally outside, I felt like an otter surfacing for air until I took my first deep breath. This was nothing like our sweet mountain air.

Cars, yellow buses, vans and lorries revved their engines and spewed their choking fumes into the air. Motorbikes and rickshaws carrying entire families hooted while cyclists rang their bells and darted into the gaps between the bumper-to-bumper traffic jams. I tried not to inhale too deeply but the smoke of cooking fires, the sharp stink of sewage from open drains and the rotting stench of rubbish was inescapable and tickled the back of my throat. At the same time the sweet intoxicating scent of jasmine flowers, the aroma of overripe guava fruit or the smell of fried curry leaves and mustard seeds sold by the many roadside vendors drifted through the air.

A cow meandered haughtily among the traffic, ignoring the concert of horns around it as children wound their way in between cars to sell cigarettes or waited at traffic lights to clean the windscreens. On the sidewalks and amongst the traffic people were teeming, crawling, running, walking, lying, shouting, sleeping everywhere. Was this a special day? How could there be so many people on this great Earth, let alone in Delhi?

Our apartment block had seen better days but it was one of the nicest in the area. Some buildings nearby were terribly run down in comparison. I fought my way through the crowds to keep up with Auntie. We turned a corner and bumped straight into a beautifully painted elephant, its head only a couple of feet beneath the tangle of electric wires weaving intricate patterns as they came together from the surrounding buildings. People kept bumping into me or touching me.

'Look away! Don't encourage them,' said Auntie. 'If you give them as much as a paisa, they'll never leave you alone.' Children were tugging and pulling at me in the maze of *galis*, some toothless or blind, some missing limbs or crippled so that they had to drag themselves along on skateboard-like contraptions. I looked down at the spots of spat-out red betel nut on the pavement and hurried past, hating myself but not daring to disobey.

Alongside the beggars were men and women dressed as splendidly as in the Bollywood films. Sapphire and violet saris, crimson and aquamarine embroidered with threads of silver or gold. I stopped and stared but Auntie quickly ushered me on my way.

All kinds of food were cooked out in the open or in the back-street *dhabas*; mouth-watering delicacies that I had never tried before. And fruit: loquats, litchis, mangosteens, kumquats, durians, passion and dragon fruit and many more that never made it to Dal Lake.

I succumbed to an orange *jhola* bag from a pavement vendor. Auntie shook her head even though I only handed over half the cash he originally wanted. She was right — the same bag was a third cheaper at the next corner.

At the end of my second week, we rode in a rickshaw down streets with palatial residences on the one side and makeshift housing on the other to a maze of shabby factories in the Old Slum Quarters. Auntie wanted to buy some silk, but here? Rats darted audaciously across the alleyways and scavenged amongst the piles of refuse left rotting in the heat. Small children played on the filthy floor whilst their mothers slaved away at sewing machines nearby. Children even younger than Tahir sat before mighty looms, their nimble hands spinning elaborate patterns in carpets to grace cool marble floors in Milan or Paris. With the factory floors stacked on top of each other, the lower levels were dimly lit with an occasional beam of sunlight spotlighting the thick dust in the air. Auntie found some beautiful turquoise silk she had been looking for.

'Where do they sleep?' I asked, referring to the children we'd seen.

'Either on the floors or in cots in rooms at the back.' She didn't seem to think this out of the ordinary. I had never seen such exploitation in my life.

★ ★ ★

As the days dragged by, the heat pressed down on the city like a giant hand. I longed for cool mountain breezes, waterways and lakes. The temperatures in the streets were a reason to keep to the apartment where the fans and five large earthenware pots filled with water made it slightly more bearable. That wasn't the only reason to fill them, though.

'Delhi doesn't have enough water,' Auntie explained, 'so it's always good to have some in the house.'

One day at lunch I turned on the taps and all that came out was a brownish splutter and we had to wait all afternoon for the supply to resume. Water had never been a problem back home. Most of all I missed my freedom, which had been taken from me the moment I boarded the train. There was no freedom in this city, in this climate. I couldn't even open a window in the scorching heat. The days dragged on endlessly.

My only escape was the roof. Sometimes I

would tiptoe up the stairs at night so that I could stare at the same moon that lit our Vale. I would try to block out the ever present din of the traffic and pretend I could smell a whiff of my pa's pipe that told me he was home. I wanted to talk to him, but I couldn't very well pick up the phone in the hallway. What could I say that wouldn't mortally offend my uncle? If I wrote him a letter, Ma would see it. I couldn't believe that she was party to some kind of marriage plan yet I couldn't totally rid myself of my suspicions. Why else had they invited me? I decided that if I heard the slightest news on that front I would run away and board the next train back home.

* * *

Each week, a letter from home arrived for me, which I took to my room, reading and rereading the lines.

20th August 1972

My city girl!
I hope you are enjoying yourself. Here all is well apart from the old trouble. One man dead on arrival. A second bled to death with a bullet in his stomach

before my eyes. A third escaped with a hole in his foot. Taken for insurgents on the border. A deliberate targeting of civilians. I pray to Indra that things won't escalate.

We went to see the new puppy in Srinagar on Tuesday (see photo). Your brothers were very excited and want to call her Sahira. What do you think? Granny hasn't been her old self lately, but I'm sure she'll buck up once you're back. We all miss you. Ma especially. You know she's only ever happy when her brood is complete. Can't wait to see you very soon. Give my love to Desh and Vitra.

Your loving Pa

At the bottom Ma had added:

Beti Jaya,
All these men. Who is there to help me now? Your brothers never have any time. Be good to Vitra and Desh. Dying to hear all about it when you're back.
Your adoring Mamiji xxx
P.S. Rajan sends his love, too.

I must have been mistaken. Ma couldn't be in on a marriage plot. The Bakharwal puppy with its fluffy coat was totally irresistible. I wanted to scoop it up in my arms immediately. But at least I would be there when it arrived. I wouldn't miss that for the world.

I wrote a couple of times. I had plenty of time for that. I tried to sound all bright and excited but life in the apartment wasn't getting any better. Uncle was starting to look at me differently as if my presence irritated him. Was I imagining things? Why had they invited me? They were much too old to have me around them. I put my time to good use and finished all my schoolwork. I started crossing off the days until I could once more be myself, when I could run free and not in fear as in the city. Four weeks turned into three weeks. Then it was two and finally only ten days before I would see the whole family again, before I could escape the stifling heat of the city and the apartment that was my cage.

★   ★   ★

The shower had been running an awfully long time. I was watching the refuse trucks in their almost impossible endeavour to manoeuvre around the obstacles in their way. They had the same trouble every Tuesday. Auntie didn't usually stay under the shower that long. I knocked on the bathroom door. No answer. I knew she was in there. I tried the door, it was locked. It was the kind of lock you can turn from the outside with a coin or a knife. There was a rupee lying near the phone. I grabbed it and managed to open the door. A thin, bony leg stuck out from under the shower curtain. She lay unconscious on the floor of the shower, a deep gash on her forehead, one arm unnaturally bent in a pale pink pool of blood and water. She was still breathing, thank Vishnu. I switched the water off and shook her gently. She came to and cried with pain.

'Jaya, where am I?'

I covered her up with a towel. I had seen Pa's patients in the same state of shock. Her swollen right arm looked broken but she could still move her fingers and her other limbs. I eased her out onto the dry floor and sat her up against the wall, a towel behind her back and another under her arm. Blood was dripping down from her face. Once she was comfortable, I called an ambulance and made her a strong cup of chai. All the while, she looked around her, wide-eyed and disorientated. By the time I put down the phone to my uncle the medics had arrived. He turned up at Ram Manohar Lohia hospital just as they were putting her arm in plaster.

'What happened?' said Uncle. 'Can't I leave you two alone for a second?' Auntie looked back even more blankly than usual. Four stitches sealed the cut below her *bindi*.

The doctors wanted to keep her in for the night for suspected concussion but Uncle Desh would have none of it.

'My wife will be fine, just fine. Our niece is staying with us. Family is best for her. She will be in good hands.'

This time I agreed with him. The corridors outside were crowded. It was very loud and I could smell sewage and waste. An hour later we eased Auntie out of the wheelchair into the black and yellow taxi. Uncle muttered something about the expense of it all as I held her good hand in the back seat. I put her to bed and she immediately fell asleep under the influence of the painkillers.

There was no way I could go home as planned in ten days. The pain of not being able to go back was at least as intense as Auntie's physical pain. This must be how Heidi felt, I decided. I missed my brothers as I never thought I possibly could. And Ma and Pa. Why did this have to happen?

'I want to come home!' I whispered to Ma on the phone.

'Yes, of course you do. We miss you, too,' there was a tremor in her voice, 'but it won't be long now and they would be completely lost without you. They have been so kind to you. It is your duty to do the same for them.'

Auntie stayed in bed for the following three weeks and talked even less than she did otherwise. It was obvious they could not manage without me. I was stuck. A month passed but there was no question of me leaving them in this situation.

At least I could phone home more often now. They had collected Sahira, our new puppy the week before and even Ma was excited.

'She pricks her ears when you call her name and I never would have thought it but your father is besotted with her! I caught Rajan pulling her tail the other day. He was only playing but Babu really told him off. He went a little far for my liking. But boys will be boys.'

I was so sad that I had missed Sahira's arrival. Would she know I was even part of the family when I finally turned up? I knew that Ma was right, I could not leave my hosts, yet I didn't really feel as if I personally owed them anything. If there had been no accident, we would have happily gone our separate ways. But something else bothered me even more than Sahira's homecoming.

'What about school?' Term was about to begin.

'My dear,' said Ma, 'why are you worrying about school? This is far more important than school. Desh and Vitra are like family and it won't be for much longer.'

What if I wouldn't be able to catch up? But I knew there was no point in saying that.

Auntie recovered very slowly and I took over all the chores there were to do. In the beginning, I had to help her wash and dress until she developed some kind of slow one-handed technique and of course I even cut up her food for her. The only good news was that I could now leave the flat to go shopping when Uncle was at work.

★　★　★

The first time I ventured out by myself I walked directly to the market which was only two blocks away. People were pushing in on me from all sides and I kept checking my purse under the fold of my sari. Three girls came around the corner, one of them carrying a baby with a festering scab on its head. It took all my willpower to look away. Sensing my vulnerability, they started tugging at my dress with much more persistence than ever before.

'Miss, miss, ten rupees. For our little brother,' said the girl with the baby on her hip, 'we are hungry and our mother is dying.'

I couldn't just walk on. I reached into my purse and handed them some coins. At this rate I wouldn't have much left for the market. Still they tugged at me. 'A little more, miss. If we don't come back with more, our father will beat us.' 'I can't, I haven't . . . ' They seemed to think they had struck gold with me and they touched my sari near my purse.

'Go away. GO AWAY!' I shouted, forcing them to beat a reluctant retreat.

I suddenly felt very disorientated. Had I really walked down this street with Auntie? There were lots of vendors and sumptuous snacks on offer but something wasn't quite right. I walked on and on, sure that I would spot something completely familiar any moment. No, now I was certain. It was the wrong street. I spied a narrow alley that must cut through to a parallel route. Yes, that was it. I hurried past the dark entrances; I could hear a baby crying somewhere. The heat was so intense and my heart beating so fast. My face glowed and sweat trickled down my back. I had no idea where I was. I turned around but going back was pointless. How would I find my way back? When I turned, two men stood in my way. I felt for my purse and walked with determined steps past them, my heart thumping ever louder. Just as I passed them one lurched at me and I smelt the alcohol on his breath.

'Come here, sweet little lady!'

The other man laughed a deep guttural sound. I ran as fast as I could. A woman emerged from a doorway. Too soon. Her brightly painted face brushed my own when I banged into her at full speed. She went flying. I didn't turn to see how she was, just shouted sorry with the sound of the man's jeers still echoing in my ears. I broke into the light the next minute and immediately recognized the far side of the market. I was safe! I sat down on the pavement and counted my blessings. For once Uncle had been right. I would be far more careful next time. I hated Delhi with a passion.

★ ★ ★

I knew how to cook and clean, how to do almost everything. Ma had made sure of that and in the previous five weeks, I had watched and helped Auntie enough to know where things were and how and when things needed to be done. I surprised them with the dishes I put together and, amazingly, after a few weeks, Auntie blossomed. She was being looked after for the first time in her married life. She was very grateful and as she slowly regained strength, she helped me as much as she could, telling me when I had forgotten something or helping me with the shopping list. I could not say the same for my uncle.

'Why are the plates on this side of the cupboard? You know we always keep them on the other side. And look at the dust gathering on the sideboard. Are you young people blind?' he grumbled.

There was no point in answering back. Auntie would smile at me when his back was turned as if to excuse his behaviour, but she would never say anything. That would have been a step too far for her. I yearned for the day when I would finally leave the confines of the flat. Then my days as a carer would be over. I vowed to never, ever leave our Vale again.

7

One morning in Ghoond, when autumn could be felt in the wind that blew down from the Himalayas and in the mist that lingered in the valley, shrouding the tapestry of gold and red forests at the foothills, when the herdsmen had finally brought their yaks and zomos down from the high pastures, safe from the roaming packs of white wolves, just in time to celebrate Diwali, the festival of lights, when fires had been lit to drive away the cold of the night and stocks were high in preparation for the long hard winter ahead, when Rajan, Tahir, Ma and Granny were still safely tucked up in their beds and Pa was out on a call, the Earth shook.

When I was fast asleep almost 1,000 miles away.

* * *

'Come quickly and watch the news!' Auntie stood before me in her nightdress, her arm still in its white cast, her long grey hair falling over her shoulders. Uncle was sitting in his dressing-gown in front of the TV, a look of shock on his face. A reporter was standing in front of a half-demolished building. I had to look twice. Our village hall! Where was Avani? The reporter pointed at parts of the collapsed roof. Word started to come from the television.

'A powerful earthquake has hit Kashmir, the territory disputed by India and Pakistan since Independence from Britain in 1947. More than a thousand people are thought to have died, with reports of casualties still coming in . . . '

I thought I must still be dreaming. I was paralyzed, incapable of taking in what the man was saying.

'Please. I have to phone!' I begged.

My fingers kept slipping off the dial, I started again and again. When I finally completed the number there was only a strange tone at the other end. I tried again. Still the same horrible sound. I passed the phone back to my uncle.

'It's not working.'

He looked at me as if I were slightly mad and dialled a local number. No problem. I ran into my room and pulled my suitcase out from under the bed and started to throw my belongings in. Uncle followed me in.

'What are you doing, girl?'

'I've got to go home!'

He put his hand gently on my arm. 'We must wait for the all clear. Even if there was a train and the tracks were still intact, the roads might be blocked. You would be stuck in a bedlam. We cannot let you go until we know that there is someone there to collect you . . .'

'Kaliq will get me!'

He opened his mouth to say something, but shut it again.

'Jaya, we must wait until we have word,' said Auntie. 'I am sure you will hear very soon. Then you can go.' Her voice of reason got through to me.

★　★　★

News came in dribs and drabs. The next few days were excruciating. I couldn't eat, I couldn't sleep. Whenever I closed my eyes images of my family and home appeared like in a wonderful movie. I even saw Sahira, the dog I had never touched, playing with them. The pictures were so vivid. There could be no doubt that they were all alive and safe. Yet there was no word from them. Surely they must know that I was nearly out of my mind with worry. The days slipped into a week and I was slowly going mad. Ten days later, Uncle was reading *The Times of India*.

'It's horrific. They say the death toll soared to 20,000 on Wednesday, making it one of the deadliest quakes in decades. Aftershocks have rattled the region, sending up huge clouds of dust from steep-sided mountain valleys where villages lie in pieces.'

I tried to picture our village. I couldn't. My mind refused to go there.

Uncle continued, 'In remote mountains, a steady flow of injured villagers continue to seek medical attention. Many have infected wounds, untreated since the tremor, and have to rely on relatives to carry them for hours on foot to makeshift clinics. Helicopters are dropping relief supplies and mule trains are pushing into areas where no helicopters can land. 'There are many people out there we are not going to reach in time,' said an army spokesman. 'Some of the injured have no chance of survival at all.''

It sounded so awful but it wasn't about my family. Our house was solid, made of stone. It had withstood the tremors, I was sure. And then I thought about Pa. His clinic would have saved so many lives but I took comfort in the fact that he must be treating the injured right at the centre of the devastation. That was why I had heard nothing, I reassured myself. If only I were there, I could have helped him. The days passed agonizingly slowly. We tried phoning but always the same tone.

'Hello.' Uncle had got through! 'This is Mr Bhatt from Delhi. You haven't got time? Hello, hello!' He shook his head. 'The woman at the other end hung up! Can you imagine? She actually hung up on me!'

There seemed no way to communicate with anyone in our Vale. I would lie on the sofa staring at the phone and only get up to help Auntie with the cleaning and cooking when she asked. Her cast now off, she resumed her old role.

No news is good news, I kept telling myself. The phone lines are down and they just cannot get hold of me.

Slowly, very slowly the full consequences of the quake emerged. Tens of thousands of people had perished and tens of thousands made homeless, their homes flattened by the gods.

I was sitting on the sofa when my uncle finally got through to the International Red Cross.

'Bhatt from Delhi here. I want to enquire about Dr Darshan Vaidya and his family. You have lists. Good. No, I'm not exactly family but like family . . . You can't tell me? You won't tell me! Now listen here, I have his daughter Jaya Vaidya here. What? You want to talk to her? She's only a girl . . . '

I moved across to take the receiver but he continued to argue with whoever was on the other end. There was a moment's silence when he looked at the receiver and then he reluctantly passed it to me. I pressed it to my ear, hardly able to hear anything above the thumping in my chest.

'Miss Vaidya. We have to validate your identity. Could we please have your date of birth?'

'Sixth of February 1957.'

'Miss Vaidya. I'm terribly sorry. I'm afraid it's not good news . . . '

Ma, Rajan, Granny and beloved Kaliq buried under the rubble of our home! Pa's jeep crushed by a landslide on a mountain track. He had been identified by Ranjana. Sabri and Tahir were missing. I sank onto the floor and started sobbing uncontrollably.

The thought of Tahir eventually made me stop. They hadn't found his body! Maybe he was still alive? It was the only thing that stopped me from throwing myself out the window there and then. Uncle dismissed this.

'It doesn't mean a thing, girl. Where would he be if he wasn't at home?' What he said made tragic sense. 'Do you think they've cleared all the rubble yet? They are still tending to the injured and counting the dead.'

67

I could never run to my mother's arms again. I would never hear Rajan's voice again. I would never lie in my bed and smell Pa's pipe smoke from below. I was alone with two old folk.

8

Tahir heard Garuda shriek in the night. Then again. Perhaps a fox? No, it couldn't be the case. She was safe and sound on her perch in the woodshed. But still, she certainly knew how to get his attention if she wanted. If she kept on like this, she would wake everyone. He listened and sure enough she let out another cry. There was nothing for it but to go out in the bitter cold. He heard his grandmother cough. She had been so unwell recently; he really didn't want her to wake up.

'Shut up, Garuda, I'm coming!' he whispered to himself.

Creeping out of his room, he tiptoed down the stairs, past the figure of Shiva with the candle burning in front of it. He stepped over Sahira, deep in her puppy dreams and grabbed his coat off the hook. It was a moonless night and he could hardly see anything as he picked his way over the familiar stony path round the back of the house to her enclosure. He didn't mind the dark. It was people who frightened him and robbed him of the words on his tongue.

There was a touch of winter in the air. The

lacked his cheeks as he pulled his coat
around him. His hand felt the copy of
i in his pocket that he carried every-
wi ere with him. After all, Jaya had told him
to look after it for her. He opened the door.
Garuda was flapping her wings madly. How
could a bird be that loud? Then the ground
began to shake.

'What the . . . ?'

And the walls of the shed came tumbling
down around him.

When Tahir finally came to, all he could see
were the hooves of the donkey, carrying him
higher and higher up the mountain path
before he passed out again.

9

My uncle left me to grieve in the privacy of my room. He smiled sympathetically at me over the dining room table and talked to me in a gentle, respectful voice. He too had lost his close friends, he told me. Auntie was quieter still, if that was possible. The tragedy must have reminded her of her own and she was too emotionally stunted to comfort someone in the present. She simply withdrew further into herself. I wanted someone to take me in their arms and comfort me.

Days slid into weeks and weeks into months. Still no news of Tahir.

'Please ring up the authorities,' I begged.

'Perhaps tomorrow,' he replied but I never actually saw him do it.

I slept as long as I could and passed the days reading Pa's letters, watching television or simply staring out of the window. I couldn't get past the first page of any of Uncle's books. I had no need to go outside, not even on the roof, no urge to do anything. I was stranded in a place I could never call home. I wished to be dead.

I threw my schoolbooks away one Tuesday,

one by one down the rubbish chute. I watched with perverse glee, when the men in turbans finally collected the bins. Stupid dreams. A waste of time. They were the reason I was being punished. Pa had taught me to worship the gods in our Vale but that hadn't been enough. Why would they have let this happen?

Whenever I could, I listened to the radio as if to hear something that would tell me it had all been a huge mistake. Ma and Pa were alive and well. My brothers were just as robust as ever. Auntie came in and switched off the news.

'Jaya, you must think of something else! You must distract yourself.'

Had she dealt with the loss of her children any better?

★ ★ ★

I wasn't good company and not much use, either. Auntie could now fully resume her duties and no longer needed my help to peel and cut the vegetables or carry the food to the table. I was too wrapped up in myself to offer to help her in the kitchen or hoover unless she asked me, which she did less and less. The old couple, set in their ways, were now faced with the prospect of having an orphaned teenager living with them permanently.

One day Uncle looked directly at me and said, 'Food prices have shot up recently. It is very difficult to make ends meet with this galloping inflation.'

I hadn't noticed any increase, but then I hadn't noticed much recently. Such strange comments became frequent and I started to feel growing discomfort. I was a burden on them. I was riddled with guilt anyway, that I should breathe, eat and sleep when my loved ones were all dead.

The odd condolence card from friends of the family trickled in. I received a note from the Scottish couple who had visited us so many years ago.

7th November 1972

Dear Jaya,

It is with great shock and the utmost sorrow that Marie and I have received word of this dreadful tragedy. We cannot bear to think about what has happened to your wonderful family and what you must be going through. We treasure the memories of our visit to your home and the hospitality lavished upon us by your mother. We feel honoured to have had the privilege of knowing your dear father as both a close friend and a gifted physician. I particularly remember the young cricketer I played with all those years ago at university. I don't know if he ever told you, but we wanted to keep him here. I offered him a full partnership in the clinic, and even organized a British passport for him but he couldn't go through with it. Kashmir was written across his heart, he said. Something I only came to understand when we finally visited.

I am sure that your father's dedication and visionary thinking will be sorely missed in your community. We talked about his plans for a new clinic only recently on the phone. He also told me how well you were doing. He was so very proud of you. You may not remember us, but should you ever need any help, please don't hesitate to get in touch.

With heartfelt sympathy,
Stuart and Marie Hamilton

Their address and telephone number were printed on the top of the card. But why would I write to them? They belonged to the world that my father had left behind decades ago; they lived on the other side of the globe.

I put the card carefully back into the envelope and placed it along with three or four others in my suitcase under my bed, where I kept all the letters I had received from Pa. Ten envelopes, each containing his beautiful handwriting, plus Ma's notes and my brother's drawings. I took one out each night and read each word slowly until I could recite them all off by heart. They were my connection with them, proof that they had existed, that they had loved me, that I was a Vaidya.

I tried to be as quiet as possible, staring out of windows at the cluttered Delhi skyline with its blanket of smog, my guilt at having survived plaguing me like a nagging tooth-ache.

My uncle started to pick on me for the slightest reason. 'Look at this glass you've left lying around. You're turning the place into a pigsty!'

He had never really warmed to me and the feeling was mutual. Now he made his feelings even clearer. Even though I had barely touched my food, he accused me of eating them out of house and home.

'Where is your gratitude? Where would you be without us? You would have perished with the rest of the family. Your aunt and I work all hours and you . . . what do you do?'

I had nothing to say in my defence, only wishing that I had been buried under the rubble with my loved ones. I tried to stay out of his way by keeping to my room as much as possible. I had started to keep a diary as a way to cope with the wave of darkness that threatened to engulf me. Mostly the entries were brief and boring:

Delhi, 21st January 1973

Got up. Streets are flooded from the massive downpour in the early hours. Helped Auntie sort the old newspapers. Hadn't been thrown away for six months. Cut out all the articles about Kashmir. Stomach pains. Wanted to stay in bed.

10

Uncle Desh beamed at me across the dining table. 'You are very fortunate indeed!'

'Fortunate?'

'I have pulled it off. The perfect match for you!'

'But I . . . I don't want to get married!'

His fist crashed down on the table. 'Where's your gratitude? You're a destitute orphan. Good families avoid you like an overripe mango. Don't you understand? You have no tree to hang from. We cannot look after you forever. You must marry! Your future husband lives on a farm in Panipat with his mother and brother. You know what they say about the Punjab.'

'That girls are so scarce there that the men are desperate for brides?' I blurted out.

To my surprise, Uncle ignored my backchat. 'No, they have more food than they can eat! You will do well there. Mandeep has been seeking a bride for quite a while now. He's a little over forty, isn't he, Vitra?'

Ancient! Horror infused me like a poisonous potion. Auntie shrugged her shoulders. It didn't surprise me that she had been in on this all along. My hands started shaking with anger.

'Well, he is in his forties,' Uncle continued, motioning to Auntie to put more *sag aloo* on his plate. 'It's a good age to marry a young malleable girl like you. The perfect age to become a father, too.' He winked at me. I felt ill.

'So, that's it?' I asked, finally finding my voice again. 'You've just decided this, without consulting me?'

Uncle looked incredulous. 'I don't need to consult anyone in this matter, least of all you! Your own parents could not have chosen better. It is an excellent prospect, given your situation.'

I was to take over the care of an old woman and her sons, and soon there would be babies to rear. Pictures flashed through my mind; images of women worn out by hard work and childbearing or dying in childbirth. I had seen enough of those in the mountains. I looked from Uncle's self-satisfied face to my auntie's blank visage with its weak watery smile, and knew that was that. No use in further protest.

In my room once more, I took the box with my father's letters out of its hiding place, reading and rereading his last letter, tears trickling down my face onto the crisp white paper, smudging the black ink. He wouldn't have wanted this. I dabbed my tears away gently before straightening out the letter on the shelf to dry for the night. If only I could talk to him, tell him, tell anyone of my predicament.

I slept fitfully, dreaming of a dark shape, pressing down on me until I could no longer breathe. I woke up gasping for breath and switched on my bedside lamp. I reasoned with myself. It was a question of duty and trust. After all, Uncle had brought my parents together. What was wrong with me? But I knew what this marriage meant for me. I turned and buried my face in my pillow. When Auntie woke me, I saw that she was steeling herself to block out any empathy. She did as her husband bade her. She always had. She always would.

I heard nothing for a few days until I almost thought Uncle's plans had failed but he returned from work one day, rubbing his hands together.

'I have some jolly plans for us this weekend. A little outing! To show you what wonderful prospects you now have in the Punjab. And the family must see you. They are most happy with your photo . . . '

He had sent my photo to strangers! Without even asking me. How dare he!

'We cannot expect your intended to come

all the way here,' he continued. 'Mandeep and his brother have a farm to run. I want you to put on your best sari and we shall go and meet your future family.' The man's name sent shudders down my spine. Uncle wiped the sweat from his brow with his napkin. 'Just the two of us. Auntie will be busy enough here.'

She looked down at her plate.

Dressed in my golden sari, and travelling on the very same railway line to Kashmir, we headed north. I peered out of the window as the countryside sped past and my destination loomed ever nearer. I longed to stay, to remain on board until I could see the mountains. Uncle soon fell asleep and his snoring was only interrupted by the frequent stops at the stations en route. A good five hours later, we stepped out in the middle of nowhere onto a platform which constituted the entire train station. There was no one there and nothing of interest to rest our eyes on. The afternoon sun forced us to take shelter under a small Shisham tree. Uncle Desh took out his gold watch and muttered something. I knew better than to ask any questions. I didn't want to set him off. After about twenty minutes, I started to wonder if we would be left there until the evening train arrived. Perhaps it would all come to nothing!

11

Ripe fields of corn rippled in the hot wind on either side of a dry track. Behind us was a stubby harvested field. I squinted at a dust storm on the horizon until I made out an old cart pulled by a mule heading towards us. A huge man with a turban and a beard stepped down. A Sikh. I tried to remember what I knew about Sikhs but my mind went blank.

'*Namaste.*' He bowed his head. 'I am Dhan, Mandeep's brother.'

He looked like a giant as he exchanged polite remarks with my uncle in a Punjabi lilt that I struggled to understand. He did not look at me once. I might as well have been the mule by his side. We boarded the cart and set off, passing through fields where women were doing back-breaking work or gathering sticks. I imagined myself joining them very soon. Then we trotted through a village where children played barefoot in the sand-like earth, the smaller ones naked from the waist down and men sat in little clusters, drinking tea and playing games.

★ ★ ★

The farmhouse was simple. On the porch hung chillies, onions and maize. A fat buffalo grazed serenely on clumps of dried grass besides a water pump. We were welcomed by an old lady with a ring in her nose. Still tall and strong, she pinched my cheek and smiled the same smile as her son. She reminded me strangely of my own mother. A group of children had gathered to inspect me. Dhan went off and the woman beckoned me in.

'A glass of *nimbupani?*' she asked.

In any other circumstances I would have loved a glass of the refreshing drink of lemon but now I sipped it indifferently, trying to withstand the gazes of the giggling children and the old woman's searching look.

Mandeep's frame filled the doorway, blocking out the light. He was even taller than his brother. My whole body froze. There was nowhere I could run. As he ambled in I saw that one of his eyes was cloudy and grey, and his beard came almost down to the long curved sword that hung from his waist. He put his hands together and greeted us and the heavy metal bangles around his wrist jangled. I noticed the grime under his fingernails. He's a farmer, I told myself. He turned his head to look at me with his good eye and smiled. I averted my eyes. He was much, much too old for me. My stomach became a pool of acid at the thought of him touching me.

Uncle and Mandeep proceeded to talk to each other. I could just about follow the gist. Something about the harvest this year. Their way of speaking was different to anything I had heard before, but I knew I could learn it if I tried. I didn't want to learn it. I didn't want to talk to Mandeep. I didn't want to have anything to do with him or his family. I wanted to run out back to the station. Any place would be better than where I was now. I would stay with Uncle and Auntie and care for them forever, do anything for them. Surely if I begged them . . .

Our hostess poured out another cup of tea for my uncle, before she shooed the children away. She eyed me approvingly and nodded to my uncle. I felt like a goat at a market. I didn't have a private conversation with Mandeep but as we bowed our goodbyes and Uncle Desh talked for a few minutes with my future mother-in-law about my dowry, his smile seemed to have faded. There was something possessive about him now. On the journey home, I tried to talk to my uncle but he put his hand up to silence me. There would be no point in appealing to my auntie. The matter was decided. After he had fallen asleep once more, I imagined myself at the side of Mandeep, his mother and brother, and fought back the tears.

⋆ ⋆ ⋆

I followed the preparations for the forthcoming wedding as if I were sleepwalking. The sixteen-year-old girl who went with Auntie to choose the material for her *lehenga* wasn't me. Soon, I would have a home, a husband, on a farmstead . . . in the middle of nowhere. I had to bow to the will of the gods now. I was entering a different life, a life of subservience with a husband I must learn to live with. There would be little other distraction in future. Not even books. Above all, I would have to be practical. Children would soon follow. Would I be able to create a happy home for them? Perhaps they were the solution. I would see things in a different light once they arrived. I would have something, someone of my own. No longer a daughter or a sister, I might become a mother at seventeen.

For Uncle, the great day could not arrive fast enough. The day when I would finally be off his hands. With youthful élan he rubbed his hands together and smiled to himself from time to time. It had given him a goal in his old age. He would have such a peaceful life without me whilst I stared into a hopeless abyss.

Mandeep featured regularly in my dreams, appearing out of nowhere, chasing me, or just staring at me with his mother and brother. One night I dreamt of a little boy, born with twelve fingers and a tail whom I called Tahir, only he died. I woke up covered in sweat and trembling. Then I tried to picture my family but they eluded me like faceless shadows. My life was taking me further and further away from them. In a train hurtling towards my nuptial night.

I ventured into the living room where Uncle, relaxing as usual on the divan, was blowing circles of smoke into the air with his cigar.

'Do you think you could ring the Red Cross about Tahir?'

'He's dead, my dear. You know that as well as I do.'

'But what if he can't speak? He's got a problem. He clams up in the presence of strangers . . . ' I started to babble.

'What do you mean, clams up? Fourteen-year-olds talk! He can't be that stupid.'

'Please, Uncle. Do just this one thing for me. I have to know before I leave. Please ask if he's on the list of missing or . . . ' I pleaded.

Uncle gave me a withering look, and then

sighed. 'I'll call them from the office tomorrow.'

★ ★ ★

I counted the hours until Uncle Desh came back from work. Surely the gods would have spared my little brother. Shiva, let there be some sign of him. He couldn't be dead; I felt it in every bone of my body. He was alive out there somewhere.

Uncle Desh's face told me everything when he finally returned. 'I'm afraid it's not good. Just as I predicted.'

My legs gave way and I collapsed onto his divan. The room was bathed in a red light from the evening sun but Uncle's face was redder still.

★ ★ ★

Two weeks later, an official parcel arrived, containing papers rescued from the ruins of my family's house. A birth certificate and passports. I had two of the latter because of my English great-grandfather, a colonel in the British army. Uncle had requested the documents for the forthcoming marriage.

'We can't have people saying you're not properly married, can we?'

86

I inspected my documents in my room. Paper fell out. Neatly folded inside my British passport was a letter from the Red Cross dated a week previously.

Thank you for your enquiry. We regret that despite extensive enquiries we have been unable to trace the whereabouts of T. A. Vaidya. He remains on the list of missing and you will be informed should there be any change of status without delay . . .

I read it a second time. Uncle had lied to me! Wherever Tahir was, he wasn't buried there. My uncle had wanted to break me. Yet if I exposed him, I knew it wouldn't change a thing. I would still have to get married; only my last days as a girl would be a living hell.

Tahir might be injured and unable to speak. Whom did he have besides me? I had to go back and find him. Pa and Ma would want me to! Even if I never found him, at least I would have tried. I still had the money for my return ticket which Ma had given me. Even if the train line was still obstructed, I couldn't sit here and wait, not now, not when Tahir was out there somewhere. I had to get to the train station to see if they were running. If I couldn't get away, I would stay in Delhi for a while. There must be something I could do out in this huge city. It was up to the gods whether I went or worked but in either case, I would foil Uncle's plans for my future in the Punjab.

I secretly packed my case, just my beloved letters, a few clothes and my shawl. I had stolen some food, dried fruit and a packet of biscuits, just like Heidi. I went to bed and waited until I thought they were asleep. On tiptoes I crept past their bedroom door, reassured to hear Uncle snoring loudly. I pulled back the chain on the front door and shut it as quietly as I could behind me. The servant boy outside stirred, looked at me and turned over. I made for the stairs, as it was the least probable route of drawing attention to myself.

Outside, the warm night air held the promise of a sweltering new day and I felt hope for the first time in ages. Uncle was eight storeys above me, sleeping peacefully in his mausoleum.

* * *

I didn't know exactly where the station was. I certainly didn't have a map. All I knew was that we had headed east when I went to the station with Uncle and east was where the sun was about to reclaim its grip on the city. I walked and walked, desperate to put as much distance between me and Uncle as possible, until dawn crept over the city and shutters were taken down from shop fronts. All around me people were waking up to another day, some in makeshift beds on the pavements or emerging from hideouts in the back alleys. Cars hooted and wound their way through the increasingly jam-packed roads. On and on I trudged, only stopping occasionally to ask my way as the streets filled with more and more people. A man with a goat on the back of his moped zoomed by. I could have gone faster if I had been fitter but I was worn out and painfully thin from the worry of the last weeks. Sweat trickled down between my breasts as I dragged my case on.

Finally I caught sight of one of those stinking old buses that had the magical words written on it: 'Delhi Central'. I knew I couldn't possibly walk the whole way or at least then I would arrive after Uncle had woken to the shame of my disappearance. His anger would know no limits, and time was of the essence. I would have to use some of my precious rupees. At least I would know my next step when I reached the station.

The station was crowded with early morning commuters. I scanned the big board in the middle of the station for Jammu Tawi. My heart missed a beat. There was a train! Today at 10:50. I would get a ticket and hide until mid-morning; I couldn't run the risk of Uncle finding me. The possibility was too horrific to contemplate. I stood in the long queue, trying to look as inconspicuous as possible, eyes averted to the ground. Not much longer now. At the front of the queue an old woman was complaining about something to the man in the ticket office. Nothing moved for five minutes. This would be the first place Uncle would come looking for me. He wasn't stupid. Still the woman ranted. I imagined getting on the train and the moment when it would pull away. He couldn't stop the train, could he? And soon, in less than a day, the Giants would embrace me once more. I knew, I just knew that everything would be all right once I was in their sight.

Directly in front of me a woman stood with a babe in arms and three boys all preschool. The youngest boy started crying and pulling at her sari until she crouched down with the baby to comfort him. The oldest boy turned around and stared at me, then stuck his tongue out at me. I smiled and stuck my tongue out too but then the boy's expression changed to alarm. I felt a hand grab my arm tightly. A man in a beige uniform and turban was saying my name.

★ ★ ★

'You slut!' screamed my uncle as soon as the police had gone. 'Did you think you could get away with this? How dare you bring shame on my name and your family?' His hand lashed out and caught me below the eye and sent me crashing back. I slammed against the wall and slid down to the floor. He stood over me, hand raised once more but Auntie grabbed it.

'Enough!' she screeched as she hung onto his arm. Blood fell onto my sari, my golden sari. I wiped my bloody nose on my sleeve.

'You lied to me. You lied about Tahir!' I spat the words at him.

He slowly lowered his arm. 'Go to your room,' he snarled before throwing my suitcase in after me.

I heard him shuffle away, only to return after a couple of minutes. Then the turn of a key in the lock.

12

Tahir stared at the men as they ate their food around the fire. There were eight of them. He sat a little way back and scooped the rice from his bowl. They had untied his hands and feet, for there was nowhere to run to in the darkness. His head throbbed terribly. They had dressed his wound and tied a cloth around his head. He must look like them now. A man with hairy ears walked over to him with a cup of something steaming in his hand, sat down on his haunches and nudged Tahir. The boy took it and sipped the sweet black tea.

'What's your name?' said the man in Urdu, in a deep, rough voice. Later Tahir found out that he was their leader. He couldn't have answered even if he wanted to. The Reckoning had finally stolen his ability to talk. The day he had been taken from his home.

★　★　★

The next day the leader told Tahir his family was dead. 'Liar!' Tahir wanted to shout but no sound came out of him. He just shook his head and tried to run. He heard them laughing behind him. He ran and ran, but then a horse came galloping behind him and a big hand scooped him up. He was too scared of falling off to struggle.

The man took him to a huge stone beside a scrub with a view of the valley, pointed and placed some binoculars in his hand. Tahir looked through them. Everything was blurred. The man shook his head, and showed him how to focus them. Then he pointed again. The boy recognized the meadows and the rocks of his home. But where was his house? Just a pile of stones and half a wall. The wall of their kitchen.

'There you see. No one could have survived that,' the man pronounced.

Tahir sunk to the ground, dropped the glasses and flung his arms up over his head.

He cried and cried until the man told him it was God's will and that God didn't like cry-babies. Which god was he talking about, Tahir asked himself and then he thought of Garuda. Perhaps she had been able to fly away as he wished he could do.

★   ★   ★

They weren't herdsmen. Tahir knew what they were. Freedom fighters. One of them

93

was always watching him. Tahir had known plenty of Muslims before the Reckoning but he had never met a freedom fighter before. They had long beards apart from one other boy who must have been about fifteen or so. The other boy told him he must join them. Hindus and Muslims must fight side by side, he said. He never saw them take the cloths off from around their heads. They were kind to him but he still couldn't talk to them. He was a good listener, though; he watched the men and took in everything they said. Night after night he slept in their camp which they moved every few days. No one must find them, they told him. He would be shot like the rest of them. The soldiers rarely took prisoners.

Sometimes they spent the night in caves. The men seemed awfully serious, always planning the route they would take the next day and talking about the murderers on their heels. They rode for days, Tahir clinging tightly to the leader as they made their way through the snow. He didn't know where he was. Everything was white. Even the Giants looked different up here. But the rebels were not fazed, they knew the area well, knew where the horses could go without sinking in too deep.

The cold was unbearable. He couldn't feel

his toes. And he was hungry. Soon there wasn't much food left. Only brittle naan and strips of dried meat. He had never eaten meat before, not even at parties. They said he could either eat it or starve. It tasted even worse than it looked. So salty that he ate a handful of snow after he got through his water. There was no point in trying to escape anymore. He would go to sleep and die in the snow.

Finally they crossed the pass and came down from the mountains.

13

I pushed the handle down and banged on the door.

'You can't keep me here!' I screamed.

No reaction. Just the noise of the lift moving. I looked around. I had to do something. I grabbed a book from the shelf and started tearing the pages out of it. Screwing them into balls and throwing them at the door. Then I sat down amongst the litter.

My meals were brought to me and I was only allowed out for a brief wash in the mornings or to go to the toilet. My thoughts circled around Tahir and the wedding. In the Punjab there would be no escape, no way to return to my homeland to find him.

After three days my uncle announced that, out of the goodness of his heart, I would once more have the run of the flat. The front door, however, would be locked at all times. From now on Auntie would only go out when he was home. One of them would always be watching me.

'For your own good, my dear.' He wagged his finger at me almost playfully.

As if his tone could make up for hitting me. 'I cannot allow you to bring shame on us again. If your intended found out about your misconduct, the deal would be annulled.'

The deal? Of course, he was making money out of me!

Uncle carried the keys to the front door on him at all times and I was still locked in my room at night, usually after the evening meal. I saved my tears for then, trying not to let them hear. I would not give him that satisfaction.

Gradually anger replaced my misery. How dare he? How dare anyone lock me in? Did he own me? Had he bought me at a bazaar? The wedding was less than two weeks away. I looked out at the night skyline. Out there, someone must be able to help me. Surely it couldn't be legal to lock a girl up. But the police had brought me back. I couldn't expect help from them. Nobody would help me. I was a girl, not a holy cow.

I took my shawl out of my suitcase and wrapped it round me and looked at my possessions. Just a few clothes and some letters. Uncle had taken my money off me; there was no way I could even buy a ticket now. I must accept my lot until I saw some chance to escape. For Tahir's sake. If I ever got away again I would have to travel light. I fingered the letters and the condolence cards. Best get rid of them. Start with the cards first, perhaps tomorrow I might be up to throwing the letters away, too. One last look at the cards. I tore up the first one from one of my teachers at my school. An older mistress who had taken a shine to me early on. In the bin it went, ripped in two. And then came the one from the Scottish couple:

You may not remember us, but should you ever need any help, please don't hesitate to get in touch.

How could they help me when they lived on the other side of the world? I tore up six more cards and went to bed.

★ ★ ★

That night the lady with bright red hair appeared in my dreams. I could still remember her in the morning. She and her husband had both been Pa's close friends. How I would love to talk to someone who knew him. The key turned. Another dreadful day of nothingness lay in front of me. I heard Uncle shut and lock the front door. Then the sound of Auntie heading for the bathroom. I got up quietly, fished the pieces of card from the bin, went out into the hallway and took the phone with its cord round the door into my room. My hand trembled as I dialled the endless number. It rang for ages. Something clattered outside. I stopped and checked where Auntie was. Then I tried again. This time someone answered immediately. I was so shocked that I nearly hung up.

'Mr Hamilton?' I whispered.

PART 2

PART 2

14

Scotland, 1973

Mountain peaks pierced the pink blanket of cloud and stars were beginning to appear above the setting sun as I flew through the heavens with Mr and Mrs Hamilton. Tahir was somewhere down there but staying in the Punjab wouldn't have helped him one bit. I was leaving my homeland and my brother with no idea of the future. The only thing that mattered was that I wasn't getting married! I couldn't help cheering inside when I remembered my uncle's face as he opened the door to my Scottish saviours. How I had peered through the bedroom door, my heart thumping like a drum. Uncle stood in the hallway, his face glowing dark red, sweat running down into the creases of his double chin.

'Mr Bhatt, we are old friends of the family. We have come all the way from Britain. We knew Jaya's father very well. Could we come in and see Jaya for a moment?' said Mrs Hamilton.

Uncle didn't say a thing. Why didn't he

step aside and let them in? He looked like a giant baby turtle who couldn't decide whether to jump into the water for the first time or not. Mrs Hamilton added, 'He would not want this union for her. Jaya doesn't want to get married. She told us so much herself. She has a choice now. We want to take responsibility for her.'

This was the worst thing she could have said! She did not know my uncle. I had no chance now! I wanted to run out to them and shatter the glass wall of duty that lay between us but there was no such luck. My uncle would call the police and have them arrested. It was like watching a film I could never star in.

Uncle was shouting, 'Impossible! This is not Scotland. Jaya has been promised. It is a question of honour and as good as written in blood! There is the matter of her *dahej*. A great deal of money is involved! No, there can be no going back, not in India!' He went to shut the door in their faces.

Dread flooded my body. I moved slowly out towards them, like you would to a cliff edge, my guts turning to jelly. I wished they had never come. Uncle would make me pay for their visit dearly. He would lock me in my room and tell me what terrible people I knew. Make my last days here even worse than the hell I was anticipating. I could feel the bile rising in my tummy. Perhaps he would marry me off tomorrow! I was going to be sick there and then on the carpet. Mr Hamilton, who had been standing quietly behind Mrs Hamilton, moved forward and put his foot in the door as he chuckled.

'Och, I see. It's the money you're worried about, Mr Bhatt. We are . . . of course willing to cover the costs you may have incurred and a wee bit more — ' he coughed, ' — for the immense sadness you must undoubtedly be feeling at the loss of your niece.' Was he mad? Uncle was certainly going to explode!

To my astonishment, Uncle flung open the door. 'Come in, come in, why didn't you say so before?' His beady eyes started to sparkle and dart to the hallway where Auntie was listening. 'Vitra! Bring us some tea. Mr Hamilton, of course we are willing to discuss the situation. My wife has found Jaya invaluable in the household.' As I slid into the living room, Uncle went to stroke my cheek but I instinctively drew back. 'I don't know how we could possibly manage without the girl, for we are no longer young as you can see. All these months we have fed and clothed her without a thought for ourselves like grandparents.'

Was this my uncle talking?

Less than an hour later, I had packed my bags and my papers. Even though I knew so little about my new companions, I didn't care. I had to get out. And then I was bowing to Uncle and kissing Auntie's hands as Mr Hamilton carried my suitcase into the lift. A pale blue cheque from the Royal Bank of Scotland was all that remained of me on the dining room table.

★ ★ ★

It was dark when we landed and there was no escaping the wind and the rain that whipped my sari when I emerged from the plane. Half expecting the bearded official to stop me from entering the country, I was surprised to find myself ushered through and on my way to the car with the Hamiltons, my British passport still clutched firmly in my hand.

'Wake up, Jaya. We're home,' said Mrs Hamilton. Home, how could I be home? Fog enshrouded the house and the dampness overcame my efforts to stay awake and take in my new surroundings.

I clung to the hot water bottle in my bed and stared into the fire, trying to suppress the doubts lurking in the recesses of my mind. I had had no other choice but to leave. Gone were my lakes and meadows forever. I felt like a lotus blossom that had been carried away by the wind.

*   *   *

A sliver of light cut the curtains. Where was I? Kashmir, Delhi? What a strange room! It was round. There was a sprig of flowers on the table in front of the window and embers still glowing in the fireplace. Somewhere far below dishes clinked. I sat up slowly. My feet touched the cool wooden floor. I slipped my shawl over my shoulders and pulled the velvet drapes apart.

The ocean! A murky grey slate stretching out to the horizon and merging so seamlessly with the skies that it was hard to tell where the one started and the other stopped. To my right, two hunchbacked trees waved at the distant lighthouse like old women on cliffs that plunged into the sea. I was in a place neither limited by mountains nor buildings, leaving me more exposed and vulnerable than ever. I sat down on my bed again. How on earth would I ever get used to living here?

I pulled my shawl tighter around my shoulders. What had Ma always told me? I shouldn't think too much. Anything was better than life with a man more than twice my age. I dressed and walked tentatively down a flight of stairs to a hallway and then down the grand staircase that led to the ground floor. Music was coming from a room where I found Mrs Hamilton sitting at the dining table, sipping a cup of tea with a fire burning fiercely in the hearth.

'Jaya, did you sleep well? Sit down, are you hungry?'

Words got stuck in my throat and tears started to trickle down my face. Mrs Hamilton jumped up and put her arms around me. Her warm, comforting arms felt so good. No one had done that to me since I had left home. Something Auntie Vitra had been incapable of doing.

'There, there. You're safe now,' she said as she pulled a crisp white handkerchief out of her pocket and handed it to me.

'Sorry,' I sniffed. 'I don't know what's the matter with me.'

'Nonsense. It must be completely over-whelming for you. How about a cup of tea and some bacon and eggs?' I could smell the odour of meat cooking.

'I'm afraid I don't eat meat,' I said, feeling more of a misfit than ever.

'How silly of me! I should have thought. Help yourself to some toast.'

I was used to eating everything with my right hand, not with a knife and fork. I had never used a knife for anything but slicing vegetables. Not wanting to show myself up, I took a plain slice.

'Jaya, there was a terrible storm here on Tuesday and I need to check on the state of the grounds. Would you like to come?'

I nodded and finished my toast.

'I hope you don't mind but I asked Mrs Craig, our housekeeper, to bring along some of her daughter's clothes. Your sari is beautiful but it's bitterly cold outside. Sheena is about a year older than you, I think, and her clothes would be better for going out in. It's only until we can get you kitted out properly.'

★ ★ ★

The jeans fitted with the help of a belt and the baggy red pullover didn't look too bad on me. A serious young woman, not a girl, stared back at me from the mirror as I pulled my long dark hair out over it.

'How bonny you look in Sheena's pull-over!' Mrs Craig wiped her hands on her apron. She had prominent cheekbones and eyes as bright as Tahir's. 'That top always made my lass look a wee bit pale but I might have knitted it 'specially for you. Call me Aileen, everyone does. It's good to have someone young in the house again. The place is much too quiet these days with the bairn gone, if you ken what I mean. Anytime you want a chinwag, I'd be pleased of the company. And if you want to lend a hand . . . ' She plunged her hands back into the pastry and chuckled. 'But you'd better have a couple of days to settle in first.'

A bairn? What on earth was she talking about? Was there something wrong with my chin? I mumbled something about coming back soon and almost ran out.

Despite my warm jacket and boots made of rubber (too big, but two pairs of socks soon fixed that) the damp seeped through my clothing into my bones when we walked out into the wind. Back in our Vale, you could dress for the cold even when the rivers froze but here it seemed useless.

From the outside the house looked like a castle with its two small towers on either side. I could make out my room in the left tower above one where someone must still have been sleeping, for the curtains were drawn. The grounds spread out in front of us with manicured hedges and a lawn glistening with rain. Out of nowhere, a drenched black and white dog shot out and jumped up on Mrs

110

Hamilton before targeting me.

'Down, Beauly, down, leave her alone!' It rolled over to expose its shaggy underside, offering me a paw in the process. I bent down to take it and stroked its smooth head.

'Meet the Lord of the Manor. He seems to love you. He usually takes to women but not quite as quickly as this. Dogs are such fine judges of character, don't you think? He's completely mad now because we're back. Beauly, it's OK! She's here to stay.'

I smiled. 'Can I take Beauly for walks?'

'Och, you'd be doing us a favour. We just can't seem to wear him out, and there's so much to do here. Come on, I'll show you around. You couldn't possibly call me Marie, could you? Mrs Hamilton makes me feel so ancient.'

My face burned even in the wind. How could I possibly call her Marie? A person of such respect for me. With his tail wagging and his ruffled fur standing upright against the wind, Beauly led the way along a path lined with low border hedges. We entered the walled garden.

'It used to be a kitchen garden but I couldn't resist putting in another flowerbed. There wasn't much to go by when we first came here. The previous owner bought the place for his wife but she died four years later of a stroke.'

'How awful!'

'Terrible. He simply couldn't bear it. Upped and left almost immediately. The house fell into total disrepair and the grounds . . . you can't imagine what they looked like! I've got some photos on the wall in my study. I tried my hand at gardening in the beginning but with no joy. The trouble is, you see, the earth here is no good at all. Not enough of it and poor quality at that. Much too rocky. I had some rich red earth shipped up from Devon and it transformed the place. I can grow plants here that would have no chance otherwise . . . Oh dear, I'm boring you, aren't I? I shall shut up immediately.'

'No, Mrs Hamilton, err . . . Marie, I mean.' It felt so wrong calling her that. I could never have done it in India. 'Pa loved plants and animals.'

'Yes, I know.' She took my arm. 'Where would you like to go now?'

'The sea. I've never seen the sea before! Until this morning, that is.'

'What are we waiting for then?'

With Marie in front of me, I braved my way down the narrow steps leading to the small rocky cove where Beauly was already sniffing around. The water was directly in front of me. It drew me towards it like a magnet. I had to feel it on my skin! Even though I couldn't swim, I took off my boots and waded into the water as Marie watched incredulously. It was cold but nothing like the freezing torrents that rushed down from our Giants. Beauly raced in and out of the water, barking at the water I kicked at him. I stooped to pick up a floating strand of seaweed and smelt it, then dipped my fingers in the sea to taste the salt. It was just as Pa said! How I wished Tahir could see this, too.

★ ★ ★

The photos on the wall in Mrs Hamilton's study of a rundown abandoned house and a rambling overgrown garden bore little resemblance to the place I was now standing in.

'Why don't you explore your new home while I see to the post?'

My new home. Emotions pressed in on me like the crowds in Delhi. How could this strange place be a home to me? I started climbing the stairs. A poster of a human skull greeted me at the very top of the other tower. What kind of a person slept here? The door was ajar and I saw that the room was round like mine. The shelves were filled with sports trophies and books, lots of books, travel guides, a couple on rugby and others on architecture. Beer bottles, all different, stood

113

to attention on the windowsill.

A young man white-water rafting peered from a photo on the mantelpiece. Like Stuart, only darker, the same stature, the same eyes, but thinner with a mop of longish, curly chestnut hair escaping from a helmet. White teeth flashed at me. Undeniably their son. Another photo showed him with his arms around the waists of two girls in long flowing evening dresses. This time with short hair and a moustache, dressed up in a black jacket with silver buttons, a waistcoat, a white shirt, a bow tie and a Scottish sarong.

Down the stairs again to the next floor, I knocked and opened the first door. A suitcase lay on a white rug at the foot of a four-poster bed facing the sea. A half-finished watercolour of a stormy sea stood on an easel to the right. Silk pyjamas, the kind you could buy at every street corner in Delhi, lay on the bed. A black bra dangled from the back of a chair. I backed out in horror and quickly shut the door. The next one was locked. The one with the drawn curtains. I tiptoed away and went down the grand stairway

A library! Book shelves lined three sides of it from floor to ceiling, with a gallery to access the higher levels. There were cushy brown armchairs with green tasselled cushions, and an intricately-patterned Persian carpet lay in front of the roaring fire. A chessboard took pride of place on a table in the corner. I picked up the beautiful, smooth white figure of the queen.

The leather-bound books on the lower level were kept behind metal and glass fronts, so I climbed the ladder to examine the others. I hesitated before touching them, and then remembered what Marie had said. Home, she had called it my home. My fingers touched the spines of the books until I found *Kim* by Kipling. I climbed back down, sat in one of the armchairs, tucked my feet up underneath me and journeyed back to India.

'Jaya.'

My heart leapt into my mouth. I opened my eyes. Mr Hamilton was looming over me. 'I didn't mean to give you a shock. I just thought it best to wake you.'

'I . . . I was going to put it back.'

'No, it's good that someone's reading them. Which one is it?'

I held up the book.

'Aye,' he said, 'if I were stranded on some South Sea island — not such a dismal prospect, actually — that's one of the few I'd take. You keep it as long as you like and help yourself to any of the others, too. They're only gathering dust.'

He sat down in the armchair opposite,

shook out his newspaper and we both read until I got up and walked over to the chessboard.

'You don't happen to play, do you?' said Mr Hamilton, looking at me like a puppy waiting for a ball.

'Pa taught me.'

'Err, well then . . . You wouldn't consider a game with an old fogey like me, would you?'

I sat down at the board. 'Black or white?' I asked before he started grinning like the boy in the photo. I didn't realize that we'd been playing so long until Marie came in just as the grandfather clock outside chimed one.

'Give her a break, Stuart. She's only just got here. And anyway lunch is ready.'

'No! I'm enjoying myself,' I protested.

'Well, just don't let him bully you.'

'No chance.' I snapped up his knight.

Mr Hamilton slapped his thigh. 'The lass has me in a corner but I'm not giving up that easily. Just you wait 'til after lunch!'

* * *

The sound of a hoover had woken me up. A door slammed. I slipped on my *chappals* and wandered down to the bathroom. When I came out again, the door to the locked room was standing ajar. I couldn't help but walk towards it. The curtains were now pulled to one side. A picture of a girl on a pony, with red-gold hair, the same colour as Marie's, smiled at me from over the fireplace. There were dolls in one corner and a collection of cuddly toys on the bed. What was a child doing here? There was no child in the house, I was sure. Over on the shelf another picture. Of Marie, much younger, pushing a child in a wheelchair. The same girl, only paler and wrapped in blankets. A noise behind me made me freeze.

'I'll do yours while you're having breakfast.' Aileen was standing there with a stepladder.

'I'm sorry.' I glanced back at the picture one more time.

'That's Lily. They lost her to leukaemia when she was six. The bairn never knew her, bless him. He was born a good two years after they lost the battle. They didn't get lucky again. That was it. No more lads or lasses after him.'

Poor Marie and Mr Hamilton. They too had lost someone they loved so much. A bond was growing between us.

Aileen picked up a teddy bear and dusted its head. 'She kept fretting, taking the lad's temperature, that sort of thing but he was hardly ever ill. He's kind of happy go lucky. Studying architecture in Edinburgh.' She

117

paused and put the teddy carefully back in its place. 'He loved making sandcastles on the beach when he was little even then.'

★ ★ ★

Mr Hamilton or Stuart as I was now to call him (impossible!) wasn't around that much, though, because his clinic in Glasgow took up most of his time. People came from far and wide for treatment. Even film stars.

One evening, we were watching a documentary on schools in Glasgow, when Stuart asked, 'What do you think of my nose?' He winked and nodded towards the presenter, a pretty blonde woman.

'Perfect!' I replied.

In the evenings he was usually up for a stroll or a game of chess. One night he got up in mid-play to warm his hands at the fire. 'He never would have stayed here, you know.'

'Who?'

'Darshan. Your father.' He shifted uneasily from leg to leg. 'I make people more attractive. That didn't interest him . . . Mind you, I did a remarkable job on that boy with second-degree burns last year if I do say so myself. But it isn't my bread and butter, and your father knew that. We got talking about his clinic in the last few months before his death. I wanted to help him out once he'd got it going. Of course, I couldn't have moved to Kashmir but I wanted to free myself up for a couple of months every year and do some vital surgery to really help people. If only we had got that far.'

Stuart understood how important a clinic would have been.

15

Marie was leafing through a book when I entered the dining room one morning. 'Have you got any plans?'

Still sleepy, I asked, 'Plans?'

'For your future.'

She was throwing me out! I was to move on. Of course. Why on earth would strangers take me in? I wasn't their daughter, after all. I should have stayed in India. At least I would have somewhere to call home now.

'Jaya, what on earth's the matter?'

I could see myself crawling back to my uncle. 'I'll go and pack my things!'

'No, you've got it all wrong! How often do I have to tell you this is your home? But we can't let you go to seed out in the wilds with us wrinklies for company. You need an education, to meet other young people. It's the least we can do for your father.'

The mention of Pa brought me to my senses.

'Now listen to me,' said Marie. 'There's no secondary school nearby and we want to give you the very best of chances. Alastair boarded and he loved it. Let's find a good school together.' She pushed the book towards me. 'Look at these. I've put crosses next to the ones we might consider.'

The first place looked more like a beauty spa than a school, with sports fields, tennis and squash courts and a swimming pool. There were science and language labs, a studio, a theatre and, finally, a table of outstanding exam results. I looked at the fees. Surely only princesses went there. 'This is crazy. They cost far too much!'

'Don't be silly, we want to do as much for you as for Alastair. What about this one? Would you consider looking at it? I mean, we've haven't asked you yet but don't you want to finish your education? Darshan told us how bright you are.'

In another life, I thought.

★   ★   ★

A beautiful Georgian mansion sat in park-like grounds and woods. We drove up the sweeping drive to where parents gathered in front of the main building, exchanging last words with their children or carrying suitcases into the building. Although I was wearing uniform (maroon blazer and hat) I felt that all eyes were upon me. I must be the only foreigner here. Stuart had kissed me on

121

the cheek and wished me good luck before heading off to work. How to say goodbye to Marie? She wasn't family after all but she made it all feel so normal with her warm embrace.

'I'm sure you'll have plenty of friends when I next see you!'

I watched her car pull away and fought the urge to run after her. I had never felt so alone, not even in Delhi.

★ ★ ★

I had never shared a room in my life before if you didn't count me crawling into Granny's bed occasionally when mighty thunderstorms sent us all cowering. I started to unpack my belongings. First out was a rust-patterned cloth with elephants to hang on the wall above the bed.

'Make sure you put your stamp on your room,' said Marie in the shop that sold Indian things.

My roommate had certainly done that already. Her belongings were everywhere. A man with huge lips stuck his tongue out at me from above her bed. I put fresh linen on my bed and on top my shatush shawl, soft and familiar. I walked over to the other bed and looked at the maths books stacked on the shelf and the half-open French book on the desk. I picked it up and stared at the strange words. *Plus-que-parfait.* The door banged open and I dropped the book back on the desk. In walked a shortish, stocky girl with a mass of freckles, frizzy white-blonde hair and a pretty upturned mouth.

'You'll have to respect my privacy if we're going to get on.'

My cheeks burned but then she stuck her hand out. I took it, too dumbstruck to say anything.

'I'm Hayley. That's Caroline's bed. We were absolute buddies. Shared for three years but she's gone back to South Africa now. I spent last Christmas there. I suppose the two of us'll just have to make do.'

Before I had a chance to say anything, she exclaimed, 'Is that a dead animal on your bed?'

'Grandmother's shawl.'

She walked over, picked it up, smelt it and let it drop back on my bed.

'Well, each to his own, I say. Did your parents drop you off?'

'Sort of.'

'Oh divorced, are they? Snap. I was dumped here years ago. Got a new brother now.'

There seemed no point in explaining. No one else had my kind of background here.

Misery stabbed me every morning. I found myself bottom of the class in almost every subject. It was all too much for me. Changing from one system to the other would have been a tall order at the best of times, but after missing so much, keeping up was nigh impossible. Maths was taught in such a completely different way here that I wondered if it could possibly be the same subject and having never studied French before, they started me on Latin which simply compounded my sense of being an utter failure. Hayley, in contrast, seemed to sail through most of the tests. Even though I devoted every waking minute to schoolwork, I wasn't making any real progress and I hadn't made a single friend. You're an outsider and not meant to be here, a voice whispered in my head every evening before I went to sleep.

I made my letters to Marie and Stuart sound bright and cheery enough, telling them about Mr Gray, whose enthusiasm for biology was infectious, and my swimming lessons. Back home I always sat fully dressed at the side of the lake, watching my brothers diving in and splashing about wildly. Miss Mackenzie had been shocked when she discovered how frightened I was of actually being submerged in water and consequently arranged for special lessons. I thought I was

124

the first girl in the history of the school unable to keep her head above water but apparently a Chinese trio had been the same the previous term.

Dressed in a black swimsuit which would never have been acceptable back home, I fought my fear of drowning. Until one day I managed a whole length all by myself!

⋆　⋆　⋆

On a windy autumn morning, Miss Evans, the headmistress, called me into her office.

'We can't access your old reports and your work is giving us cause for grave concern.'

'Everything's so different here,' I answered feebly.

She sighed. 'I'm afraid we have certain standards here, Jaya. Unfortunately we can't make exceptions. I hope you understand. We expected your work to be better considering your entrance exam results so we shall be keeping a much closer eye on you from now on. If there's no sign of improvement, we may have to take certain steps.'

⋆　⋆　⋆

'Where's my shawl?' I asked Hayley, who wandered in with a towel around her head.

My shawl always lay on top of my bed.

'Your what?' she said, wide-eyed.

'My shawl. It was there on my bed this morning.'

She shrugged her shoulders. 'Search me.' She threw herself on the bed.

Shrieks resounded from below. I ran over to the window to see the caretaker fishing something brown out of the pond down below. Girls were standing around laughing. I turned round to catch a fleeting smirk on Hayley's face. I couldn't believe it. She had thrown my most precious possession out the window.

'You bitch!' I marched over and slapped her face, then rushed down the stairs without waiting for her response. Tears fell into the sink of the laundry room in the basement, as I set about washing out the stinking brown water. It would never smell of home again.

16

Tahir's body ached. His legs almost gave way underneath him when he dismounted. A woman with a blue headscarf led him away. He could only understand snippets of what she said because she didn't speak the kind of Urdu he was used to. She showed him where he could wash. He was so happy to be able to scrub the dirt away and when he looked down at his feet, the water was black with grime. The aroma of food wafted towards him. He found steaming hot vegetables and rice on the table. He ate so much that he thought he would be sick but still he kept eating. And the woman simply smiled. For the first time in weeks he felt clean, warm and safe, and he slept on something soft.

Over the following months he learned to hide whenever a passing tradesman came into the village.

'If they find you, they will kill you. Or they will make you talk. And then you will wish you were dead. Nothing must endanger the cause. Do you understand? Nothing!' said Omar, whose passion was frightening. He told Tahir that his god had made the Earth shake because the people had done nothing to save Kashmir. 'Allah will strike again. For we have learned nothing! Kashmiris of all faiths must join together to save our Vale. We will only be safe when we have freed people from the oppressors. Pakistani or Indian, both want to bleed us dry!'

Tahir shivered. What if Omar was right? What if the gods expected him to do something? The boy began to understand that there were many terrible things in this world, but that there was something you could do about them.

17

'How about a trip to Edinburgh?' Marie suggested when I escaped to the Mains at half term.

'Love to,' I replied when all I wanted to do was hide away in my room.

Edinburgh was like a black and white negative in the drizzle. Rows of gloomy run down terraced houses greeted us on the drive in but at least they were not the sprawling ghettos of Delhi. No beggars lived on the streets apart from one old man I saw sleeping on a bench in a dirty coat with holes in his shoes and a half-finished bag of chips in his hands. And children passed but they never asked for money. A few of them didn't look well off but none crippled or wasted. There were faint exhaust fumes in the air but I could feel the sea breeze. I could almost imagine living here.

'Boys are so boring to go shopping with,' said Marie as she put her arm through mine. 'Enough of school uniforms. We're getting you something pretty!'

She could hardly contain her excitement when we found a beautiful crimson dress that pulled in at the waist and made me look . . . well, I had never worn anything like it before. Then I looked at the price tag.

'I've never had a dress that cost this much before!'

'Don't be such a spoilsport!' Marie said as she handed over a wad of notes. As we sat in the Italian restaurant afterwards Marie beamed. 'It's been such a great afternoon. Let's do this more often, Jaya. It's the kind of thing I miss with only menfolk around.'

She needed me, too.

★ ★ ★

One afternoon I wandered back from a ramble along the cliffs, breathless and clutching a bunch of wild flowers when suddenly Beauly, who had been happily trotting along next to me, tore away from my side and ran towards a red MG parked outside the house. I stepped inside, put the flowers down carefully on top of the table in front of the hallway mirror and was just unbuttoning my duffle coat when I heard a deep manly laugh.

'Get down, you old softie!'

I found Beauly standing astride a figure on the sofa, trying to lick his face. I froze. I had never been alone in a room with a young man before. The man turned to look at me with that unmistakable grin. Stuart and Marie's son. He had long wavy hair and a beard and he was much more grown up and muscular than in the picture in his room. He looked me up and down for a moment and I felt myself blushing. My hair must be all over the place from the wind, I thought.

'Hi, I'm Alastair,' he said, pushing Beauly down and springing to his feet so I had to look up to him. 'Mummy's been going on and on about you and the old man says you play a mean game of chess.'

Marie burst into the room. 'Alastair! You're back!'

He kissed her on the cheek. 'You've been hiding my new sister from me.'

What a thing to say! Surely, Marie would put him right but she simply glowed with happiness. He had the same effect on Aileen for when I heard him chatting to her in the kitchen afterwards, her voice had a bright ring to it.

$\star$ $\star$ $\star$

Jazz music resonated down the stairs from his room while Alastair unpacked. Over lunch, he looked at me with those amber eyes. 'How are you settling in?'

Strange men didn't address me directly where I came from. 'I love it here,' I managed to answer.

'St Medan's brilliant, isn't it?' I opened my mouth to answer but he had already turned to Marie. 'Laurie's sister went there.'

'That's right. What's she up to these days? Didn't she do a gap year in Santiago . . . ?'

I stared at the fine dark hair just above his knuckles and was so wrapped up in trying not to spill my soup or do anything else foolish that I didn't realize he was talking to me until he repeated, 'Tennis . . . d'you play?'

'Me? Well, I used to at school but I haven't played for ages.' My mind flashed back to the courts in front of the mountains. I looked out the window. It was still glorious yet surely I couldn't play against a man.

'That's good news. The op put an end to the famous old Hamilton serves.'

Stuart nodded. 'My knees. Can't run about like that anymore. Alastair plays for the university team.'

Why was a tennis champ wasting his time with the likes of me? Still, I didn't want to appear unfriendly, so after lunch we went out to inspect the tennis court.

'It's still playable despite the cracks in the surface,' Alastair said as he produced two racquets, some balls and a net from the shed at the side of the court.

'I grew up messing about on this.' He returned my serve gently and placed his shots with such precision that hitting them back should have been as easy as picking ripe mulberries except my days with a tennis racquet in my hand were an awfully long time ago. After about half an hour I said, 'Sorry, I missed that one again. Shall we stop? You must be getting very bored.'

'No. Your backhand is decent considering you haven't played for a while and anyway, I want to have someone to slam the ball against!' He jumped over the net, placed his hand over mine without even asking and adjusted my grip. His fingers were warm and firm. A man could never have touched my hand like this back home. I was embarrassingly conscious of how close he was to me. He sprinted back to his side and went on to show me how to put more spin on my slice. We stopped as the wind picked up and I came off feeling exhilarated but tired. I hadn't been put through my paces like that for a long time. But it wasn't the only thing. This wonderful man was taking me seriously. Me, an Indian girl from the mountains.

As I headed off to have a shower, Alastair called after me, 'I'm going for a spin tomorrow . . . if you fancy coming.'

Tennis? Did he want another game so soon? Marie appeared on the landing and must have read my confusion. 'A drive, he's going for a drive.'

Where I came from girls didn't get into strange men's cars. Girls were never alone with any man except their brothers. Suddenly everything slid into place. He's like a brother, an older brother, I told myself. It doesn't mean a thing here and I wanted to go so much that I would have told myself anything. Marie smiled and said, 'Mind you're back for dinner. Alan and Ruth are coming. Where are you going, Al?'

'Thought we'd just head west. Drive to a couple of lochs.'

Dear Brahma. What was a loch? 'Count me in,' I heard myself saying.

★ ★ ★

The road wound in and out of the hilly coastline until we turned inland and drove for miles across swathes of rugged landscape and gentle hills. Then mountains! Nothing like my guardians, more like their younger brothers. But mountains all the same. Alastair stopped the car next to a lake at the foot of the range. He pointed to the highest. 'That's Ben above Loch Linnhe.'

Ah! So a loch was a lake. 'Ben?' I asked.

'Ben Nevis.'

As I drank in the sight, Alastair got out and started putting the roof of the car down. When we set off again the feel of the wind in my face and my hair was liberating. This was so much fun. Next stop was a ruin on the banks of another loch that stretched out of sight like a massive river. Alastair spread out a red chequered blanket on the grass and produced a basket of food from the boot.

'Where did you get that from?'

'I know where Aileen keeps the goodies!' The wind had dropped and the banks of the loch reflected in the water like a watercolour. I took a sip of elderberry juice.

'Can you see Nessie?' he asked.

'Nessie?'

'The monster caught here in prehistoric times. They've got photos to prove it. A head and a series of humps. She's a real magnet for tourists!' he said.

'She's not a monster. She's a serpent,' I explained.

Alastair raised his eyebrows.

'A Scottish serpent.' I told him how Nag made the water turn turquoise.

'Well, you've certainly put a whole new slant on Nessie. Tell me more about your valley and the gods.'

'Shiva lives in the cave of Amaranth. She's made of ice and only fully formed in the holy month of *Shravan*. Pilgrims walk for days to see her. We wanted to go as a family when my brothers were bigger . . . '

I stared out at the water, which wasn't turquoise but patchy blue and black as the clouds raced over the sun that spotlighted the ruin. I didn't want to talk about Tahir and Rajan but it felt soothing to describe the place where I had grown up. A drop of water fell on my cheek and then it started raining lightly. The weather changed from one moment to the next in this country. Alastair put up the roof of the car before the skies opened and drenched everything. On the cosy drive home, I thought how wonderful it was that there was someone I could talk to. Gods like Nessie made a big difference, too.

18

Months passed and Tahir began to learn their ways. His hosts in the settlement were quiet folk who huddled around the fire at night and sang songs to keep their spirits up. When the days became longer, the rebels said goodbye. Tahir was sad to leave the blue-scarfed woman but he didn't belong here. He didn't belong anywhere anymore. He had come as a boy but now he was a man. He no longer needed the soft motherly touch of a woman anymore. This time the horses and donkeys carried the heavy load and they walked until the first cave where they left most of the supplies.

'We can come back,' said Omar.

This time Tahir had his own horse. Riding was easy, speaking was still impossible. A horse was not his only new acquisition. The leader gave Tahir a gun and showed him how to use it. Tahir shot the bottle on his third attempt.

'Good, very good. You're a natural. See if you can hit a moving target,' said the older man and pointed. 'Up there. That bird.'

Tahir couldn't do that. He wouldn't be

here if not for Garuda. The gun made him strong but still the words melted on his tongue. Omar pushed him to one side. 'You're no better than a girl,' he snapped and snatched the gun from his hands, took aim and fired. The buzzard plunged, flapping its wings madly, to the ground. Omar told him to fetch the bird with its beautiful feathers and proud curved beak. It was still warm in his hands. Had Garuda suffered before she died?

★ ★ ★

In the days that followed the men became nervous. They knew something he didn't. They whispered behind his back and fell silent when he approached them. Tahir was frightened but he had no one else to turn to when they took him to the border control point and no way of asking, either. They watched from a ridge through binoculars. Hours passed. What was so fascinating about a checkpoint? Omar nudged his arm and passed him the glasses. The soldiers were dancing like cockerels about to fight. Marching slowly, then fast, twirling their rifles and flipping them from shoulder to shoulder.

'Change of guards,' Omar explained.

How many years had they trained to pull

that off? If they could do that surely they were able to pick him off at a great distance with their guns? That night when they gathered in the caves, Omar's hands were shaking and when he spoke, his words tumbled out so fast that Tahir had to lean closer to understand him.

'Tomorrow is perfect. No moon and the start of the festival. There will be hoards of people crossing the border.'

They stayed in the cave all day and left under cover of darkness. Perhaps it was special tonight, thought Tahir. Perhaps at the start of the festival, they danced at midnight. But then the leader placed a huge gun in his hand. Looking back, that was the moment when Tahir should have left. When he had any choice in the matter.

'We need every man tonight. You shoot when they shoot. Do you understand?' said Omar.

Tahir nodded. As long as he didn't have to shoot a bird. Omar told him to lie low behind the boulder and left him there. Then the loudest bang and a yellow flare lit up the sky. His ears hurt and something round flew right past him. He looked down. A man's head lay there, his blood-soaked turban half unravelled. Smoke filled the air. Men were screaming. Soldiers firing madly about them.

Tahir shot into the air until he had no bullets left. Something sliced his cheek and sent blood spurting down him. He ran for his life.

★ ★ ★

The wound left a scar. A dark red trench in his cheek, where the bullet had grazed his cheekbone, narrowly missing his eye. They started talking to him as if he were a man, perhaps because Omar never returned from the raid. Captured or killed, no one knew. Tahir didn't tell them that he had only shot into the air. He was even more frightened because he knew what they expected of him after this. Next time he would have to kill someone, he was sure. He couldn't tell them that he would never be able to do that, couldn't even talk let alone beg them to let him go. They would never listen anyway. He shut his eyes and thought of Jaya.

19

The wind howled and the rain was trying to paw its way in through the window when Alastair found me on the rug in front of the fire in the library. He bent down, grabbed *Pride and Prejudice* from me, surveyed the cover and then handed it back to me.

'Who reads Austen these days?'

'I do and you won't have to put up with me much longer. I'm going back at the weekend.'

He stoked the fire vigorously. 'Be bloody dull when you're gone.' Then a smile lit up his face. 'Tell you what, I'll drive you back. What d'you say?'

Why would he want to put himself out for me? 'If you're sure.'

He carried the chessboard towards me and plonked it down in the middle of the rug. 'Now put down that stupid book.' He lay down on the other side of it and propped himself up on his elbows. 'You can be white.'

Beauly came in and collapsed next to me in a welcome gesture of support. It soon became apparent that Alastair was following some hidden strategy. I would take one of his pawns only to lose my bishop to him a couple of moves later. The pressure was intense and although I fought as best I could and held my own over long stretches, he had as much stamina in chess as in tennis.

Aileen brought in some tea and biscuits but we hardly noticed her presence. The game dragged on for a couple of hours until we were only playing by the light of the fire. I had lost most of my pieces. Did he have to win everything? He was looking insufferably smug when I spotted my chance.

'Checkmate!' He had left his king exposed.

He sat up, moved his king to one side, dithered and then put it back. His brows knitted and he thought for a long time. I knew that there was no way out.

'Damn!' He swept the pieces from the board. Beauly barked and I froze.

He sprang to my side and put his hand on my shoulder. 'Sorry, I just really hate losing.'

I started to collect the marble figures. Once all was back in place, I noticed he was looking at me.

'Well, I never!' He scratched his head just like his father. 'Who would've thought that you're that bright underneath it all?'

★   ★   ★

142

We drove in silence down the narrow country lanes with their steep hedges before cutting across the highlands, without encountering more than a couple of cars on our way. Mist licked the bottom of the hills with low-hanging clouds chopping off their tops. After the Sunday roast I was feeling drowsy. When we hit the dual carriageway, I must have nodded off for the next thing I knew, we were taking the familiar slip road off it again. In less than half an hour, we would be back at St Medan's. I dug my fingernails into the palms of my hands, but instead of taking the road signposted to Aberfeldy, Alastair ploughed on in the other direction.

'Where are you going?'

'I used to come down here sailing with friends years ago. Thought we might see if anything's changed. We don't have to get there until five. You're not in any rush, are you?'

'I don't mind if we never get there,' I blurted out. He didn't say anything so I just stared out the window. We drove down a small winding road until we got to a small lake. There were a number of tiny sailing boats skimming the water in the breeze, each with a solitary occupant, a child. We got out of the car and started walking. Hayley and Miss Evans appeared in my mind's eye. The knowledge that within an hour or so I would have to endure them again for another two months was unbearable.

'What's up? Come on, you haven't said a word about school all break. Are they bullying you?' asked Alastair.

I didn't know how to put it in words.

'Look, if school's such a nightmare, get the folks to take you out,' he continued. 'As soon as possible. You don't have to put yourself through much more of it. You're old enough to leave school. You could become an apprentice; start your own business. Whatever. Don't let them push you into anything.'

'No!' I found myself saying. 'I want to do something else.'

'Well, that's good to hear. What?'

I swallowed hard. 'I want to study medicine.'

As soon as I said it, everything changed. I'd finally put into words what had been locked inside me since Kashmir. It was as much a part of me as the spots on a snow leopard. It was not only about me. It was me. Alastair stood back and looked at me. I had never told anyone this before, not since I left Sonamarg and Pa.

'So what's the problem? If you want something, go for it.' He sounded more like a father than a brother. 'Why don't you just

144

knuckle down to work then? Is it the language?'

'Don't be silly,' I rallied. 'We spoke English at my last school, sometimes even at home — in fact my Hindi must be getting quite rusty now.'

Alastair stood there, the wind catching his wavy long hair. I felt so strongly about this man; two weeks ago, he had been a total stranger, now I could tell him things I wouldn't tell another soul.

'I used to be good at everything. I knew what I was working for and Pa believed in me. Then the earthquake happened. It's been so long. I have no idea if I can catch up or if I am even in any state to. Can you imagine what it's like to lose your family?'

Alastair shook his head. 'No, but I can see that you've lost your confidence, too. Jaya, don't let what happened to them crush you, too. You don't want to look back when you're old and think if only . . . You can still do it. You can become whatever you want.'

My plans felt real now that someone finally knew about them. I nodded. The boats all met in the middle of the lake and an image of the *skikaras* on Dal Lake flashed through my mind. The wind carried the muffled voice of the instructor's loudspeaker out over the water to us.

Alastair placed his hands gently on my shoulders.

'You don't have to be afraid of anything now. You have us. The old man and Mummy adore having you around. Nothing's going to happen to you now, do you understand? You've got nothing to lose.'

I nodded.

'Enough secrets, I'm starving.'

How could he possibly be hungry again? When I passed through the school gates with Alastair at my side, something had changed. I had someone who knew my secrets. Alastair was my secret weapon.

20

I surveyed the coastline on the drive up to Peterhead in my Christmas break. My heart did a funny kind of turn every time I thought of Alastair. I couldn't wait to see him again and tell him that I wasn't a total failure any longer in class. Nothing to shout about but at least I was treading water instead of sinking to the bottom of my year. All thanks to him. I imagined the two of us sitting in front of the fire and hearing all his news, too.

'We're a bit low on red wine,' said Marie. 'I don't know if we'll get another delivery of Languedoc before Amanda arrives. We'll just have to take whatever we can find in town to tide us over.'

'Amanda?' I asked as we overtook a transport of pigs.

'Alastair's girlfriend.'

Girlfriend! It took a moment for this to sink in. 'What . . . what's she like?' It was an effort to keep my voice steady.

'Och, I've never met her but I know they'd been friends for quite a while and you know how one thing leads to another.'

I didn't know how I kept a smile on my

face as Marie chose this or that delicacy that Amanda might like. Afterwards I made straight for the beach, stamping savagely on seaweed before shooing Beauly away. He slunk off to inspect a dead crab but soon raced back and shook himself, spraying me with water.

Why hadn't Alastair told me? I felt betrayed that I had emptied my heart to him. Amanda made me face up to my feelings for Alastair. How could I not love this wonderful man? His wavy hair, his grin and the way he took me seriously. But now it was obvious that he had only been acting like a brother to me, not even really that. He was only being kind. I was a Kashmiri, as different from him as my country. We were separated by a cultural rift so wide I couldn't begin to understand what went on in his mind. I stared out at the horizon before sense kicked in. Even if we got on, he was far too old and could only ever be at best a brother to me, nothing more. A seagull flew low over my head. I clambered over the rocks and set off along the beach to the lighthouse. Beauly came up to me with a stick in his mouth. When I finally obliged, he couldn't have been happier.

On coming back, I feigned a headache and lay down on my bed and buried myself in

Anna Karenina. I must have nodded off because I dreamt of walking Beauly across a glacier. I threw a ball, then heard a surprised yelp and a glimpse of his black and white tail as he slid over the edge of a crevasse. I sat bolt upright. It took me a moment to realize where I was even after all those months, but then it dawned on me that Beauly was fast asleep in his basket in the hall. It was all in my mind.

★　★　★

A huge Christmas tree towered over the Mound and strings of lights lit up one side of Princes Street in Edinburgh. The Grassmarket sparkled blue and white, reminding me of Diwali, as Marie and I made our way across it. We bought a pipe for Stuart and a leather wallet and pullover for Alastair. There was talk of a party on New Year's Eve. We stopped off at a delicatessen and came home laden with bags.

'Father Christmas is waiting for these,' said Marie as she disappeared off to her study.

Ah, I knew that their god of Christmas was kind and jolly. Holly hung over the doors and Aileen saved three Christmas cakes from the brink of burning. Stuart dragged a tree into the hall which we set about decorating with red baubles and silver tinsel. I wondered if we would worship it on Christmas Day.

Yet, the most important person still hadn't turned up. I missed Alastair's teasing. I had got a grip on myself but I couldn't stop imagining Amanda. Tall and leggy and most likely blonde.

On Christmas Eve, Marie was wrapping some perfume for Aileen in the sitting room when I heard a car pull up, then barking and a commotion. I looked out the window to see Alastair making a great fuss of Beauly. What had happened to his hair? His head was almost shaven.

Marie stood back and tutted. 'At least you don't look like a hippie.'

He came in and it took all my self-control not to stomp away in disgust. His beautiful hair butchered. This must be Amanda's doing.

'Hi!' He pointed at the mistletoe above me and kissed me on the cheek with a glint in his eyes. I thought how impossible such behaviour would be in India. He seemed very pleased to see me but not as pleased as I was to see him. With or without hair, the hallway still brightened with his presence.

★ ★ ★

150

I found a beautifully wrapped box containing some long, dangly emerald-coloured earrings at the end of my bed. How did they get into my room? Alastair looked so innocent when I came downstairs in my dressing gown. There was a red parcel waiting for me under the tree.

'Why am I getting all these presents?' I asked but Stuart just laughed.

'We're just so happy you're here,' said Marie.

My heart was brimming. How was it possible to feel so much for these people? I unwrapped the present. A radio with a built-in cassette player!

★ ★ ★

I had never experienced such happiness since I had left the Giants. Alastair spent a lot of time with me and once when we were alone after we had had a glass of wine, he went to hug me. I pulled away.

'What's the matter?'

'You can't do that.'

'Why on earth . . . ?'

'It's different in India. Very strict. Men don't hug women before . . . '

'But you're not in India anymore.'

'My uncle nearly married me off before I came here.'

151

'What . . . ? You're kidding.'

He sat down on the settee. He looked at me. 'How is that possible, Jaya? You must be only seventeen.'

'Sixteen actually, I thought Marie and Stuart . . . ' He shook his head and so I told him about my betrothed in the Punjab and how I had run away. He was quiet for an awfully long time but I didn't regret what I had said. His parents knew, why shouldn't he? It wasn't anything I should feel ashamed about.

'But you didn't, did you?' he asked.

'No, I didn't.'

'Is there anything else I should know about you?'

My heart thumped loudly. My brother. Should I tell him? I looked into his eyes and I saw a good person, someone who only wanted to be a friend or perhaps a better brother.

'I think Tahir's alive.'

'Tahir?'

'My younger brother. He was nowhere to be found on the list of the dead.'

'Jaya, I hate to say this but that doesn't mean he's alive.'

'It does for me and I won't rest until I know his fate.'

'But you've got a new life here with us now.

It might be a wild goose chase. You have to accept what happened.'

'Alastair, he's my brother!'

'But you've got me now.'

'Alastair, you're not my brother.'

'True,' he said.

Hogmanay was approaching. Pa had taught us to sing 'Auld Lang Syne', and in Kashmir we too welcomed in the New Year at midnight with friends. Had we just done this to please Pa? I was beginning to doubt my memories which were slowly fading like the footprints of the shatush in the snow. I fought back my homesickness like the urge to vomit.

'Amanda's coming this evening,' said Marie casually but it sounded like a storm warning to me. 'I'm tickled to be finally meeting her,' she added, looking slightly frazzled. 'Would you mind helping a little bit? Aileen will only be coming tomorrow and there's such a lot to do.'

'Of course not.'

I would rather have cleaned all the toilets in Delhi than prepare for Amanda. Still, I put the sheets on her bed and made sure everything was in place in the guest room that happened to be just under Alastair's room. I imagined him creeping into her bed in the wee hours of the morning and gleaned meagre comfort from the thought that they

153

would be uncomfortable in the single bed. I dreaded meeting her, knowing that I would look incredibly unsophisticated beside her.

Finally, a petite figure jumped out of a huge car and ran straight into Alastair's arms. 'Al!'

They kissed for an incredibly long time. I pulled away from the window, braced myself and went down into the hall. Alastair's arm was around her waist. Amanda's oval face was perfectly framed by her cheeky brown bob. I looked into huge brown eyes. 'Hi, I'm Amanda.' Alastair flashed me one of his stupid grins. I did my best to smile back. Amanda seemed at ease as Marie ushered us into the sitting room. Standing there like a ballet dancer, Amanda admired Marie's painting of the heather-covered highlands over the fireplace.

Alastair looked happy. Amanda blended in perfectly. She was so much more like the Hamiltons than I was and, much as I fought it, I couldn't help liking her. She was utterly adorable. Of course she would be. Alastair had chosen her. She didn't demand caviar but tucked into Christmas cake. Quietly spoken yet interesting, she was studying literature, and I found myself talking to her about *Mrs Dalloway*, which I too had discovered in the library. Alastair draped his

154

arm lazily around her shoulders while I tried to concentrate on what she was saying.

A party was just the thing I needed to banish my jealousy. I took particular care getting ready; I didn't want anyone to be ashamed of me even if I wasn't Scottish. I put on a tiny bit of make-up but nothing too obvious and wore the earrings I'd been given for Christmas with my crimson dress. The low neckline made me feel uncomfortable. But there was nothing I could do about it now. Then I remembered what Ma had once told me: 'If you walk in with confidence, you'll make every dress look good.' I would do her proud, I decided, and behave like the good girl she always wanted me to be.

'Jaya! You look so bonny but there's something missing. I know just the thing.'

Marie walked over to her jewellery box and produced a string of pearls.

'They're not really me,' I said. Much too ladylike, I thought, but when she fastened the clasp they set off my golden skin. Stuart said I looked gorgeous but Alastair frowned when I came down the stairs. He must think it's too revealing. Oh well, you can't please everyone, I thought. My cheeks glowed and by the time the five of us had piled into the car, it had started to snow lightly.

'We might have to spend the night there!'

Stuart joked as we turned into the drive that led to a grand manor house.

Lit up like an Indian palace, many gleaming cars were parked outside. Once inside, we milled about amongst friends of Stuart and Marie, and their children. Amanda grabbed my arm after Alastair saw one of his mates.

'I don't know about you but I don't know a soul here,' she said.

Alastair was looking around at her. His friend followed his gaze but she merely waved at them and wandered off with me. I had meant to hate her; now she was the next best thing to a real friend. Alastair's taste in women couldn't be argued with. Amanda took two glasses from the tray suspended in front of our faces containing an orange fizzy drink that smelt good. After Amanda swigged back the contents I took a sip. It was slightly bitter but quite pleasant, and I emptied my glass in time for her to say, 'Come on, let's dance.'

Despite its grandeur, the house felt festive and cosy and the rhythm of the music went straight through me. I didn't mind when Amanda excused herself to dance with Alastair because Hamish, a friend of Alastair's who wore a startlingly white shirt together with a kilt, had joined me. I felt so happy and free. I could do anything I wanted here, I mused, even dance with a man. Alastair and Amanda wandered off to the buffet. The light from the room caught the snowflakes outside. But it was hot inside. When the nice man with the fizzy wine passed, I helped myself to another drink. Hamish laughed and took one, too. This one was different; just as fizzy but clear and dry, and the bubbles went straight up my nose.

Alastair and Amanda were dancing again, her arms around his neck. I didn't want to watch them but wandered on with Hamish by my side. He handed me a new drink as soon as I downed the one in my hand. It was nice of him to look after me. I bumped into Marie; Stuart was talking to a man who was pretending to hit an imaginary golf ball.

'Are you enjoying yourself, my dear?' said Marie.

I nodded enthusiastically. Stuart laughed loudly about something with the golfer.

'Shall I show you around?' Hamish took my arm.

We walked on. Such a marvellous place; so warm, so welcoming. The people around me got larger and then receded. My steps felt light, as if I were walking on rubber. These people must be incredibly rich, even their floors were special. It was so pleasant here, I felt free and light. I looked over at the buffet, faintly remembering that I had been hungry, really quite hungry when I arrived. But now? The last thing I wanted was food, in fact when I thought of food I started to feel a wee bit queasy. People were talking all around me, looking at me, smiling. What nice people! Someone was pointing out of the window at the snow outside.

'You must see the conservatory, it's magic,' said Hamish.

He was right. It was a white wood and glass dream, with plants that would have looked more at home in Delhi. They cast deep shadows on the blanket of snow outside. The doorway to the conservatory was beginning to tilt at strange angles. I sank into a plush armchair as the room swayed. Hamish was now holding my hand and coming much too close. What would Ma say to this? Us being quite alone was improper. Things may be different here but I didn't like it, either. The music seemed far away and I wanted to tell him to move away but couldn't seem to find the words. I needed air, not someone staring at me that closely. I had to get out. The room started to turn like the merry-go-round I had once ridden on in Jammu. Instead of glass walls, I saw tall mountains. No, the mountains were outside. I got up and stumbled towards the French windows, fighting the impulse to vomit on the floor. I had to get out, breathe fresh air, and get to the mountains. I tried to open the doors; I was going to be sick, here, in front of Hamish. I couldn't open them. I wished Hamish would leave me alone. A hand was on my shoulder.

'What the hell did you do to her?' snarled Alastair. I didn't hear anything else.

Hamish was now on the other side of the conservatory. Alastair helped me into my shoes, opened the door and led me out. Cool air fanned my face and snow pressed in through the side of my shoes. He guided me away from the lights; I saw a wall and leaned over it, just in time. All the while, Alastair stood behind me, running his hand lightly over my shoulders. He gave me a handkerchief to clean my face, bent down and gave me a handful of snow.

'Are you all right?'

I tried to nod but I was shivering.

He took his jacket off and draped it over my shoulders. When I had cleaned myself up, he put his arms around me and pulled me to him. I didn't bother to resist this time.

'What was all that about?' He stroked the crown of my head like my father used to. Hot tears streamed down my face. He gave me another tissue, and I looked at him. People started flooding outside, loud and excited.

'Come on, it's nearly midnight!' Alastair took my hand and dragged me towards them. They were counting backwards from ten. A bell sounded and he turned to me and kissed me lightly on the cheek. 'Happy New Year!'

Marie and Stuart came up and hugged me before Alastair broke away as Amanda came rushing towards him. He kissed her on the lips and then everyone joined arms and started singing. Hamish too was kissing some girl. I felt shaky but better. Alastair was watching me from where he stood. As our eyes met, I knew it was all right, he wouldn't tell anyone. Most importantly, I had been the first one he had kissed in this brand new year!

★　★　★

Next day I didn't surface until sometime after one o'clock and descended the stairs feeling fragile, only to bump straight into Alastair. My cheeks burned but he just looked at me with that stupid grin on his face.

'Can't remember what happened yesterday. Must have had one too many. Come on, let's have some brunch.'

Amanda left the next day in her Mini, with Alastair telling her to drive carefully. There was now a good six inches of snow on the roads. I turned away as they kissed goodbye, but I couldn't help hear her parting words.

'See you soon, my darling.'

★   ★   ★

I was lounging on my bed listening to the top twenty charts when I heard a knock. Alastair came in and sat down next to me.

'Alastair!'

'What? Oh, sorry.' He jumped up and sat on the windowsill. He set off an avalanche of conflicting emotions in me. I turned the music down. How could I tell him that he shouldn't even be in my bedroom when he basically owned the place and I liked him being here? Why was he up here bothering me when he had Amanda? I still hated his short hair. Had she made him do that? He looked around at a loss for a minute at what to say.

'I wanted to tell you something,' he started.

'If it's about Amanda . . . ' a spark of anger made me reply.

'Amanda? No. We've known each other for ages. Long before I met you. It's not about her,' he said dismissively as if his love life had absolutely nothing to do with me. The spark ignited an angry fire in me which I was barely keeping under control. 'I've been thinking a

161

lot about you. I'm glad you told me about Tahir and it was stupid that I said what I did. It's just that . . . '

'What?'

'Well, I didn't want you thinking about going off to India.'

'To Kashmir.'

'Kashmir — India. Whichever. It's too far. You belong here now. You managed to escape a half-blind old man and you should just settle down and get on with your life here now. You're lucky . . . we're lucky to have you here at all.'

I felt myself softening towards him again. 'I think about my luck every day but it won't stop me looking for Tahir.'

'No, I didn't think it would, but at least I told you how we see it.'

'Have you told your parents about him?'

'Of course I haven't!'

'So it's more like how you see it.'

He smiled and shrugged his shoulders. Did he know how I felt about his girlfriend, I wondered.

'Well, I'd like to share something with you. Something I haven't told anyone else.'

Not even Amanda? Now I was listening.

'You know about Lily's death, don't you?'

I nodded.

'Up until now I've been all they had to pin

162

their hopes on. Until you came along, that is. Now you're here, it's made me think. How you fit in and take the focus off me a little.'

'Alastair, what are you trying to tell me?'

'I want to write. I've always wanted to write. Only I could never tell them because I don't know where it's taking me. So I've been trying to finish my studies and find out as much as I can about the history of the Scottish clans. I've already penned the first couple of chapters of what should be a trilogy. Don't laugh.'

'That's fantastic. Tell me more!'

21

The last thing I'd been expecting in the first lesson back at St Medan's on a sleepy Monday morning when my brain was still in festive mode was a test. I dreaded English anyway. After all I was Kashmiri not British. Miss Angus, a short stout woman who stood very straight to make the most of her height, was feared by all as she ruthlessly dissected our essays with her sharp red scalpel. Now she stretched up and started writing something in neat italics on the board: *A Situation That Changed my Life.*

'You have one hour starting from now.' She sat down behind her desk. The blank piece of paper stared back at me like a wall of ice as I tried to block out the noise of nibs gliding across paper, filling lines and covering pages. What on earth were they writing about? What had they experienced in their safe little lives, in their safe little houses, in their safe little country? The clock on the wall told me that I had already wasted five minutes. The classroom had a view of the medical centre. What had really changed my life? I wrote my first sentence: *I knew I shouldn't have*

followed my father into the house, but I had
to see what the screaming was about . . .

Words started to tumble out of me as if
someone was writing through me. The pages
filled themselves. All too soon the bell rang
and Miss Angus said in her clipped way,
'Time's up, please finish the sentence you're
writing.'

I didn't quite get to the bit where I was
driving away with Pa, but I had written down
what made me want to be a healer. They
could make of that what they wanted. There
wasn't anything else I would have wanted to
write about. I left the classroom and stepped
out into the cold January air.

A week later, the essays were handed back
with their cruel red surgical wounds. All
except mine.

'Jaya, would you mind coming to the front
of the class?' Miss Angus asked.

This is it, I thought. I did my best and now
I was going to be disgraced in front of the
whole class. What a great way for the New
Year to begin. As good an excuse to be kicked
out as any, I thought.

'Jaya, did this actually happen to you?'

She was calling me a liar! 'Of course it did!'

'Well, I felt I should enquire. However, I
must add that a vivid imagination is not the
worst thing to have, when putting pen to

paper. Now, my dear, would you be so kind as to read out your essay to us?'

The class stared at me just like the blank piece of paper last week, only they were even more intimidating. There was nowhere I could hide, nowhere to escape being made a laughing stock. My cheeks glowed fiercely as I began.

'I knew I shouldn't have followed my father into the house but the screams wouldn't stop.'

'I'm afraid the girls at the back won't be able to hear. Louder, please!' said Miss Angus.

I coughed and started again. When I finished, the class looked at me in silence. Then Jane, a prefect with thin brown hair, started to clap, a couple more joined in and then the whole class broke into applause. My cheeks were now on fire.

'That was a remarkable piece of writing, Jaya. You really should put it in the school magazine. Girls, why don't you follow her example? Write from the heart and it will show in your work. Well done!'

22

'Come on, let's go!'

Beauly bounded down the hall, tail wagging like a huge feather duster before we made a beeline for the beach. Seagulls screeched in delight above a sparkling blue bay and the sun shone down on my head like the feeling in my heart. I was home for Whitsun and now was what mattered, not my past or my dreams. Beauly must surely have been a crocodile in some other life, so still did he stand, half-submerged in water waiting for me to throw a stick. I threw him one, stripped down to my swimsuit and waded into the sea. Beauly swam a little way out with me. I wasn't only floating on water. I swam and I swam, taking the occasional break to turn on my back and look at the sky. Beauly, now back on the beach, started barking.

The Mains nestled on top of the cliffs in Marie's glorious garden against a backdrop of purple heather-covered hills. So unspoiled with no one around apart from Beauly. I shut my eyes; saw the mountains in my mind's eye as clearly as if I had seen them only yesterday. And Tahir. Anything could have happened to him. 'No!' a voice in my head shouted. He would always be alive for me unless I had evidence to the contrary. What did he look like now? As a young man. The water was warm on the surface but little currents of coolness caressed my legs and stomach as I ploughed my way steadily out. Tongue lolling out of his mouth, Beauly was now sitting down. He would wait for me, I was sure. I turned onto my back and let myself drift. It was so pleasant to be moving, so calming.

Beauly started barking. He was little more than a dark point running back and forth. Someone else was in the water. Swimming into my solitude. I couldn't make them out from this distance but it was time to turn around anyway. I had drifted a little way down shore.

It was a lot harder to swim back in. There was a strong undercurrent that was dragging me gently but firmly further out. It was so hard to make any progress at all. Like swimming on the spot. The shore wasn't getting any closer. At this pace I would never make it. The figure was swimming out to me. I could make out his hair. Wild and curly like Alastair's . . . It was Alastair, plying his way through the water, using the current to get to me. It was much easier for him; the water was sweeping him out. I tried to meet him. This

168

was so frustrating! Oh no! I was dragging him into this, too. I was on the verge of panicking. Within a few minutes he came close enough to shout.

'Are you all right?'

The sound of his voice did much to contain my fear. A few more strokes and then he drew level with me.

'Come on, we can make it.'

He pulled my arm a little, gave me a moment to catch my breath; we swam and swam. We weren't getting back but being carried further along the shore away from Beauly. We were being carried towards the rocks.

'It looks further than it actually is,' Alastair shouted.

Tears clouded my vision. 'I don't think I can go on any longer!'

'We're nearly there!'

I was gasping for breath and I could feel a cramp coming on in my foot. I was going to drown! The rocks were looming up in front of us. Tall, steep and slimy. Alastair told me to hang on to a jagged edge that was sticking out.

'It'll stop you getting slammed against the others.'

He heaved himself upward and slipped. Then he tried again. This time he managed to get himself up out of the water, but there was blood everywhere. His elbow was bleeding badly. He reached down towards me. I couldn't grab his hand! It was a few inches too far out of my grasp. I pushed myself up with the remnants of my strength but plummeted down again, salt water filled my nose and mouth. Gasping for breath, I resurfaced.

Alastair shouted at me, 'It's like break-point, when you've got to reach the ball to keep in the game.'

My feet found a small rock. I took a deep breath and propelled myself up. He grabbed my hand, it slipped, but he lunged forwards and tightened his grip around my wrist, pulling me with all his might. I came up out of the water, scraping my knees on the rocks in the process. He pulled me away from the edge and I collapsed on the smooth warm rocks. My arm hurt and we both lay there panting and shaken. My wrist really hurt, and my knees stung badly as water splashed over us. All was still while we struggled to catch our breath.

'What the hell did you think you were doing?'

I sat up and looked at him covered in blood. He was furious. I had waited so long to see him. Here he was by my side and I had almost just caused us both to drown.

'I'm so sorry. I . . . I wasn't thinking. I was so happy . . . ' I burst into tears. He was by my side; he didn't have to move much. His cold wet body, the solidness of his muscles, was pressing against me as he put his arms around me.

'I thought you were going to be carried out and I wouldn't be able to get to you.'

I could taste his bare skin, hear his heart beating. I was suddenly conscious of how little I had on. This wasn't right. I pulled away but then reached out and touched his hand.

'No, it's all my fault. I was so stupid. Thanks, thanks for saving me.'

His face broke into that familiar grin. 'Well, who the hell would I play tennis against if you were gone? Come on, we've got to collect Beauly. He'll be going mad with us out of sight.'

We clambered over the rocks and started walking back. It wasn't easy terrain to cross. The tide was too far in so that we had to make our way up along the cliffs. We were dry now, and the sun was quite strong. If I forgot the last half hour, it would feel so good with Alastair by my side and the sun in my face. I ignored the pain in my knees and held my injured arm with my other. Beauly ran

171

towards us, his hysterical welcome for once utterly appropriate. Alastair had stopped bleeding. We cleaned ourselves up in the sea water, dried ourselves, got dressed and entered the house through the kitchen door.

My wrist was painful for the next few days and tennis was completely off the cards, but I thanked the gods, including the Christian one, that nothing worse had happened, especially to Alastair.

23

I lapped up Stuart's talk of his clinic as if I were listening to Pa.

'Stuart, darling. Have some more roast potatoes and stop talking shop. You'll send Jaya to sleep,' Marie protested.

'Sorry, Jaya, I do get a little — '

'No! Do you think I could come along to the clinic one day?' I asked.

'I'd be delighted! What about tomorrow?' He grinned at me.

★ ★ ★

With its flat triangle of a roof and ornate entrance, the clinic squatted on the crew-cut lawn like a Japanese temple. Once inside, everything gleamed around the fountain in the middle of the foyer. A blonde nurse, with ruby lips and the whitest teeth I had ever seen, smiled at Stuart.

'Good morning, Dr Hamilton.'

'Everything under control, Monica?'

'Just fine, Doctor.'

'What about Mrs Davis? Did she scream again when she saw herself?'

'No, this time around she knows the swelling will go down in a month or two. Her only concern is that she'll look good for her son's wedding in July. But she got upset when the TV broke down. We called the man in on Sunday evening to fix it, Doctor.'

'Good. Give her a box of chocolates and whatever else she wants. She should get a discount anyway, with all the custom she's sent us.'

'Here's your post and the files.'

He sifted through the letters, whilst I looked around. The door to the waiting room was open. Oil paintings hung on the walls. A solitary lady was sitting on a huge, white leather armchair, a glossy magazine on her lap.

'What's the matter with her?' I asked when we got to Stuart's office with its huge mahogany desk. There were pictures of patients on the wall behind him, before and after their treatment.

'She needs a face lift. If she agrees, you can stay for the consultation.'

I was given a white coat and stood by as Stuart explained how the scars would be hidden behind the woman's ears.

'In about six weeks, friends will start saying how amazing you look and asking where you spent your holidays. Five or more years

174

younger at least. These two clients underwent the same nip and tuck.' He handed her some photos. I noticed how he didn't use the word patients; it really was all about business.

I saw nurses in tight-fitting blue and white uniforms tending to the patients in rooms, which would have graced a luxury hotel. Wine-red wallpaper, matching carpets and even a minibar. A man sat on his bed, watching rugby on TV, his nose and half his face heavily bandaged.

When we drove back in the evening, I knew how right Pa had been. It wasn't our kind of medicine.

★　★　★

'Hi, I'm Kate.'

The most gorgeous-looking girl with long, blonde, curly hair and a wide open, almost surprised look on her face, turned up at the Mains. She settled all doubt about Amanda and why Alastair hadn't said a word about the latter lately. Kate was tall and chewed gum with a passion.

She entered the front hall and said, 'Wow.' Alastair took her hand and led her into the sitting room. 'Wow,' she repeated and all I heard was a series of wows until the door to his room shut behind them. I couldn't help wondering if she took her gum out before they kissed.

At breakfast she chatted non-stop, interspersed by a high-pitched laugh at regular intervals as she recounted total drivel. Gone was the calm of Sunday brunch and I knew Marie well enough to sense the boredom behind the expression she feigned when Kate droned on about some well-known actor.

'Imagine your old man going off with another bloke! There's not much you can do about that, is there? Apart from a sex change!' She broke into a titter.

Unlike Kate, Marie laughed without a sound passing her lips. 'Well, I'm so sorry but I have to answer some letters,' she said.

'Yes, darling, you've just reminded me of . . . ' and Stuart beat his own diplomatic retreat.

Alastair caught his hand in Kate's long blonde mane, twirling the thick strands into curls, seemingly oblivious to the awkwardness.

'Must go,' I said as brightly as I could, without bothering to explain myself and left the room without looking back.

Kate insisted on watching *Crossroads*, a soap opera, in the sitting room in the evenings. I watched two episodes with her, but that was my limit. Even Beauly gave Kate a wide berth, pushing his shaggy frame against my shins or actually sitting on my feet. Because I avoided Kate's company, I didn't see much of Alastair, either. I didn't care if he noticed. How could he bring such an annoying bird-brained creature here?

24

Tahir had never seen so many soldiers on one spot. A whole battalion on skis milling about like ants on the Siachen Glacier. At 22,000 feet, India and Pakistan stood their ground on the highest battlefield on Earth. There wasn't much to fight for, Tahir thought, as he looked at the inhospitable terrain. Men shouldn't be up here. That much was clear. The gods didn't take sides when they showed people their limits. Yet the two nations would stop at nothing in their scramble for Kashmir. Both sides braved the altitude, freezing temperatures and strong winds for months on end. More troops were killed up here by the weather conditions than by combat and numerous fingers and toes were lost to frostbite.

'Sitting ducks! We'll teach them a lesson they'll never forget. Surprise them when they're asleep,' Mustafa told Tahir.

The two of them were dressed in white so that the soldiers wouldn't spot their mission to place explosives at a strategic point. A single detonation and the avalanche would do the rest. Tahir knew they'd have to act quickly otherwise they would die up here with the soldiers. He had a crashing headache and he couldn't breathe properly as the glacier swayed before his eyes. But they would have to wait for nightfall to carry out Mustafa's instructions. He mustn't fall asleep, whatever happened. He looked at the dazzling whiteness and thought of how he used to be able to hide away from people and their sick ways. He weighed up his chances of making it down to the green carpet of the valley without anyone noticing.

★ ★ ★

It had started snowing so heavily so that you couldn't see the person in front of you in the dark. He had always been a good skier. He heard the swish of the wood underneath him as he whizzed away. He was acting on instinct, trying to put as much distance as he could between him and what was about to happen. His heart was beating in his ears and he was breathing much too fast, his lungs trying to extract the scarce particles of oxygen from the air. A rock loomed up in front of him, which he only managed to miss by a hair's breadth. He heard the dull bang above him. And then a deafening never-ending thunder. He turned around but all he could see was a wall of white.

25

On the first day of my final school exams, I woke up with my throat on fire and stared in horror at my reflection in the mirror; my eyes were puffed, my face swollen. I reported to the nurse.

'I'm afraid you're going to have to stay in the sick bay,' she said.

'No! I just need something to calm my throat down. A couple of aspirins should do the trick.'

'Miss Vaidya, we can't have you walking about the school, giving this to the others. It might be scarlet fever.' Sister Belinda approached me, thermometer in hand.

'You're not going to stop me!'

'I can't let you go, Miss Vaidya. I'm not allowed to. I shall have to ring Mr Knight.'

When she got through to him, I grabbed the phone off her. 'Mr Knight, you've got to help me!' By now I was so worked up that talking felt like swallowing barbed wire.

Sitting up in bed in the isolation room at the sick bay an hour later, I set about answering the first question on evolution.

***

Now that the exam pressure had relented and I was off antibiotics, I felt good again. My skin glowed and my hair was sleek. I was determined to enjoy what might be my last summer at the Mains, for I had no inkling of where life would be taking me after this. I had come to terms with the fact that although I had given it my best shot, the bout of scarlet fever had quashed all hope of becoming a doctor. Alastair was in Stockholm, working on a library designed by his firm in Dumfries. It was a massive project which offered him a permanent position on his return.

'Dumfries. It's better than I hoped. I was afraid he would stay in London.' Marie pulled out a weed from in amongst the rose bushes. She wasn't the only one cheered by this thought. But he would probably come back too late for me. Who knew where I would be by then.

***

Sure enough, Alastair showed up the day before my results were due. It was wonderful to see him again, especially with no Kate around but my mind could think only of the coming day. I wanted to travel to the school to find out immediately where my life was going. And I would be able to see everyone one last time. Over supper I declared, 'I have to go to St Medan's. I can go alone, take the train and bus. Celia always does it.'

Marie frowned.

Alastair let out a hoot of laughter. 'Don't be stupid. It would take you all day to get there and back. I know where Celia lives and it's much nearer. In fact, I don't know if you'll make it back before nightfall, the trains and buses being what they are around here. No, I'll drive you there myself.'

Although I resented Alastair's bossiness, I gave in easily because the next day no longer seemed as forbidding as before.

★　★　★

After only a couple of hours' sleep, I felt worse than if I had stayed up all night. I stood under the shower for ages, trying to put off the moment when I would start this day. I went down to the kitchen to hold onto my mug of tea like a life ring. I couldn't eat a bite; my stomach was tightly zipped up. Alastair came downstairs, taking the steps three at a time, just as noisy as always.

'Hiya, sweetheart.'

Why was he calling me sweetheart in that

general all-encompassing way, like some bus driver?

'Fancy a fry-up?'

I shook my head as he covered the bottom of the frying pan in bacon. Three eggs followed.

'George told me to let you know about his birthday party. Everybody's welcome. Even school kids.' He winked at me.

I glared back so he shrugged and worked his way through four pieces of toast and the entire contents of the frying pan. Once he had washed everything down with two mugs of tea, he clapped his hands together.

'Ready?'

Just as we were leaving, Marie appeared in her dressing gown and slippers. 'Good luck!' She took my hands in hers. 'Medical school isn't good for everyone, you know. It's such a hard slog and does it ever end? Just look at Stuart, he got up at six and came back at nine last night.'

She had a point.

Alastair piped up, 'Anyway, you can always marry some rich old gaffer.'

I gave him a withering look. We sped along the lanes that led to the wide road to Miles Davis trumpeting through his new speakers — the only things I ever heard Alastair boast about. I was grateful that this time the music drowned out any chance of conversation. I looked out at the countryside. How often had I travelled this way? I asked myself, as I ticked off the familiar landmarks. This time, I took in every detail, on my walk to the guillotine. I recognized each turning, willing the car to slow down so that I could put off our arrival a little longer. If only we could travel at a mere twenty miles per hour instead of the steady sixty-five which Alastair was cruising at. Then the walls and gate of the school grounds and the cars, some parked, some still converging. Familiar faces, nervous waves, boyfriends grasping the sweaty, cold trembling hands of my friends, parents trying to smile brightly at other parents as if it were just another school event, talking about the bad summer when all the while their eyes kept darting to the main entrance.

Phoebe, a girl I always sat next to in biology, was standing all by herself. I ran up towards her, and we caught up on the last few weeks until we dried up and shuffled our feet in the gravel. Alastair came forward and put his arms round us both.

'Come on, you two. Anyone would think you were back at school!'

He herded us forward as a crowd gathered in front of a notice board besides the statue of Saint Medan with her cloak and sword in hand. Even though it was still August, there was already a tinge of autumn in the air, and the light cast sharp shadows on the ground. A grey squirrel bounded across the far edge of the lawn and skirted up an old oak tree out of sight; it was quick but not as quick as the brown ones that glided over the rocks in our Vale. Blackbirds rustled in the foliage and as I looked at the grand old building with its leaded casement windows, a lump swelled in my throat. I had had wonderful times here after my poor start, been given a unique chance; no matter what the results turned out to be, I was in a much better position than before. The people here had accepted me, even though I was different. I had become one of them and made friends I would keep all my life and now I had to leave. It all seemed so safe, so sheltered here now. Now it was decision day: I would walk along whichever path the gods chose for me.

★　★　★

Mrs Smith, the rotund, middle-aged secretary with blue rinse in her white hair, bustled out of the reception with some papers in her hands. She pinned the results to the board, then turned around. 'Good luck, ladies!'

Girls began to surge forward to finally be

put out of their agony. I hung back; couldn't bring myself to see what I already knew: that I would never be that good. I was shaking all over, and still I waited in line as girls hooted with joy, or turned to their loved ones to disguise their sobs. Phoebe was jumping about as if she was on a pogo stick. I remained rooted to the spot. Alastair pushed me forward. 'Go on!'

All I wanted was to walk down the drive and never look back, but I stepped forward. The names were arranged in order of merit and, as I scanned the lines, panic gripped my throat. I hadn't gained a single qualification! It had all been for nothing, I had messed up. How come? I had gained so many points in the modules. Nothing counted if you failed the exams! Alastair pushed me gently aside.

'Look, you're up there!'

Before I had time to locate my name, he turned round and whisked me off my feet, twirling me around and around.

'You did it!!!'

When he put me down, I finally saw that I was second of sixty girls, with As in all the sciences. I was stunned but Alastair was absolutely beaming. Before I knew it, he pulled me towards him and kissed me squarely on the lips. I pulled away in shock even though it was the most delicious feeling ever but what if someone saw us? Boys didn't kiss girls, not in public, yet no one seemed to notice us or how I glowed with pleasure and confusion. The grounds, the crowd, my friends faded around us, but then Phoebe bounced over to me.

'You jammy so and so! How did you manage physics? Warwick, here I come!' Without waiting, she bounded off again.

The rest was a blur with most of the girls chatting and smiling and hugging each other as parents resumed their polite conversation, and then it was farewells and promises to see each other soon. As I sat in the car again with Alastair in blissful silence, one thought overrode everything else. Medical school, here I come.

26

St Andrews, 1975

Could this grandest of ancient student halls really be where I was going to live? I walked through the massive wooden front door of St Salvator's to report to the caretaker, who looked as if he had come with the building. A sleek-haired student, casually sporting the kind of clothes that reeked of good taste and money, was engrossed in conversation with him and I expected them to show me the door like a trespasser. Instead, the old man smiled.

'Welcome to St Salvator's, Miss Vaidya. We've been waiting for ye.' He handed me my keys. 'Ye'll find your room on the second floor. Your post box is over there behind ye. Best check it regularly. Ye never know what ye might find.'

My name in bold gold letters for all to see! My hand shook as I opened the box. I took out the envelopes and held them in my hand like a rare blue lotus blossom.

'Horacio, I cannae get away at the moment. Can you show the lassie upstairs?'

'A pleasure.' The student bowed flamboyantly, and picked up my case. 'Follow me.'

I had been assigned a double room with a splendid view of ancient elms and the chapel. I tore open the letters, which included an invitation to meet my tutor, a note from Josh Summers, a second year student who wanted to show me around that evening, and an overview of Freshers week.

My roommate Elizabeth had chosen St Andrews for one reason alone. Students had the privilege of playing on the most famous golf course in the world for a mere pittance and so she duly kept a whole selection of golf clubs in a bag next to her bed. At least she kept it there until I nearly broke my ankle tripping over it one night. In the beginning her talk of birdies, eagles and albatrosses made me think she was an ornithologist. She had virtually grown up on a golf course in Dorset, where her father was president of the club. She talked me into joining her on the Castle Course one afternoon, but soon took me to task.

'You've got to concentrate on the game, not on the view!'

★   ★   ★

Real life kicked in all too soon after a mad, never-ending round of parties and events of

189

Freshers week. It was purely a case of bum glue; sitting and learning for hours on end and all the harder when I saw the amount of time those studying the Arts had. In my scarce spare time, I wandered around the town, picturing my father strolling down the cobbled streets past the ivy-clad walls and sandstone houses with his books in hand. If I was closer to the gods in the Himalayas, then this was as close as I could get to my father in Scotland. He had sat in the very same lecture theatres. I was at *his* university.

27

Professor Donahue asked me for my diagnosis and my voice came out so feebly that he retorted, 'Come now, Miss Vaidya, you can hardly help the patient if she cannot hear you.'

A murmur went through the small group of students gathered around her bed. The elderly woman looked in considerable pain; one purple leg covered in yellow festers lay on top of the sheets. Her eyes were clouded and watery and her nightdress was stretched tight over ample rolls of flesh. In the steadiest voice I could muster, I said, 'I'm sorry, Professor Donahue. It looks like a problem with the circulation. Probably caused by diabetes.'

'Looks like? Probably? The patient doesn't want to hear guesswork!' He almost threw the results of the blood tests at me which luckily I grabbed.

The woman winced and shifted position as her trembling nicotine-stained fingers reached for a glass of water. The students went quiet as if they were holding their breath. Some looked at the professor, others at me. I could feel my cheeks burning. I took my time and perused the results in the uncomfortable silence. Why did he have to put the patient through this? Now I was angry.

'The colour of the limb and the fact that the wounds will not heal points to circulation problems caused by diabetes. This is confirmed by the blood tests.'

'Correct. Make a note of how you should present the results to the patient in future.'

I wished I had time to sit down at the woman's bedside and talk to her instead of talking about her as if she were merely a piece of rotting meat. The staff though did their best to make the patients feel good. Some of the nurses were bossy but the smooth running of the wards hinged on their commitment and the gruelling long hours they put in. They knew the ropes and were usually kind and supportive of us novices, but I once saw Sister Anna make mincemeat of a junior doctor who missed the five o'clock deadline and had to order a taxi to take a blood sample to the lab.

I wore my scrubs with pride and breathed in the smell of disinfectant like fresh mountain air. Although the facilities had seen better days, the hospital was light years ahead of anything I had experienced in Kashmir. I hoped that things had changed there now; that new clinics had been built with the money that had flowed in after the earthquake. Would anyone build a mountain clinic if the reports were true that people still were subsisting in makeshift housing in areas far from where they had lived for generations?

28

'Where's that shy lassie who first came into my kitchen two years ago?' exclaimed Aileen at Christmas.

I glowed and so did everything around me. Food tasted better, colours were brighter and everything looked wonderful even though it was grey outside. When had I been happier since I left Kashmir? Stuart, however, seemed to have aged five years. He was paler, his brow had fallen and there were dark shadows under his eyes. He was thinner and, more often than not, I found him asleep in the library, newspaper in hand, his glasses perched precariously on the tip of his nose. One day I came across Marie with a cigarette in hand on the bench overlooking the bay. I had never seen her smoking before. She stubbed it out like some naughty schoolgirl.

'Are you OK?'

'Totally fine,' she replied.

'And Stuart?'

'Oh you know, all that driving and work doesn't get any easier at his age.' I didn't press her. If she wanted to talk to me, I was there. But they both wanted to hear my tales of student life. Things were different in St Andrews but not that different, we established. I caught up on all those early morning starts, all those late nights and the nights I hadn't slept at all. What a luxury, to be taken care of, to be spoiled for a while with food on the table and my washing done for me. But I couldn't stay long; I had to be back at the hospital for my clinical over New Year. Alastair wasn't coming home this year. He was too busy.

'He's gone off to Italy on a writers' retreat, whatever that is. Apparently he's been working on a book for years. He was offered a place there on the merit of what he'd written. It sounds amazing but I must admit I don't know why he can't just write at home. All a bit hush, hush,' Marie confided.

So he had finally told her. I was happy that he was happy. I was sure he had someone there, waiting for him when he came back. I had been so busy, had had no time or thought for anything or anyone. Only back at the Mains did I really miss Alastair again and wonder what he was up to. He had probably sensed that I didn't need him like I used to. Our relationship had been a bit one-sided before but I had now grown up. Our lack of contact wasn't bad, I decided. Like real brothers and sisters, there were bound to be times when we kept more in touch than others.

Beauly, who had now turned twelve, had aged along with his master. He spent much of the day dozing in front of the fire, his legs occasionally twitching as he chased rabbits into the bracken of his dreams.

Christmas came and went and just when I had got used to the peace and tranquillity, I had to go back. Marie seemed particularly sad to see me go this time, and I almost regretted planning my clinical until good sense told me I needed to get it over as quickly as possible especially as this time of the year didn't really mean that much to me. What better time to do it?

★　★　★

With most students away, St Andrews seemed deserted. There was no escape from from the emptiness I encountered when I got back from the clinic at night when the residences took on a kind of eeriness as, apart from a couple of medics and a handful of international students, there seemed to be only me there. Without its students the town seemed deserted and shrunken. I had an invite for a party on New Year's Eve but I didn't know the people very well so I found some excuse.

Basically, I was too tired from the shifts at the hospital and I didn't see the point of celebrating without my friends.

On New Year's Eve, a thin layer of snow lay in the dark streets. The damp and the cold made me feel even more tired after my shift at the hospital. As I trudged on back, I started to regret that I hadn't got my act together, that I was such a wimp to stay home by myself. Like so many girls who planned their lives around their boyfriends, said a voice in my head. I wished I could get on the next train to the Mains. What was I doing here by myself? Still, I would languish in the bath and have a frozen pizza or whatever else I could dig up. Then, I would snuggle up in bed with a good book.

A tall hooded figure was waiting outside the door of the hall.

'Jaya?' The voice was unmistakable.

'Alastair, what on earth are you doing here?'

'Happy New Year!'

I had never been more pleased to see him. He scooped me up and whirled me around, then carried me in and plonked me down in the deserted, carpeted entrance, before retrieving his big leather bag. He had a beard, a deep tan and there were a few lines around his eyes. I went to touch his beard.

'Sorry about that, didn't get round to shaving.'

'No, I like it. And you're so tanned.'

'Well, now we go together, don't we?'

'How did you get here?'

'There were no more buses so I took a taxi from the station. And before that the train from the airport. I haven't been home yet.' He wiped away the drop of water that was running down my forehead. 'I wanted to catch you tonight. But if you're going out . . .'

I shook my head. 'No, I messed up. I turned something down and now I'm at a loose end.'

'Come on then, girl. What are you waiting for? Get dressed. We're going out! Is there anywhere I can freshen up?'

I showed Alastair the shower and then put on a simple black dress with my emerald-coloured earrings. He emerged out of the bathroom bare-chested and incredibly brown.

'You look great!' he said as he donned a clean shirt. I wasn't the only one, I thought. 'Come on, we've got to hurry if we're going to get a table somewhere,' he added.

When we got outside, it was snowing lightly and the sea was especially dark and ominous as the waves crashed against the rocks. I started to shiver and he put his arm around me. We walked through the slushy streets trying to find a restaurant nearby. No chance, everything was fully booked, every available seat taken. It was the same story everywhere we went; the town didn't have endless venues after all. I was just thinking what I could possibly rustle up for the two of us back at the residences, when a waitress in the last restaurant said, 'Hang on a minute' and reached for the phone on the wall over the bar. She shouted something above the chatter in the broadest Scots I'd ever heard.

She turned to us. 'They still have a table over at a country house near Kingbarnes. But you'll have to hurry.' We nodded. 'Aye, I'll send them right over.'

It wasn't easy finding a taxi, and by the time we finally reached the place I was still shivering from the wait. Alastair ushered me in through the massive oak door. There was a huge hearth at the far side of the hall and Christmas decorations hung from the beams. We were shown to seats at the end of a banquet-like table. People were in evening dress and some men wore kilts. It was a little difficult to talk above the chatter and the music, but we had so much to catch up on.

'How's your book going?'

'It'll probably come to nothing. I can't talk about it yet but it's easier to write in winter when the building sites are closed for weeks on end.'

'What happened to Kate?' I couldn't help asking.

'Oh, that silly girl ran off with a lawyer.'

'Great news!' We both smiled. 'Why didn't you stick with Amanda? I thought you went together so well.'

He didn't answer. Instead he asked, 'What about you?'

I told him about life on the wards.

'There doesn't seem to be a mountain too high for you to climb.' He took my hand in his. 'Come on, let's dance.'

'Kashmiri wedding dances are my speciality, I'm afraid. I don't know how to dance like that!'

'Then it's about time you learned. It's a bit like tennis.'

It was so easy to fall in with what he was doing as if we had done this countless times before. I had forgotten how good he was at nearly everything, how good it felt to be close to him. Too good, I thought and was almost relieved when we sat back down to the next course.

Alastair was knocking back drink after drink. I had a couple myself but I had learned my lesson on my first Hogmanay with Alastair. Just before midnight, the crowd went out onto the wall overlooking the moonlit expanse of water. They started to count back from ten to zero. Fireworks went off and as I gazed at them, I thought there was no better place to see in the New Year than Scotland. Alastair looked down at me, pulled me close to him and planted a soft brotherly kiss next to my lips as we bade the old year farewell. I kissed him back but this time my lips found his. An electric current ran through me, his very presence seemed to fill my body. He tasted of wine and delicious Alastair. I didn't want this to end. My heart and body were responding in a way my mind could not. Eventually he pulled away and looked at me once more. How could I? He was my brother. I was Kashmiri. It was so wrong, wasn't it?

He put a finger to my lips. 'Shush, it's OK.'

We stood there in the cold as the surroundings came back into focus and the others broke out into 'Auld Lang Syne'.

'Don't worry — we've both had a drink or two. I won't remember a thing in the morning. Look.' And he swigged back his wine.

★ ★ ★

I had never seen Alastair drunk before. This time I was the one who guided him back to my room, who supported him up the stairs. He collapsed onto my bed and I took his shoes off and covered him up. It was strange to be looking after him for a change. I sat in the chair opposite. Why did he make me feel safe and confused at the same time? Marie and Stuart flashed up in my mind. Hopefully Alastair was right. This would be all forgotten in the morning. I surveyed his handsome, tanned familiar face, sleeping like a child in my bed and withstood the impulse to climb in beside him and cuddle up.

29

Norwich 1981

Annabel, my medic friend from St Andrews, told me about an opening for a junior doctor at the Norfolk and Norwich University Hospital and the chance to share a house with her and four others on the river.

'Why do you have to go so far away?' asked Marie.

'I'll be back as often as I can,' I promised. East Anglia was hardly any distance away in Indian terms.

'The lass knows what she wants. Good for her, I say,' said Stuart, putting his arm around Marie. The sight of them together made me less guilty about leaving. Beauly lay at their feet, wagging his tail half-heartedly before closing his eyes once more. These days he slept most of the time and when he did go for a walk, his hips seemed to be troubling him and the grey around his snout betrayed the fact that he was now getting on a little.

★　★　★

Life at the house in Norwich centred round the big wooden kitchen table. When we shunned the canteen, we ate takeaways or tucked into ready meals when shifts allowed. All of us suffered from a dire lack of time, let alone sleep. You sat and talked with whoever was about at the time.

I was in the thick of it! Doing what I loved, except that I never seemed to have the time to do the job properly. Just when I was on top of things, my bleeper would summon me elsewhere and I would be rushing from one ward to the other. Precious time was eaten up filling in forms and writing reports in the tiny glass cabin that served the six of us on duty at a time. I felt totally inadequate. How could I attend to the patients properly under these conditions? I balked at the enormity of what lay ahead. How would I react when I had to make that life or death diagnosis?

I couldn't afford to make any mistakes. I found myself holding a two-week-old baby with the mother looking at me as if I had held a million babies before or sewing a nasty gash on a man's forehead. The hours were long; much too long for the pay, but it was still a wonderful feeling to know that I was supporting myself for the first time in my life.

The nurses at Norwich were used to having juniors on the wards and were very patient with me, even when I made mistakes like filling in the wrong form but I was once praised by a senior doctor for diagnosing a heart defect in a patient with none of the common symptoms of Noonan syndrome. Most importantly, I got to work in the different departments and get a taste of my specialist area. Dermatology was definitely not my kind of thing; you had to wait too long to see the results, too much trial and error for me. I was torn between surgery and gynaecology. The latter had been the decisive factor in my choice of career yet surgery was immediate, life-changing and life-saving, requiring a level of skill that was both terrifying and thrilling. So much went on in the operating theatre; I listened to the soothing words of the anaesthetist as the propofol took hold of a petrified girl, watched the precision of cutting, and the brutality of the chief surgeon's words on throwing down his scalpel and snapping off his gloves. 'Time of death, 8:32.'

★　★　★

In the middle of examining an obese teenage girl with all the symptoms of acute appendicitis, an alarm went off. Somewhere on the floor, someone's heart had stopped. I ran down the corridor, frantically searching for the light that would tell me where the patient was. My heart was beating wildly, too. Keep calm, I told myself. A nurse pointed down the corridor past a row of plastic chairs. I almost fell over myself as I staggered into the room. A team of nurses was already collected around the bed. A man lay spread-eagled, his flabby chest and stomach exposed, red-faced and perfectly still in a urine-soaked bed.

A nurse drew the curtains around his bed. Nothing was blocking his windpipe and I couldn't detect a pulse. I shouted for his notes and the rescue trolley. Someone grabbed the red defibrillator from the wall. The nurses pulled the bed away from the wall. It had to be detached before I could implement electric shock treatment. Sweat trickled down my forehead. A nurse passed me the wires which I placed on his chest. His whole body jerked once, then again as the current shot through him. No reaction. No fucking reaction! Nothing. I placed my palm on his chest and started to pump. No reaction. I moved to tilt his head, pinched his nostrils shut and bent to blow into his mouth. His eyes stared blankly at the ceiling and he tasted strongly of nicotine. Still his chest refused to rise of its own accord. I scanned the notes as I gave it one more go, then started pumping again. My hands hurt with the effort. I felt a rib crack. I looked at the nurse, who shook her head.

'It's over. There's nothing more we can do.'

My lips tasted of nicotine as death stared me in the face.

'It's his second heart attack. We saw him after the last one in winter. I remember him joking with us a lot. He went to cardiac rehab. He couldn't give up the ciggies. Came in last night complaining of chest pains.'

I'd hit a wall. There was no bringing him back. I was a doctor and someone else was paying the price for my incompetence. I closed his eyelids and took myself off to the loo. I had thought everything was possible, had thought I was capable of working miracles ever since I saved that baby girl. I put my head in my hands and cried. When I came out I felt a hand on my back. I turned to look at Dr Saunders, the consultant physician.

'There's always a first time.' She handed me a tissue. 'We don't even get to ten per cent of cardiac arrests in time. It happens to us all.'

'But what's the point?'

'The ones who do pull through, of course! Stop beating yourself up. We're only human.

It's not always up to us. No reason to throw in the towel. Come on, I'll go and see if nurse can muster a cuppa.'

30

I was singing at the top of voice to the radio when Robert popped his head round my door.

'What about knocking?' I said.

He tossed a letter on my bed. 'I did!'

The crisp cream-coloured envelope lay there full of promise. Who could be sending me such a nice letter? I opened it carefully.

Mr and Mrs Charles Hopkins
request the pleasure of your company
at the marriage
of their daughter Amanda to
Mr Alastair Hamilton,
son of Dr and Mrs Stuart Hamilton
on 7th August 1982
at 2pm at York Minster
and the reception afterwards
at Hazelworth Castle.

At the bottom of the card Alastair had scribbled, *I took your advice.*

No! Why hadn't I blurted out how much I loved him when he kissed me? My facemask cracked. Tears dripped down and stained the card. Dear wonderful Alastair, who looked after me when I needed him, Alastair laughing and reaching for my hand, Alastair taking me seriously from the moment we met, Alastair asleep in my bed where he belonged. No! From now on he would be someone else's. I stashed the invitation behind the books on the shelf and tried to banish it from my mind.

⋆　⋆　⋆

But Alastair always was on my mind. What should I do? Write him a letter, phone, get on the next train? No, it would be so embarrassing. He was in love with amazing Amanda. Two special people; totally made for each other. I would make the most terrible fool of myself and it wasn't as if we would ever be able to forget about it. He was my adopted brother and I would see him every so often at the Mains, would witness his happiness and have to be happy for him like any sister should. I stared out of the window at some birds flying over the ward building opposite. English birds I didn't know.

I went out to discos with my flatmates and danced until I dropped. Anything not to dwell on Alastair. I took up aerobics with Annabel even though our shifts forced us to miss about half the classes, and went day-tripping on the Norfolk Broads with Robert, who had a car. Not a hill let alone a mountain in sight. I had never seen anywhere so flat.

Nothing really took my mind off Alastair for very long. I simply couldn't bring myself to reply to the wedding invitation. Perhaps he would think it had got lost in the post or perhaps he didn't think about me at all. When you're really in love, the last thing you think about is other people.

The thought of losing Alastair made me think about Tahir. If I had ever had a chance with Alastair, it was entirely my fault for not following my instincts. My gut feeling told me to go back to Kashmir and look for my brother — a voice that came and went in my head, never completely drowned out by my new life. Wasn't I desperately needed in our Vale? Here I sometimes had to deal with the self-induced consequences of the Western way of life, drinking, smoking and overeating. Back home there was everything from serious undernourishment to bullet wounds. Wasn't that the reason I had come this far? I was Kashmiri, not Scottish or English, no matter what my papers said. I had to go back to my roots. I would make a few enquiries. It was early days and I shouldn't expect any immediate replies but there was no harm in asking. It was pleasant enough here as things were but I really didn't see any point in putting off my return any longer than necessary, especially as I doubted whether I would see much of Alastair in the future. I hadn't heard from Marie and Stuart for a while, then out of the blue a letter from Marie came.

The Mains, 15th June 1982

Dear Jaya,

Hope you're well. I'm afraid I have sad news. Beauly was out with me on Tuesday for a short walk. Must have spotted a rabbit because he gave chase, bad hip and all. Then he keeled over and when I got to him, he wasn't breathing anymore. A wonderful death for a wonderful dog and he did reach the ripe old doggy age of fourteen, I keep telling myself, but I miss him terribly. I don't think another dog will ever replace him. Didn't want to upset you but thought you'd want to know.

Let's talk when you have time.
All my love and from Stuart,
Marie xxx

Beauly had been all the company I needed in

the beginning. He was only a dog, I told myself but it felt like losing a real friend. How then must Stuart and Marie feel? Once I had wiped away my tears I reached for the phone.

'It's rather quiet here now. I know you'll miss him, too,' she said. 'Oh, there is some good news, though.'

Has the wedding been cancelled? I almost blurted out.

'Alastair's secured a book deal with an option on his next two novels.'

'That's fantastic!'

'Yes, and he's taking some time out from his job.'

I gave in to the happiness I felt for him. He was doing what he wanted even if it was with Amanda by his side.

★　★　★

Good news came the day after. I had been offered a position in Srinagar! A leper colony would give me invaluable experience. They agreed to pay for my flight and supply accommodation on top of a meagre salary. Enough to survive on in Kashmir. This was what my life had been leading up to until now. I would be able to apply my knowledge in my home country where I was much more desperately needed than here and I could finally start my search for Tahir in earnest. Perfect timing. There was nothing to keep me here now.

★ ★ ★

'The tests came back positive yesterday. Stuart's got cancer, prostate cancer,' said Marie in a quivering voice when she rang me again two weeks later. My world shook for a second time in my life. I searched desperately for something comforting to say. 'You can usually live with this kind of cancer for years,' I said.

'Yes, that's what they told us at the hospital.'

I replaced the receiver and slumped onto the scruffy sofa in our sitting room cum kitchen. Impossible! On the table in front lay a pizza crust next to a half empty beer bottle and a brimming ashtray. My first family was gone. Wasn't that enough? Were all the people I loved meant to be taken from me? How could I lose another father? Had I been tempting fate with my letters to Srinagar? I couldn't leave my new family, especially not now. I simply couldn't. The whole thing was giving me a headache. I would write back and tell the head of the leprosy station I couldn't come until . . . No, I would write back and tell Dr Ahmed I couldn't come at all. There would be other offers ... I hoped. I just wished I could talk to Alastair. Or better still anyone who loved Kashmir like I did. Poor Alastair. How could I be thinking of myself especially in this situation? I sat down and wrote him a letter, finally accepting his wedding invitation.

31

A hot stab of homesickness struck me as I cycled to the hospital a week or so later. When would I ever see the Giants again? A juggernaut turned round the corner without indicating. I swerved, narrowly avoiding gliding under its belly. Pay attention, girl! My head was throbbing by the time I locked my bike up outside the hospital.

It was Miss Black's third admission this year. Broken bones every time. She was in her eighties and couldn't have weighed more than a ten-year-old. Her ankle, however, was like a balloon.

'What happened?'

'She slipped on the bathroom mat. I found her there this morning,' said the woman with the blue rinse perm. 'I'm her niece.'

'We'll have to do an X-ray. It might just be sprained,' I said in a loud voice because Miss Black was hard of hearing. I knew that with her history of osteoporosis, there was little chance of her getting away that lightly. Poor thing.

Sister Laura pulled back the curtain. 'A Mrs Hamilton called. Wants you to ring her back when you have the time.'

She wouldn't ring me at work without a really good reason. Dread seeped through my veins. As soon as the patient had been wheeled off to radiology I rang back. Marie's voice sounded quietly desperate.

'Jaya, he's taken a turn for the worse. He didn't want me to bother you before but now things are really bad. He wants to see you. Alastair is already here. Can you come?'

This was much too soon. It couldn't be true. He was meant to go on for ages. He had looked fine last time I saw him, considering. There must be something I could do. They must be mistaken. I wasn't going to let him go, not without a fight. I finished my never-ending shift, threw a few things in my case and took a taxi to the station.

★　★　★

'Hey.' Alastair looked fragile, not like him at all. He pulled me to him at the station and put his chin on top of my head. I could hear his heart beating. We stayed like that for a moment before he picked up my case and put it in the car. I thought of the time he'd come to St Andrew's. How happy we'd been, the fun we'd had and then the kiss. It was branded onto my mind, no matter how hard I tried to see him as my brother, no matter how much I tried to reconcile myself to him getting married.

'How is he?' I said as we passed a deserted croft.

'Bad, really bad.' His voice cracked and he reached for my hand. It was warm and familiar. I held it tightly until we turned into the Mains. The house looked beautiful in the July sun, the garden in full bloom. It was hard to imagine that anything other than a holiday spirit awaited me inside.

Marie was much thinner than when I had last seen her. Guilt flooded my lungs. She had been right. Norwich was much too far away. Too far away to get back at weekends. Too far away to have seen much of them these past months. But Marie wasn't thinking about herself, even then.

'Jaya, come here, let me have a look at you. You look good, so professional. Don't you think so, Alastair?'

'She looks lovely.' And he smiled for the first time.

I made to go straight up to Stuart, but Marie put her hand on my arm. 'We've made a bed up for him in the library. He feels more part of things downstairs. But he's sleeping now. Come into the sitting room.'

We drank tea in front of an empty fireplace,

which at this time of the year was usually adorned with a huge vase of flowers. Alastair stared out the window whilst we talked, as if he couldn't bear to hear what Marie was telling me.

'It could be weeks, perhaps only days. They don't want to subject him to chemo. His heart won't take it. They let me keep him because I said you'd be here.' She smiled pleadingly at me. 'He wants to be home, he's had enough of hospitals. He wants to be with us.'

★ ★ ★

The desk and chessboard had been pushed to one side and on a bed in the middle of the library lay Stuart, like the negative of a treasured photo, his cheeks caved in, his skin a taut plastic bag. Even though I came across patients in a similar state on an almost daily basis, this was different. This was my beloved Stuart. There could be no doubt how near the end he was. He raised one shimmering, blue-veined hand and beckoned me to the bed. I sat next to him and took his hand in mine. It felt like an injured sparrow I had once found on the lawn.

Stuart's voice was as feeble as everything else about him so I had to bend towards him to hear him. A tube came out of his nose and there was a stale smell about him.

'I knew you'd come,' he whispered.

★ ★ ★

I found Alastair outside on the bench by the hunchbacked trees afterwards and sat down next to him.

'Fucking cancer!' he said and his strong shoulders started to shake.

I put my arms around them and rested my head against his. 'I'm here now.'

★ ★ ★

The kindest thing was to keep Stuart on morphine but sometimes he drifted into a horrific landscape of dreams only marginally better than the pain that he had to endure without it. I was helping him, but he was giving me a greater gift: letting me accompany him on his final journey. I was being given the chance to say farewell to this second father of mine.

Being with Alastair made the situation bearable. Together we helped each other, taking turns in sitting with Stuart and keeping Marie company. I found him one evening on the beach skimming stones on the water. It was a balmy evening and it was still light enough to see the stones and seaweed under the water.

'He couldn't keep his eyes open a moment longer,' I said. 'His breathing's a bit shallow but I'm sure he'll have a peaceful night. Marie's watching a film.'

Television was something that Marie had never been very fond of before. Now she kept it on all day and collapsed in front of it whenever she could. Alastair and I sat down on the rocks. The clouds had turned pink and gold above the horizon.

'Not much longer until the big day,' I said. We hadn't talked about the wedding before.

'It seems light years away right now. I can't imagine him not being there,' he replied.

I took a deep breath. Suddenly it was as clear as the water before us. I knew that when Stuart was gone there was nothing left that would hold me here. 'Alastair . . . '

'What about you?' he said before I could continue. 'What's it like being a real doctor?'

'Everything I thought it would be. And bloody hard work, too.'

He laughed. 'I've never heard you swear. You've really become British now. You're finally where you wanted to be, aren't you?'

'For the moment, yes. But I'm going back.'

'What d'you mean?'

'To Kashmir.'

'Why? Have they found Tahir?'

'No, of course not. I'd have told you.'

'Would you? You haven't told me much recently.'

'That's rich coming from you. I didn't know about you and Amanda until I got the card.'

He looked taken aback. 'You can't just up and leave. Not now! Especially not now. You belong here!'

'Alastair. Kashmir is where I'm meant to be. I've always known that.'

'But things have changed. You've become such a part of . . . What about Marie?' He paused for a second and looked straight at me. 'What about me, for Christ's sake?'

'You don't need a sister anymore. Alastair, you've got Amanda. Let's not fight, not at a time like this. I can't think about the time after . . . after this. I'll talk to Marie. I know she'll understand but Alastair, I don't think I'll be able to make your wedding after all. They're desperate for me to come and work at the leprosy station in Srinagar as soon as I can.'

PART 3

32

Kashmir, 1982

Images flashed through my mind as the plane gathered speed on the runway: Stuart's coffin being lowered into the grave, then covered with flowers. Alastair holding Amanda's hand as he looked over Marie's head at me. Marie's last words when I left her. 'Stuart was so proud of you. You know that, don't you? Now go and do what you're meant to be doing.' Alastair's sombre, brotherly kiss at the train station with Amanda at his side. The sight of the two of them waving goodbye. I felt the plane leave the ground and sank into a deep, dreamless sleep.

I climbed refreshed and strangely at peace with myself into the small propeller machine at New Delhi. Even the turbulence didn't bother me. When we finally broke through the cloud, a crown of white-tipped mountains welcomed me back.

I stepped out on the tarmac and everything gleamed in the bright, clear light of my childhood. It wasn't just a dream! Everything was just as vivid as I had remembered it to be. The fresh mountain air was tinged with the scent of a million flowers and the smiling, beautiful faces of my fellow Kashmiris seemed so familiar. I was home. As undeniable, as tangible a feeling as the Giants above me.

What about Tahir? He would be a young man now. He had Pa's graceful build, I was sure, but would I even recognize him? I sneaked glances at anyone who vaguely fitted the bill, which was quite awkward because staring at young men was definitely improper. Even if I did see him, could I just go up to him? Would he recognize me or turn on his heel and run? Would he even be able to speak? All this fretting was beside the point. I had to find him first.

DR VAIDYA

A man was holding up my name as I emerged from customs. My heart skipped a beat. I had left as a schoolchild and was being welcomed back as a doctor. This meant so much more to me here than in Norwich.

We sped away from the airport through the outskirts of the city until we reached Nagin Lake and the leper colony. Could this collection of ramshackle buildings possibly have anything in common with a hospital? I

226

asked myself. I must have walked past this place many times as a child and never registered its existence. Established in 1882 by the British, little had been done to move it into the twentieth century. Its only saving grace was that it was located next to the serene lake, so typical of the dichotomy of squalor and beauty I had often witnessed on our visits to Srinagar.

The man showed me to my room in an old building just outside the grounds. It was far from comfortable but at least I had my own sink and running water, and there was a shower which I would have to share with six other nurses. The man told me that Dr Ahmed would like to see me when I was ready.

'How will I find him?' I asked.

'I can come and get you in an hour if it pleases you, Dr Vaidya.'

'That would please me very much,' I answered before he bowed and left.

⋆   ⋆   ⋆

I put up a photo of Marie and Alastair and draped my tapestry of elephants over the table. It felt like arriving at St Medan's except that when I looked out of my window, I could see my beloved mountain crests above the lake with its mantle of water lilies.

The stench of rotting flesh hit us as Dr Ahmed, the short dignified consultant in charge, opened the door of a room in the mud block.

'It's their last stop,' he explained. 'Their families often dump them here at night. Leprosy still carries such a stigma that they'll do almost anything to deny the fact, even when it's staring them in the face like this.'

An old man with a striped woollen hat on his head sat on a pile of blankets, holding the bandaged stump of his arm with his good hand. Two holes were all that was left of his nose. He looked back at us with blank eyes, his head tilted to try and make out who was standing in front of him.

'Good morning, dear Singh,' said Dr Ahmed in Urdu. 'Did you have a good night? I have a new intern with me today, Dr Jaya Vaidya. She is very capable and will help us no end.'

The man's face broke into a toothless smile to which Dr Ahmed said, 'Yes, such good news today. Now don't you worry. Nurse'll be over presently.' He turned to me and said in English, 'If they'd just got him to us when he first noticed his fingers going numb, he would still be labouring in his rice paddy or sitting at home being tended to by his twenty or so

228

grandchildren. Instead he will never see his home or family again. They don't want to see him. They have made that very clear by their absence. There has been no sign of them since he turned up, blind and crippled six years ago. He's not infectious but they still don't want him back. A tragedy,' he sighed. 'Antibiotics are the first thing we give all of them here. It's that simple! Unfortunately, though, we cannot reverse the damage wrought beforehand.'

Dr Ahmed marched on to the next hut where an old woman smiled at me from the floor, no toes on her swollen feet, her fingers ended at the first joint. Behind her, pots and pans hung on the wall. Was she even able to cook? Did any of her family come and take care of her as was the case in Indian hospitals? It didn't look like it. She looked as abandoned as her neighbour. I couldn't help feeling relieved when we were back out in the sun. A tall man, who should have been in the prime of his life, hobbled slowly past on crutches. It was obviously very painful for him to walk. Startlingly thin, his stomach ballooned under his soiled white *pheran* and although I couldn't see the state of his feet in his shoes, they pointed inwards.

'We try to do what we can for them but the

powers that be regard them in much the same way as their families — out of sight, out of mind. We're on a very, very tight budget,' Dr Ahmed said in resignation. 'I've been here for fifteen years now and my pleas for more resources bounce off a stone bureaucratic wall. No one cares about these people.'

Dr Ahmed went into the next room and ruffled the hair of a young boy who sat on the bare floor. He was perhaps eight or nine years old with sad big eyes, all hope taken from him before his life had really started. His bent stump of an arm held a bowl as best it could while his other was scraping out the grainy mush from inside. If he was lucky, he might be able to beg for a living in the dusty lanes of Srinagar. What would I be able to do for him? Why was I here? I hadn't really thought much about my work when I accepted the job. I just saw it as some way of getting back to Kashmir but now the misery and despair hit me. I wouldn't be able to heal these people, just halt the carnage that their disease had inflicted on them. I would attend to their ulcers and rotting wounds until they no longer wept pus and bled onto their bandages. But what happened to these people afterwards?

★ ★ ★

Gone were my carefree days of wandering about a city at night. Here I made sure I was never out after dusk and wore a scarf at all times in public. Under its guise it was difficult to tell if I was Hindu or Muslim. Most importantly I did everything not to attract the attention of the Indian soldiers, who ruled our roost. It was better not to roam the streets alone but luckily Zulfah, who was one of our nurses, was always pleased to have company and fill our outings with lively chatter and gossip about people I had never met.

★　★　★

One night the dogs woke me. They seemed to be terribly excited. I pulled on my clothes and made my way with a torch to the hospital gates. A nurse had got there before me and was bending over a young girl in her teens. I took a closer look at her. The virus looked as if it had entered a pact with malnutrition to finish her off before daybreak.

After we carried her in on a stretcher, I put her on a drip and administered a massive dose of antibiotics. She was still breathing when Dr Ahmed appeared two hours later. Soon afterwards I snapped off my latex gloves and left her with a nurse by her side. I found my way back to the room by the mauve glow over the mountains as the early morning prayers from the Hazratbal Mosque resounded across the water. My senses were sharper than ever after the night's events. The song of a thousand thrushes, finches and golden orioles filled the sweet morning air when I lay down on my bed. I tossed and turned and then my family home came to mind. I was back; I could easily go and visit even if it was just ruins. I needed to see for myself what was left. Homesickness was creeping up on me but was it really wise to go and rip open old wounds? Sleep had become impossible. I felt that the dawn was calling for me to go out and meet it. I gave in and got up.

Once the idea had wormed its way into my consciousness, I couldn't dismiss it. The only way to get on with the future was to live with the past, said a voice in my head. You must go as soon as possible! No, another voice replied, I just can't face it and that's that! But of course it didn't go away. The mulberry tree under my window. The rocking chair on the porch, the sweeping view of the valley, the solid stone walls. Deprived of the previous night's sleep, I succumbed to dreams of Sabir in the kitchen and our jeep parked in front of the house with apple trees surrounding the place. Still I withstood the pull of the mountains until my dreams became inhabited by ghosts living in a house with gaping windows, crumbling walls and petrified trees. There was nothing for it but to visit at the first possible opportunity.

★　★　★

The journey in the taxi was spectacular as ever but I spent it holding my breath in dread. Up, up we drove along the roads which had changed little apart from some reinforcement here and there to secure what the earthquake and the elements had damaged. There were gaps in the forest with countless tree trunks lying where they had fallen, devoid of leaves and rotting. Houses stood like partially crushed cardboard boxes or piles of rubble on which weeds and stringy grass grew.

Our house! Unmistakable even from a distance, even though only a few walls were still standing. I got out of the taxi and walked around to what used to be the kitchen. Above me, just blue sky and a branch of the mulberry tree reaching inside what used to be my bedroom. With no house dwarfing it, the tree appeared much more majestic than I remembered. All the other walls had simply given way and been cleared to one side in the search for bodies. Would I have survived? No, the roof would have crushed me as it had Ma and the boys. There was not the slightest trace of our old woodshed. Instead rosehip bushes thrived where it used to stand and wild blue flowers sprouted from between a couple of moss-covered rocks. Pa would have liked that.

Swallows raced overhead and an eerie silence surrounded the place where I had spent my wonderful childhood. No young boys' shouts, no animal cries, no mother busy in the kitchen, no sign of Pa returning from a call. Not even the dot of a pilgrim on a mule in the far distance on the path to the Cave of Amaranth because it wasn't the right time of the year for that. Unmoved by the earthquake's aftermath, the Sind River meandered down to join the Jhelum as always while I searched for traces of my family. Nothing, for the winter storms and destitute survivors had long since carried away the remnants of our belongings. Just some overgrown rubble and my memories.

Then I remembered that Rajan had once carved his name high up in the mulberry tree. The taxi driver must have thought I was mad as I climbed partly up the wall and used the lower branches to find the spot. RAJAN. There it was! I kissed the letters. Proof that he had lived here, that I had once had a family. I took a photo.

Where were their bodies? By the time I had discovered their fate, they had already been disposed of, probably in a mass grave near the village, buried within a day as was the custom in our Vale. This was the closest I could get to a family grave. Now I had seen it there was nothing left to stay for. All around, apple trees drooped heavy with red, gold and green fruit. I picked two of them and gave one to the driver who was waiting at the bottom of the drive.

33

The visit affected me more profoundly than I'd thought. Doubts flared up at moments when loneliness threatened to overwhelm me. What if Tahir had perished years ago and the only two people I really loved were on the other side of the world? What if I didn't belong here anymore? Surely I was more Scottish then Kashmiri now? I came to accept that there was no short cut to feeling at home. I would have to get to know my country again in a new way, would have to put down roots where old ones had been severed.

Nagin Lake wasn't far from Dal market. One day I decided I would get there really early to see the vendors gathering at dawn just as I had with Kaliq. The market was usually over by eight anyway which was why I hadn't made it before. So I set my alarm the next day with a mission to reacquaint myself with my old haunts and get some fresh produce in the bargain, all perfectly possible before my shift.

Time had stood still in the best of ways, I thought, as I spied my first group of vendors forming a star in the mauve morning light with the tips of their *shikara*. It didn't take long for them to agree, for customers were slowly arriving at the lake. I bought some rice, carrots, celery, tomatoes and a bunch of flowers before sitting down on a bench underneath a chinar tree by the water to enjoy the sight of my people going about their morning errands. To my one side, a couple of elderly men were sharing a water pipe in an otherwise empty tea house on the lake front. Three women in *burqas* walked past and a *shikara* full of buckets of flowers caused a family of ducks to swim off to a more peaceful spot. A boy was talking to one of the tradesman. A woman in a red floral *pheran* and headscarf hung back a few steps behind. I remembered haggling with the vendors as a child under Kaliq's watchful gaze. Oh, to be here with someone I knew. The boy's voice got quite loud until he finally turned and held up a bag of precious nuts. The woman stepped forward, smiled and took them from him. Our eyes met. An electric current passed through me. Avani! A huge smile lit up her face as we ran into each other's arms.

'What are you doing here?' she exclaimed.

'I've come back to work as a doctor!' I couldn't help feeling two inches taller.

'What does your husband in the Punjab say to that?'

'No husband,' I said, 'not in the Punjab, not anywhere else. It's a long story. Do you have time for some *kava?*' Kashmiri chai, a delicious mix of almonds, cardamom seeds and cinnamon, was one of the highlights of coming home.

'Of course I do.'

Her boy was looking at me wide-eyed.

'This is Madhav Junior, our first son,' she added, 'after three elder sisters.'

Avani, a mother of four! She must have had children before I left when she moved to Madhav's village.

'How about some lassi?' I asked Junior and he nodded enthusiastically.

Drinks in hand, we settled down on a bench at the side of the lake and the boy gulped down his drink before running off to watch a fisherman sorting his nets next to the aquamarine water. We sipped our *kava* in leisure as Avani listened to my story as if I were reading from *A Thousand and One Nights*. My life must have indeed taken a very strange turn for her.

'Now I'm here to stay,' I concluded without mentioning anything about my new brother. 'What about you? Are you happy? And Madhav and the girls?'

238

'Happy? It is a hard life but we cannot complain. Madhav is out all hours on Wular Lake where we have a small house. We shared it with his parents but both of them have passed away. His mother only two months ago. Jaya, do come and visit. I would love the company and the girls would love you, I'm sure.' She took my hand. 'Your father, your mother, your brothers . . . I am so sorry, Jaya. We lost Aila. You remember her, don't you?'

Of course I remembered. She was the baby of Avani's family and I had so envied Avani for having a sister.

'But compared to your loss . . . '

'Thank you, Avani.' I couldn't deal with pity at that moment. 'I've been very lucky,' I said, 'and I've got used to being by myself.'

'But what about Tahir?' Her voice dropped to a whisper. 'Hasn't he ever contacted you?'

I must have looked thunderstruck because she asked in disbelief, 'You know nothing about him?'

My heart exploded with happiness like a fireworks display. 'Where is he?' I pleaded.

'If I'd known where you were, I would have told you myself.'

'Told me what?'

'He's a killer!'

A killer. Tahir. My little brother. What on

earth was she talking about? Who had he killed?

'He's a terrorist.'

'I don't believe you!' I almost shouted.

She put her fingers to her lips and looked around. 'I'm so sorry, Jaya, but it's true. I swear on my children's lives.' She looked at me and slowly got up. 'Jaya, I'll be back at the market next week with something for you. I hope you can come.' I couldn't bear to reply.

★　★　★

I spent the week hating Avani and her lies. There was no way that my little brother, who wouldn't even swat a fly, would end another man's life. Why was she making up such evil rumours? Was it envy, jealousy? Our family had always been wealthier than hers. Still, I dreaded our next meeting.

★　★　★

The following Friday two of her daughters flanked her side; pretty dark girls, almost young women who looked so much like their mother. She sat down next to me while they wandered off with their baskets.

'Read this, dear Jaya.'

It was a newspaper cutting from the

Kashmir Times. A faded black and white picture of a group of most wanted terrorists. Tahir, like a younger version of my pa, was wearing a scarf around his head and he sported a long unkempt beard as well as a fine moustache just like Pa's. Somehow, though, it didn't suit him at all. I looked at the two grim faces besides him. There must be some terrible mistake! What was he doing with these men? Worse still, what would Ma and Pa have felt about having a killer for a son?

'They're apparently responsible for ambushing a truckful of Indian soldiers on their way to an outpost on the Pakistani border. Two soldiers dead and six in a critical condition. I don't know what happened after that.'

I was slowly taking in what she was saying. I looked at the date: 5th April 1980. Perhaps there had been even more fatalities, more murders since then.

Struggling for words I finally asked, 'Has there been any news of him since?'

'Only rumours. And I'm not sure if people are just trying to keep the memory of him alive. He's a hero for some, you know.'

Here I was trying to save lives whilst Tahir was putting a bullet in people! Shame washed over me, shame for my brother, shame for the way I had acted towards Avani.

'Thank you for bringing this. I'm so sorry, Avani.'

She dismissed my apologies with a wave of her hand and hugged me instead. 'You promise to pay me a visit soon, won't you?'

I nodded as my mind swarmed with demons.

34

I must find him, talk to him, persuade him to
. . . give himself up? Was there no way I could
attract his attention, make it known to him
that I was in Srinagar? No, it mustn't get out
that I was his sister. I was stumped and
grateful for any distraction at work, but
especially for news from Marie.

Dear Jaya,

*How are you, my dear? We miss you
terribly and can't wait for you to come
back at Christmas. Things are a little too
quiet at the Mains so I've gone ahead
and got Bunny. Not an actual rabbit, I
assure you, but a cross between a cocker
spaniel and a setter. I know I said I
would wait but I simply couldn't resist
her when Alastair took me to the dogs'
home. He said he couldn't leave me here
all by myself when he went. So here she
is now and she's beautiful! She's quite
timid but adores me as much as I do her,
and follows me about as if she'd been
here all her life. I'm afraid I'm turning
into one of those old women who let*

their dogs sleep in their beds. Well, not
quite, but she does have a basket in the
bedroom . . .

What a good idea of Alastair's, I thought, and
felt a pang as I remembered that it wasn't just
work that was calling him away. I read on;
Marie was excited she was actually going to
make the wedding cake herself. Of course, a
wedding was the best thing ever for her.
Something to keep her busy, something to
look forward to. I was pleased I was this far
away. Thank the gods for more reasons than
one that I too was busy.

★   ★   ★

Every morning I made sure the patients were
as comfortable as possible, checking they had
no new infections, instructing the nurses to
change their bandages and give them all their
medication. Once I got to grips with the
routine of things, I wanted to do more. Jiji,
the boy with the stump of an arm and an air
of sadness about him, would often follow me
around as I went from mud block to mud
block. I didn't try to shake him off. It was a
bit like having some friendly pup at my side
— he rarely said anything, just watched me
with doleful puppy eyes. I could sense a lot

more going on in his head than he let on. There must be something more I could do for someone so young now that the decay had been brought to a standstill.

I sat down one day and showed him a children's picture book that Dr Ahmed had brought in from his own abundant family. In the beginning he looked at the pictures of the adventures of Binji the elephant with his sad eyes. I didn't know if it was the fact that he had probably never opened a book before or that I was paying him attention, but I could see a miraculous transformation in him. He started to laugh at the pictures as he traced the pictures across the page with his good hand. I made a decision; I would teach him to read.

From then on we tried to spend an hour every day in the sun at a table in front of his room, tracing the letters of the Urdu alphabet. Writing them again and again on some paper I had managed to acquire for him, mouthing their sounds until they finally made a word. Of course, he was lucky that his right hand was still intact and so his damaged arm would hold the paper in place as he repeated the exercises with an intensity that was astounding. Within three weeks he had mastered the alphabet and within two months he was happily reading any children's books I could get hold of from the nurses. From then on we had a happy boy on our hands, the only problem being to find enough children's books to quench his seemingly insatiable literary appetite.

★   ★   ★

I took a rare break to Adipur on Wular Lake where Avani had spent her entire married life. The thatched hut in a small settlement a stone's throw from the water was made of mud. It was spotlessly clean and tidy and very cosy with *nandas*, pretty woollen mats, covering the floor of the two-roomed abode which housed the five of them. She hugged me when I arrived and entreated me to 'Come in, come in!'

The bedding covered in *gubbas* (intricately embroidered blankets) made comfortable places to sit.

'Madhav is still out on the lake and I've sent the girls to the water to do the washing so we can have a good chat.'

'And little Madhav?'

'Oh, he's at school. It's not far. We're lucky because he can walk back with the other boys.'

'What a lovely home!'

Avani put her hand on her stomach and

smiled. 'It's going to get a bit crowded when number five comes along.'

'You're expecting again?' I said half in admiration, half in concern.

'Yes, there'll be no hiding it once the Holi festival is upon us. I want to give Madhav another boy. What about you, Jaya? When will you get married?'

'Oh, I'm married to my job,' I said but the words seemed to ring hollow.

My life may be what I had chosen but there was no denying that it lacked all that Avani could boast of. At that moment Madhav came through the door, a brace of fish hanging from his hand. He was tall and handsome as ever, if a little weathered for the years gone by, yet he was still her prince, and for a second fleeting moment in our lives, I wanted to change places with her.

★ ★ ★

I thought about Tahir all the time. Even at work. How could he? Pa had tended to the freedom fighters when he was called upon but he wouldn't have helped anyone or actually committed a crime. He had merely done his duty as a doctor. The fact that Pa loved the place he had grown up in was our great inheritance but Tahir had completely

misunderstood Pa's vision. After the earthquake, something truly terrible must have
happened to him. I racked my brains over
how to find him. Well, I certainly wouldn't
find him here in the leper colony but if I
could work my way further up into the hills,
work as a real doctor, even specialize
eventually, perhaps I might have a tiny chance
of meeting him.

It wasn't as if I could stay here forever.
Where would it get me? There was no doubt
that I was making an impact on these
people's lives but at the same time it was a bit
like treading water. The very nature of leprosy
dictated limits. For the most part I did little
more than what a fully-trained nurse did. I
craved the immediacy of truly healing
someone completely, the kind you could get
as a surgeon and needed to grow as a medic
just as much as I needed to find Tahir for my
own peace of mind.

The nurses were giggling and messing
around in the room next to mine early one
morning, being so loud that I couldn't help
eavesdropping.

'Heard about the new head of the local
hospital?'

'No, what about him?'

'He seems to be changing things.'

'Like what?'

'Can you believe it? They've just taken on two new doctors and . . . '

'And?'

'They're women!'

'Change, you think things change for no reason there? They're more likely desperate!'

My heart pounded. This was my chance! But I had to talk to Dr Ahmed immediately. I owed him that. So I plucked up all my courage and approached him.

'I wish I could offer you more money,' he replied with a sigh.

'It's not about money, Dr Ahmed!' I couldn't mention Tahir nor tell him how frustrated I was. I knew that if I stayed here much longer I would grab the first chance to escape with both hands. 'It is time for me to consolidate my knowledge. I want to specialize eventually and I may have that chance at the State hospital. Of course I will stay until you find a suitable replacement,' I said as the shame of walking out on him glowed in my cheeks.

He nodded in resignation. 'It's what happens to all our doctors sooner or later. They never stay long: always move on to better things.' A young girl in a wheelchair with no feet rolled past us. 'Tell me, what are your plans?'

Guilt made me speak up. 'My father was a

doctor up at Sonamarg. He always wanted to build a clinic in the mountains. It's why I've returned.'

My words sounded ridiculous, my dream of a clinic just as unrealistic as Pa's. I had no money, no resources and I had become a stranger in my own country. On top of that, the situation in general had deteriorated in Kashmir. Its wealth had been further sapped when a spate of incidents between protestors and the army kept the tourists away. Kashmir's problems were becoming as forgotten as the plight of the lepers.

Dr Ahmed gave me one of his rare smiles. 'Where there's a will there's a way! That would be enough reason to let you go, if any. Look at us! We should have packed our bags long ago. I shall see what we can do about a replacement but I can't promise anything. These are difficult times. Good doctors are a blessed commodity round here.' He put his pen down and looked at me. 'And you are one of them.'

★ ★ ★

The hospital was indeed still recruiting and Dr Ahmed organized my successor faster than even I had expected. A young man from Bombay returned to the land of his grandfathers. An ideal position for this was his first post since completing his studies. When I finally told Jiji, he gazed at me with brimming saucers of eyes.

'I'll come back and visit and bring you a book each time,' I promised. A tear ran down his cheek and clung to his chin as he tried to muster a smile.

35

The rundown charm of its nineteenth-century colonial architecture was not the reason why patients flocked from all over the Vale to the hospital. The sick had little choice and were often far worse for wear from the long journey they had taken upon themselves.

When I reported to the guard at the entrance on my first day, he handed me a heavy bunch of keys.

'What are these for?' I asked.

'For all the doors.'

'All of them?'

'Yes, please sign here and remember to lock them behind you, Dr Vaidya.'

I wondered if I were entering a high-security prison instead of a place of healing as I made my way to the front of a queue of people to unlock the ward I was on. The long dark corridor stank of iodine and the rich aroma of food brought in by family members. There was also a faint scent of coconut oil which patients put in their hair to make it shine.

On seeing me, a nurse in a brilliant white sari jumped to attention and saluted me. I couldn't believe it. I wondered if the months in the leprosy station had aged me more than I knew. In Norwich the nurses had adopted a kind of parental attitude to us greenhorns. Here I was, a respected doctor with authority, far above the nursing staff; this was to be my first taste of the steep hierarchy that governed this microcosm.

Dress was very important. The nurses themselves wore different coloured caps denoting their position within the regimented order, and I was so grateful to the matron who, when serving me a cup of incredibly sweet milky tea, pointed at my *kameez* over drawstring trousers.

'What's the matter?' I asked. 'No one wears a white coat here.'

'I do not mean to be disrespectful, Dr Vaidya,' she said, blushing deeply, 'it's just that they may not think you are a real doctor.' At that moment, another doctor in a beautiful red and green sari, the loose end of which was draped over dark glowing skin like a vibrant veil, passed by.

'Ah, I see what you mean!'

My next free day saw me buy two new saris and a packet of jasmine tea for the matron.

Other differences were more serious and made me feel quite desperate at times. It was difficult to find injections and needles in the untidy cabinets, and even the disinfected scalpels in the operating theatre lay in a disorderly pile. Stretchers and beds were rusty, mattresses ripped and apparatus lay in various states of disrepair. Wheelchairs were made of wood and bicycle tyres and artificial limbs had been skilfully improvised from any material at hand.

The surgeons' green overalls, which had been washed by hand over a stone, were left out on the dusty roof to dry. The pungent whiff of the sanitary facilities was especially unpleasant on my early morning shifts and I was all the more shocked when I saw a cleaner use the same mop and water for the toilets as for the operating theatre. Perhaps the iodine was indeed strong enough to do both jobs, I kidded myself, for the stench certainly implied as much.

Parents shared beds with sick children and there was no privacy or silence in the unrelenting din of the crowded corridors with relatives and bedding blocking the way, and nurses even had to shoo away the dogs which often lay in the accessible areas when they rolled the bed of a new admission in.

I soon gave up attempting to draw comparisons between the facilities in Srinagar and Norwich. The two images were irreconcilable.

★　★　★

In Kashmir you didn't go to hospital for the mere event of a birth. There needed to be some obvious danger before women would consider giving birth anywhere else than home. Medical treatment cost money, money which most people didn't have. Women were accompanied to any examination by their husband, their mother or a sister. On my second day on the ward a young woman in the late throes of labour was screaming for all she was worth as I examined her. I had to send her mother and sister outside as the sisters came to hold her down. It took me only a couple of minutes to realize that forceps weren't going to get us anywhere. This was a breech birth and the baby was stuck firmly at the top of the birth canal, a Caesarean being the only option.

'Get her ready for the operating table!' I ordered.

Colour drained from the nurse in charge. 'Both theatres are occupied!'

By the time the surgeon pierced the woman's swollen belly, it was too late. Perfect as he was, the boy's umbilical cord was wrapped tightly around his neck. The surgeon shook his head as he handed the baby to the nurse. He turned to me. 'I'm afraid someone

255

will have to break the news to her. A hysterectomy is waiting for me.'

My stomach turned. I wanted to run away and cry somewhere by myself. But there was no escape. All part and package of my duties. I attended to two or three other patients until the mother regained consciousness. The woman started crying uncontrollably as did her mother and sister. They screamed and wailed and their cries and lamenting could be heard for hours afterwards. I had to attend to other patients but no one moved them on; no one paid them the slightest bit of attention. The afflicted seemed unaware of anything around them and the unaffected left them to their very public business of mourning. It was a scene I was to encounter again and again in the course of my work there.

When I finally got back to my room which I shared with another doctor in the compound, I felt as if I had fallen into a deep dark pit. Surely this wouldn't have happened in Norwich? I wished I had someone to talk to. Why didn't I heed the signs and find a comfy position near Marie? It was all so desperate here. I dragged myself to my next shift in the evening and saw the arrival of six babies, four boys and two girls, all bonny and healthy, all of them previously at risk. Three spent the first couple of days in incubators but nothing to worry unduly about. Their births made the world of difference to me.

On passing the main operating theatre, I witnessed a surgeon showing a basin to the people gathered there. 'I'm afraid it was past saving,' he said to the man sceptically eyeing its contents. 'This uterus is much too shrivelled to do its work anymore.'

The man nodded, the surgeon bowed and then returned to his work. I went over to the nurse, who had just sprung to attention, and asked her about the man.

'Her husband. The patient knew it had to come out but he had to see it with his own eyes. Otherwise it would be a bit like stealing, wouldn't it?'

⋆ ⋆ ⋆

The burns unit was very large in comparison to the one in Norwich and regularly treated children with first- or second-degree burns from the unattended *kangri* baskets of scorching coal. Even graver was the state of a two-year-old who needed skin grafts because of an overturned oil lamp. We saved her life but could do nothing about the red shrivelled skin that stretched across one side of her face. She was only one of many we treated for similar accidents.

I once entered a room to see a patient lying naked on top of the bed, her whole body one massive burn.

'What accident caused this?' I asked my colleague. Dr Tann gestured for me to follow him out.

'It wasn't an accident.'

'What do you mean?' I answered.

'She narrowly escaped being cremated with her husband.'

I just couldn't get my head around it. There were still places nearby where families burned the wives of their departed! Surely this had been relegated to distant history. The poor woman stayed with us for almost a year. It took months until the risk of infection was finally banished and we could bandage her burns. I never found out where she went afterwards.

Tuberculosis was rampant in Kashmir. For most people it was a slow death sentence because they sought help much too late. TB didn't only affect their lungs. It put people into wheelchairs as their spines crumbled with the disease or attacked their brains. Those who made it to the hospital were the lucky ones. They received treatment and medication and if we got to them in time, they walked out of the hospital and returned to their previous lives with nothing more than a few weeks away from home. But the problem was often that they felt well when they left and so didn't continue taking their medication. Instead they sold it on the black market, only all too often to fall ill again and die.

★   ★   ★

One of Marie's letters let me know that the wedding had been cancelled. What on earth was I doing here if that was the case? My heart soared for a brief moment before I read on. It had only been postponed; something to do with Alastair's work. Something important. Marie didn't go into detail and who cared anyway? I was thousands of miles away. Alastair loved Amanda and the rest would take place in due course. I had to accept that it wasn't my business anymore and that I was destined to go through life alone.

36

Tahir came to love his gun over time. He had to oil it and clean it and look after it, a bit like Garuda, who had meant more to him than any single being on this Earth besides his family. He savoured the feel of the cold metal, the smoothness of the wood and the distinct smell of the bag he kept it in. He swore that he would be able to pick his rifle out in the dark by its smell alone. When he had it with him, he didn't need to explain himself. People respected him and listened to him even if he said very little. And he didn't have to be afraid of people, either. They couldn't just creep up on him and overpower him. No, his gun had saved his life on at least two occasions now.

The first time he stumbled across two Pakistani soldiers on the Norwa Pass; he downed them before they even tried to stop him, let alone ask for his papers. It was self-defence because if they had realized who he was, he would have been a dead man. He couldn't have talked his way out of the situation, not him; he couldn't talk his way into or out of anything. If he hadn't had his gun, they would have picked him off like a buzzard swooping down on an unsuspecting adder. The second time had been much closer, when the police had actually stormed the house in the village in the Karakoram foothills. You don't go storming houses without a reason. They must have had a lead. He had hidden behind a curtain and shot his way free without even a scratch. He wasn't sure if he had killed them; he just remembered the exhilaration as he galloped away on Shalo, his horse of the last six years. Stupid people, they should have got his horse first of all.

He had dreams like any other man, to settle down, with a respectable girl on a homestead far up in the mountains, away from those who would always choose to interfere in his life. Perhaps he could tend animals. Living off them and racing falcons in summer — the only other thing he could imagine outside of his present life. He would have a large family, lots of children who would listen to him. And as head of the family, he would preside over meals and teach his sons to love the land. But he only wished for that occasionally.

In real life, his comrades were his family. They had accepted him in a way he had never felt before. Had made a man of him. It hadn't been easy but he had fought hard to become one of them. Now they looked up to him as their leader, as the chosen one who would lead them to freedom and in doing so liberate the Vale from the oppressors' grip. The gods would bless him for it, he was sure, and children would be taught about his heroic deeds long after he was dead. There were missions much greater than personal happiness and he had found his the day the gods had crushed his family underfoot. He could not undo what he had done since then or more explicitly, he had no wish to turn the clock back.

37

Mr Stoke was recovering from pneumonia when I entered his cubicle to check up on him at the end of my nightshift. I was listening to his breathing with my stethoscope but his wife just carried on talking. What to do with *Grasmere* when they returned home? I wondered what she was talking about until she mentioned the mooring that they had to pay for. A houseboat. They couldn't bear to sell it until they were quite sure that they would never come back and until things were sorted with their daughter in Dorset.

The words tumbled out before I had time to consider them. 'I could take care of your boat until you come to a decision. I'm not looking for anything permanent . . . not down here.' I was fed up of thinking, eating and sleeping hospital in the campus-style accommodation complex. Perhaps that was why I still felt so unhappy — like some misfit neither at home here nor anywhere else for that matter.

No, there was also the problem of sharing a unit. Aida — one of the other women doctors — and I were often on different shifts and it was difficult to relax when you had to either keep quiet because she was sleeping behind the paper-thin walls or she, on the other hand, was inadvertently waking me up. I yearned for a place of my own, somewhere I could really make home.

Mrs Stoke frowned and turned to her husband, who looked as if he had just put down a heavy bag of shopping. Then his whole body shook with an endless grating cough.

'I am sorry,' I said. 'I don't know what got into me.'

When he finally got his breath back, he said, 'What a grand idea. It's just, I'm afraid it's too small for a family.'

'I'm single,' I replied.

'Perfect! You see,' he paused a moment to catch his breath, 'we came here with the army decades ago and thought we'd landed in Shangri-La. When we were sent home, we promised to come back. Bought *Grasmere* the very next summer and once Delia, our daughter, had grown up we stayed. She used to come out occasionally before she had her family. Now her own children are grown up themselves and no one's really interested anymore.' His eyes moved to the window as if he was trying to fight something back and Mrs Stoke took his hand. A moment passed and then he looked at me. 'I know you'll love it. It's a home away from home. We wouldn't want any rent, just something to cover the mooring.'

I moved in a month later.

Dear Marie,

Thanks for your letter. It sounds as if Bunny has completely taken over the Mains. I wish I could see her just as I wish you could see my boat. I know you'd love it! It's twenty minutes from the hospital on a quiet part of Dal Lake and made of cedar wood with intricate patterns carved on the outside. Inside, the Stokes have installed a perfect little kitchen, a dining table with fitted seats and a bedroom complete with double bed!

Life on the lake suits me perfectly. It calms me down, especially after a long shift at the hospital and I never feel alone because the neighbours have taken quite a shine to me, especially since I helped their girl, who cut her foot on a piece of glass. They seem a wee bit in awe of me, because I'm a doctor from Scotland yet a Kashmiri like themselves. All I did was dress her wound and give her a shot for tetanus before sending her on her way.

Next thing I knew her mother asked me to join the family for a meal. They're always asking me now but my shifts are even longer than in England and rarely leave me time for anything else. Yesterday, though, their youngest child, a boy of about four turned up on deck with a steaming bowl of vegetable korma and saffron rice.

On warm summer evenings I sit out in the fading light amongst the jasmine, oleander, clematis and tomato plants Mr and Mrs Stoke planted and watch the water and the mountains melt into a bath of blue and purple. I certainly don't need a TV! From my bed I can watch the shikaras making their way to market or dragging a floating garden behind them. There are fishing boats in sight and at eight thirty every morning, a school boat full of giggling girls in dark green uniforms passes very nearby.

Has a new date been set for the wedding yet?

Will you go for a swim and think of me? It's one of the things I can't do here.

All my love

Jaya xxx

I was proud of having actually asked about

the wedding in a down-to-earth kind of way. I had decided, at least in my mind, that it was time to put the past behind me and act like a grown up woman. After all, I had my own pad now. In due time Alastair sent me a copy of his book with a blue shiny cover but no mention of his forthcoming wedding. I thanked him and replied that I would read it the moment I had time.

For the first time in my life I was living alone and enjoying it. I could come and go as I pleased, at least within limits, because of the unrest and military presence on the streets. You couldn't forget the Indian army easily. I made sure I always took the well-lit main road to the hospital and tried to avoid being out after dark as far as possible.

Sometimes when nothing moved apart from the slap of water on the side of the boat, my thoughts strayed back to Alastair and naturally to Amanda. Surely they must have set a new date by now or even the wedding had actually taken place. Yes, that was much more likely. It was so strange that I had heard nothing more but then it seemed that every third letter in and out of Kashmir went astray. I expected some poor postal worker had swiped the wedding one and then tossed it in the bin when it contained nothing other than photos. What a grand affair their wedding must have been. I imagined a Scottish wedding in the middle of York with all his friends from home and work. Had he worn a kilt? Of course he had and Amanda would have looked stunning in whatever dress she had picked or had especially made for her. She certainly lacked neither the money nor the looks. I shook my head. Why was I picking at the scab that was starting to cover up my feelings for him?

Out on deck early one morning I heard a cry from the reeds behind me. I couldn't see anything and so I poured myself another cup of chai from my samovar teapot and took another bite of my donut-shaped bread. There are so many sorts of chapati and naan in Kashmir, especially eaten at breakfast.

I caught a movement in the corner of my eye. Something black and bedraggled was dragging itself up out of the water — one of the many water fowl that nested on the lake, I thought, but jumped off the boat to investigate all the same. As I got nearer I made out a tiny black kitten. Wet and gasping for breath, it was shivering violently. I looked around; there didn't seem to be any sign of another cat or an owner for that matter. I had a sneaking suspicion that someone had tried to drown it. It mewed loudly. I picked it up and took it back to the boat. Once it had been put out on deck in a breadbasket lined with a dish cloth in the sun, the now fluffy kitten didn't seem to have the strength to go anywhere for the time being. Still I couldn't hang around and look after her. I figured that she would be long gone by the time I got back from the twenty-four hour shift ahead. I had done what I could but as an after-thought, I left a saucer of diluted goat's milk next to the sleeping minx, locked up the boat and went on my way.

By the time I got back, tired beyond all description, I had completely forgotten about her and indeed there was no sign of a cat when I unlocked the cabin door. I had just put the kettle on and was heating up some eggplant stew when I heard a meow at my feet and two bright yellow eyes looked at me. Now that she was perfectly dry, she was simply adorable. The tip of her tail and three of her paws were white and she wrapped her body around my legs. It was all I could do not to trip over her. I assumed she had just come for another bowl of milk so I gave her a little more. After I had eaten and lain down on my bed she spent half an hour stalking and running at me, then jumping up in the air in a kind of dance, her teeth and claws needle-sharp so that my hands were soon covered with tiny scratches. I couldn't help laughing out loud when she attacked me once again. The end of the game saw us both sleeping soundly in my bed, something I tried to avoid with only partial success from then on. She was as bold as brass and knew what she wanted from the word go.

Despite intensive enquiries to try to find her real owner, she never left from that day on. Shaila grew into a slinky madam who always waited at the helm of the boat to welcome me back when I had been away. She was the nearest I had to company at home and she made me look forward to coming back.

I was woken by footsteps above my head. My heart hammered in my breast. My mouth went dry and I started to shake all over. No one needed to climb over my boat to get anywhere. I slid quietly out of bed and into the kitchen. Thud, thud, whoever it was, they weren't trying to keep their presence quiet in any way. I opened a drawer and took out a knife. I wouldn't give in that easily. I looked at Shaila, who was still slumbering on my bed and dithered about my next move when there was a clearly audible knock on the cabin door. Did they expect to be let in and hosted? Then a deep voice in Urdu: 'Please open up. A man is dying.'

Was this a ploy? How did they know I was

a doctor? But if they really needed a doctor . . . I turned the lock and opened the door, knife still in hand. I couldn't quite make out the figure in front of me in the false dawn light, except that he was wearing a scarf around his head and sporting a long fuzzy beard. Then I saw the gun in the man's hand pointing straight at me.

'Please put down that knife. We wish you no harm but my friend is lying there badly wounded.' He gestured towards the cart and horse that was waiting on the bank of the lake with another man in the driver's seat. 'We cannot go to the hospital.'

I threw a coat over my pyjamas and climbed out to look at him. I could hear the man moaning when I peered into the cart but it was too dark for me to see anything so I asked, 'Can you bring him in?' I lit the gas light and threw a clean sheet over my bed. The two of them carried the third man carefully down the steps and laid him gently down as blood dripped on my rug in the process. His leg had been bound up tightly and his arm was in a sling. I pulled out my black bag and plunged a needle into his leg. He moaned but then was quite still. It took me the good part of an hour to extract the bullets from his leg and construct a makeshift splint for the arm he had broken when he fell in what must have been some kind of attack. A gun was trained at me the entire time. I didn't need to ask who they were or even what had happened. They could only have been freedom fighters but at that moment, I was a doctor, not a judge. When the treatment was over, I stopped them just as they were about to pick up their still unconscious comrade and mount the stairs again.

'Do you know this man?' I pointed at Tahir in the faded paper clipping. The man with the gun looked at me suspiciously. His face, which had previously showed signs of gratitude, turned to stone. I knew that I would get no answer from him but still I continued. 'If you do, tell him . . . tell him his sister is here. Tell him I want to talk to him!'

Later after I had cleared up the mess and my pulse had returned to normal, I warmed my hands on a cup of chai and wondered if I were any nearer to seeing my beloved Tahir.

38

Autumn slipped into winter and ducks and swans waddled past the boat on the frozen lake, which displayed a brittle beauty underneath a leaden sky. The windows of the boat were frosted over and I snapped icicles off the roof above deck. I went to bed early just to keep warm because the gas burner on the boat wasn't making that much difference, and studied medical journals by the light of an oil lamp, with a hot water bottle and Shaila under the bed covers. In the mornings, I warmed my hands on a *kangri* basket of coals that my neighbours had deposited on deck.

The market was off the water for weeks. As it wasn't the season for vegetables, the gathering on the banks was very small and over early anyway. The aroma of roasted chestnuts lingered in the air on my way to work, tempting me with their promise of warmth and comfort.

Tiredness was something I always had difficulty coping with and all the more now in the cold. After a long shift I would often stumble through the badly lit roads with only two things on my mind — the thought of my deliciously warm double bed and the welcoming meow of Shaila. On one freezing November morning, I made my way down past the mosque on Ganderbal Road over a blanket of virgin snow that had been falling since the wee hours of the morning. A horse-drawn *tonga* distracted me from the steps behind me.

'Stop! What are you doing?' I turned around to see a soldier pointing a gun at me. He looked incredibly young — a man child in uniform. Were they recruiting children now? I pulled my coat tighter around me and then it dawned on me. That was why there were no fresh tracks in the snow. There was a curfew on.

'What have you got there?' He prodded me with his rifle. 'Hands up!'

Up they shot. 'I'm sorry. I'm a doctor.'

This situation wasn't going well for me. I had treated women who had been raped by soldiers. He prodded me again.

'A doctor, eh. You're a woman! You'll have to do better than that,' he jeered.

Oh dear Shiva, I had my ID on me somewhere and my keys in my inside pocket. 'If you'll just let me show . . . ' I went to open my coat and that is the last thing I remember.

* ★ ★

I came to in a cell with about twenty or so inmates, built at the most for ten. They were sitting on mats on the floor and on the few seats available. I was lying on the floor and my head throbbed terribly. I reached up to feel a huge bump and a sticky wound just under my hairline. He must have bludgeoned me over the head. I was lucky that he hadn't shot me. I sat up. What was I doing here? They must know now that I was a doctor. I tried to stand up but toppled over into the arms of another inmate.

'Steady! Sit back down, my dear. Are you all right?' she said.

I nodded but that just made my head hurt all the more. 'I've got to get out of here. I'm a doctor!'

She sat down next to me and took my hand.

'Don't get so worked up, memsahib. There's no point. Allah is watching over us and nothing happens very fast around here. Let me get you some water.' She walked over to a barrel of water in the middle of the room and scooped up a mug.

I quenched my burning thirst, lay back down and fell asleep despite the rank stench of vomit and faeces coming from the three buckets in the corner of the cell. When I next woke most of the others were asleep. They lay there side by side like tree trunks being transported down the Jhelum. My head was better but I was starving. As the guard outside was snoring loudly in his chair, a gun resting lazily across his lap, there was nothing for it but to wait until the morning.

I was sent home by noon with a warning but no apology. A phone call to the hospital had established my identity. There was no lodging a complaint, not against the military. I couldn't jeopardize my future. I washed and disinfected the gash on my forehead and cut strips of Elastoplast to bridge the gap. It stung badly but the shock of what had just happened was far worse. I stayed awake in my bed that night and listened for intruders, something I had never done before. From then on I would never walk the streets of Srinagar alone again if I could possibly help it.

39

'Dr Vaidya, please take a seat.' Prof Lone looked every inch the experienced and powerful surgeon he was. Why had he called me into his office if not to reprimand me for the incident in the police cell? 'You have been with us for four months now.' He cracked his knuckles, sat back and . . . smiled. 'We have decided to reward your hard work and dedication with a residency. The opportunity to specialize isn't given to every doctor who joins our prestigious ranks but in your case . . . '

I was being given the chance to qualify as a surgeon!

From that day on I spent my shifts in the operating theatre wearing the green clothes and hat of the operating team like a badge of honour, trying to glean every morsel of knowledge and technique by watching and assisting the other surgeons.

In the beginning it was only a matter of passing them the instruments but as time went on, I even progressed to occasionally assisting the anaesthetist. My heart quickened when I saw how our team fought to heal a patient or battle for their lives. I was eager to learn the art of incision but I also had to learn to deal with everything that surrounded the operating theatre. Breaking the news of a fatality to the families never got any easier, nor the way to combat the sense of failure when an operation left the patient in an even worse state than before yet I was still convinced that a surgeon's skill would be what was needed more than anything else in the hills. Even if my clinic never came about, I would be much more needed in this region than before.

I knew it would be twice as hard and demanding to combine study with my daily work and clock up the hundreds of operations before I could finally hold the scalpel in my hand, but I was single-minded about this most important step in my career.

*　*　*

The extreme winter weather didn't last long. It was milder down here in the heart of the valley than where I had grown up. Spring finally came and breathed life into the lake. Swarms of waterfowl arrived and tiny birds nestled in the fluffy pink clouds of almond trees on its banks. The excited chatter of the latter was quite deafening in the morning. The fragrance of the blossoms from creepers, bushes and shrubs filled the air. Water lilies and lotus flowers were beginning to fill the lake and the *shikaras* created lanes as they cut through on their errands. Shaila was often away at night and I tied a tiny bell around her neck to try to reduce the offerings of birds she proudly left on deck almost every morning. It wasn't warm enough to sit up on deck in the evenings but when I was free during the day, I spent hours up there reading my books and watching life on the water. The boat was berthed in a secluded spot with a spectacular view of the lake. I cooked when I could as it was my way of relaxing after the tension of the operating theatre, my favourite dishes being *samosas*, vegetable *tandoori* and *shrikhand* (mango) pudding. My shifts alternated between operations and duty on the wards and I was glad of the variety of it all. In two years' time it looked like I would be carrying out routine operations: Caesareans, appendixes, those kinds of things under the surveillance of the chief surgeon. When my life was on track I was always most content.

★   ★   ★

I don't know why I hadn't seen the note which had been pushed under my cabin door the night before when I came back, except that I only had a meal and bed in my mind. I read and reread the note.

Dear Jaya,
It is true. I am still alive and would like to see you, dear sister. Go to the great temple on Saturday at 7am and a man will take you to me.
Your loving brother,
Tahir

My brother! Tahir was truly alive! I sat down, my hands shaking. Dread and ecstasy filled my heart. I had been waiting for this moment forever, it seemed to me. Now everything made sense. My coming back, my profession which had brought me here. I would see him; he would listen to reason, I was sure. We had always had such a special relationship, as if we knew what each other was thinking. I didn't know how I would save him but if he renounced his past crimes, there must be a way. What did he look like now? I examined myself in the mirror. Would he recognize me now that I was an old maid and a real doctor?

What if they found out? If the authorities ever caught on to the fact that I was his sister, that would be the end of my life in Kashmir. The mildest of consequences would be the end of my career. I was risking my good character and at worst my life. But Tahir was all that mattered at this moment. There would be a reason for his deeds, something I could understand and come to terms with. He couldn't have changed that much. Not my Tahir, I convinced myself, as I walked towards the temple that Saturday.

★ ★ ★

A little before noon I got off the cart and followed a man with a limp until we reached what looked like the ruin of an old stone dwelling in the foothills. Now I was starting to have doubts. What if he wasn't my brother? I was dealing with terrorists here and no one had the slightest idea where I was. They could slit my throat and dispose of my body without trace. Perhaps they needed a captive doctor, someone who would always treat their casualties in their bloody war. I might never see Srinagar or Shaila or even Alastair for that matter again. He would have had me sectioned if he knew what I was up to! I suddenly yearned for him as never before. I wished I could talk to him, ask his advice. But then he had always been strictly against my search for my brother.

Two kestrels sat on their perches outside

the shack and then a solitary figure emerged from the building, slender and proud like my father. There could be no doubt.

'Tahir!!!' I cried and ran towards him.

The man with the limp lifted his gun but Tahir waved at him and caught me in his arms.

'Tahir!' Tears ran down my face but he pushed me away gently. Was he embarrassed? I surveyed his face, the same unmistakable eyes, but now framed by worry lines and exposure to the elements. He looked at least ten years older than I knew him to be. Where was my funny little brother? He was carrying all of Kashmir's troubles on his shoulders.

'Come, Jaya, come inside. Let us talk.' Inside, a pot simmered on a stove and he offered me some tea. The tea tasted bitter. 'You saved Ramed,' he said. 'He will not be able to fight for a while but he is recovering.'

'Tahir. I didn't save him to fight. Why are you fighting? Is it true? Are you really terrorists?'

He turned on me like a cornered scorpion. 'What do you know of life here? I have been watching you. I know all about you. How you left Kashmir and now have a new British family. You have become a doctor but at what price, Jaya? You have become one of them!'

'But Tahir, Pa wouldn't want you to kill. Pa

saved people, he helped the freedom fighters but only because he was a doctor.'

'Do you think we kill through choice? Jaya, wake up, Kashmir has been in the suffocating grip of outsiders for too long! If we had been left in peace, this would not be necessary.'

'But it's not necessary, killing and bloodshed is never necessary. There's always another way. There are talks and negotiation and peaceful protest.'

He laughed a deep laugh that made me feel so small, so useless. 'You think that we would stand a chance if we followed our great brother Gandhi. You seriously think that that would have any effect at all when the great nations of this Earth are conspiring together to keep us powerless.'

'Tahir, even if you're right, it doesn't justify what you're doing. It never will! Your deeds will never add up to anything more than those of a mass murderer. Tahir, listen to me, you can still change. You can still take the peaceful path. No one would recognize you if you just became a normal citizen and settled down. I could make enquiries. People support you enough to stand by you and protect you.' Even as I said the words, doubt shone through my hopes like a comet on a collision course.

'Jaya, you talk like one of them. I am a hero

for my followers. I would lay my life down for this cause. Kashmir will be free one day.'

My words left as much impression as a summer shower on a parched field. I told him a little about my work and a brief account of my years in Scotland but I could see that my tale was merely reinforcing the idea in his mind that I had somehow become a traitor. He could no longer distinguish between me and the people he thought were plotting against Kashmir's rightful destiny. I sensed that any mention of Alastair would merely aggravate the situation but at that moment I felt so much closer to my brother in Scotland than the one before me. I left behind a man I could hardly call my brother with good conscience yet our common blood would always defy reason and on the journey home, I hoped desperately that we would meet in a benevolent future where our differences would no longer matter.

40

We had no idea what was going on in downtown Srinagar on that fateful Tuesday in early March. I was taking a tea break when I heard some shouting. I looked out of the window towards the hospital gates to see a group of men carrying what looked like a blood-soaked body into the grounds. The guardsman jumped up to let them in. The man had been shot in the eye but was still miraculously alive.

Shot? Shooting happened in the mountains or they were in incidents in the news. Not here. A cold fear gripped my throat. And then the casualties started coming in with what seemed an endless stream of horrific, senseless wounds.

Rival gangs of political extremists were rampaging through the heart of the city with so-called supporters of Indira Gandhi's Congress Party clashing with the ruling Conference Party. The rioters used stones and burning objects against each other, overturning cars and setting fire to tyres in their vendetta. The police and military fired into the air and resorted to tear gas or charged with sticks to disperse the rival factions. Inevitably, terrible injuries resulted from over vigorous intervention.

The wards were crammed with the wounded and patients were even laid out in the corridors. Open wounds, burns, broken bones and bullet wounds. One woman died a day after she was admitted of a heart attack. This must be what Pa had gone through, I thought. This was war. None of the medics could be sent home and we ran out of the basics like bandages and plaster casts and the blood banks were soon depleted. When supplies did arrive by truck from beyond the Vale, we had a brief reprieve. We were operating around the clock and the terrible point was finally reached when we ran out of anaesthetic. In my new position, I witnessed a man having both legs amputated because they had been shredded in an explosion, with nothing to help him endure the cut of the knife or to silence his shrieks. I burst into tears even before he was wheeled out of the room.

During one weekend alone 600 people were hurt, 75 of them seriously and the riots continued on the following Tuesday, with 400 injured and thirteen fatalities. The authorities imposed a twenty-four-hour curfew. Nothing moved in the city apart from the troops on the streets. Luckily, I was stranded at work but what would come next? Civil war? When the curfew was finally lifted, I stayed with a matron called Zillah at the doctors' quarters and continued attending to the victims of the worst violence that Srinagar had seen in over a decade.

Three days later, I picked my way through the barricades and debris back to the lake. Nothing on the Dal Lake spoke of the turmoil on the streets behind me. A boat was pulling a floating garden to its new location up shore as if nothing had ever happened. The trees on the bank were a mass of pink blossom and the houseboats languished in the sun in full view of the snow-topped Giants. I was barely aware of the beauty around me. My only thoughts were of catching up on my blessed sleep. I squinted through the sunlight, hoping I'd see Shaila curled up on deck. Then she would run over, curl herself around my legs, purring. It wasn't my cat that I saw. Instead, there was a man sitting on my boat. Why would anyone try to intercept me? My stomach clenched and tears of self-pity sprang to my eyes. Not this now. I was too exhausted. These were not times to take risks. I would have to turn and head back to the hospital. All I wanted was to go home. The man turned and I stopped dead in my tracks.

'Christ, you look tired,' he said.

'Alastair, what . . . what are you doing here?' My heart missed a beat.

'What kind of a welcome is that? Give me a hug!'

'I can't . . . Not out here. This is Kashmir. You never know who's watching.'

We disappeared below deck and I gave him the biggest hug ever. He smelt of sweat and Scotland and delicious Alastair. My heart was flipping somersaults and all the troubles of the past days melted away. I felt so ridiculously safe in his arms. He held me and didn't seem to want to let me go until I finally pushed him away. After all, he was married . . . I looked at his hand. So he was one of those men who didn't wear a ring.

He turned full circle and whistled. 'This is nice. How did you end up here?'

'I'll tell you later,' I answered. 'Alastair, why are you here?'

He looked as if he were fighting something. 'Because I was worried about you, because I missed you and because I wanted to know what you were up to. You could look a little happier to see me. Getting a visa was hell and it wasn't that much fun getting here, either.'

If only he knew how hard I was fighting the

wave of joy that was washing over me. Why would Amanda let him come? In fact, why wasn't she here?

'It's an awfully long way to come just to find that out. You could have written or phoned. Where's Amanda? Is your wife here, too?'

Alastair's winced. 'She isn't my wife. We . . . I had a change of heart. I realized it wasn't work that made me put it off the first time. I couldn't go through with it . . . '

Neither of us spoke. My heart was hammering so loud, I thought Alastair must be able to hear it. Did I dare hope?

'She's a lovely girl but my heart just wasn't in it. Not all the way, that is. It was awful, as you can imagine, and her father and brother had some choice words to say to me . . . but I know I did the right thing. For both of us. She was glad in the end actually. Anyway, can we talk about something else now?'

'So . . . you're not married?' I wanted to make absolutely sure I had heard him right.

He looked straight at me. 'That's what I've been trying to say. Can't you understand my Scots accent anymore?' He grinned.

The ice around my heart melted in one glorious warm puddle that spread to my tummy and the rest of me. It was all I could do not to throw myself into his arms. Instead,

I crossed my arms. 'You could have let me know, surely?'

'I didn't think you minded one way or the other.' His gaze didn't move from me. I had to look away and fussed around with making some tea whilst a million thoughts raced through my head. I poured him some *kava* and we drank it in silence. I was too tired and my heart too full to say anything more than, 'I'm really happy you're here, Alastair.'

He placed his hand, warm from the cup, over mine. 'I know,' he said.

41

What happened in the capital robbed Tahir of his sleep. More misery, more suffering for his people. How much of this could they take? When would it finally end? This was surely a sign, a sign from . . . the gods, from . . . Allah? Whoever it was had never mattered to him. Just that they were watching over him, directing his life, telling him something. The message was clear as the water in Lake Krishnasar. Now was no longer the time to wait. Now was the time to act. The white *sahibs* had brought misfortune on his people and had lost their innocence long ago when they put his country on this bloody path. He did not need to spare them to achieve what had to be done.

★ ★ ★

'Alastair, you can't stay with me. An unmarried woman with a male house guest is scandalous and barely legal.'

'Tell them I'm your brother,' he said with a twinkle in his eyes.

'They'd never believe that.'

'I was only pulling your leg. I've checked into the Grand Mumtaz Hotel.'

I'd never seen such luxurious accommodation when I visited him the next day.

'Isn't it a little expensive?' I asked him as an army truck thundered past. He smiled and ordered two lime sodas on the hotel terrace.

'It's on expenses. It's all research. I'm thinking about setting my next book here.'

'Oh, Alastair, I didn't get round to reading your first book yet.'

'Don't worry, apparently enough other people have.'

'That's wonderful!'

'I wasn't expecting it to do so well. I finally handed in my resignation last month. The most wonderful thing is that in future I won't be bound to any particular office anymore.'

I dared not respond to the hopes he was awakening in me but why else was he telling me this?

Although I had one day off after the unrest, I had to work long shifts for the first week he was there, which was really frustrating. Eventually I managed to get five days off, which was the first proper break I had taken since I started working. Alastair turned up at the boat in a Land Rover at seven in the morning.

'I want you to show me your childhood

haunts. I want to see it through your eyes.'

It was so good to get away from the summer capital with all its tensions boiling and an incredible feeling to be sitting up high with someone I cared so much about at my side once more. Not that this Land Rover bore much resemblance to our old one. It was brand new and on a par with the hotel he was staying at. He had lost nothing of his driving style as he sped past the chinar trees out of the city across the open countryside, through fields of wheat and rice, until we started climbing up and up on the familiar winding tracks. I directed him and he had an expression of wonder on his face. Having him here to share my paradise was perfectly splendid. The whole sweep of the Vale lay at our feet. When we finally stopped, we got out and Alastair shook his head slowly.

'The lakes down there are like a string of pearls. I've been to quite a few places on my travels but nowhere like this.'

'Where we're going is even better,' I replied and grabbed my rucksack.

We must have walked for three hours before we finally spied Lake Sheshnag. It was exactly as I remembered it to be. On the far side of the lake, green slopes plunged vertically into the heavenly water and we were the only players in this magical scene.

'It really is the deepest turquoise I've ever seen. I suppose the bit about the serpent must be true then, too.' Alastair bit into a red-striped apple. 'Even this tastes different. What is it about this place? I swear it's cast a spell on me.'

'A golden eagle!' I pointed at the bird circling far above us. It spiralled down and briefly hovered over us in blatant curiosity.

'It's huge!' Alastair exclaimed.

'Yes, I don't think I've ever seen one this close, either.'

'Perhaps it's a sign,' he said before the eagle resumed its quest for lunch.

I didn't ask what he meant but wished time would stand still as I took a sip of mango juice. After a little while Alastair began to tell me about the Mains and Marie's newly discovered passion for photography.

'She's been on a couple of courses, one in Wales and another in Spain. She's bought all the equipment and turned one of the spare rooms into a darkroom. There are strings of photos hanging all over the place. She's getting rather good at it. Says she'll be able to take all the pictures of any children I might have.'

What a thing to say now that the wedding had fallen through, I thought. 'Why doesn't she come out here? I'd love to see her and she would find so much to capture with her lens!'

'You're right, only I would be a wee bit worried if she came out here at the moment. It's bad enough you being here as it is.'

Did I detect an edge to his voice? He must have read my mind because he quickly added, 'I can see why you love it here, though,' he looked around, 'and the important work you're doing. It's just . . . '

'What is it, Alastair?'

'Well, there's another reason why I'm here. It's taken a while to sort out the estate but the old man's left you the clinic.'

42

'I thought you'd be happy,' Alastair said.

I reached for his hand and took a deep breath. 'I'm very honoured. But . . . you'll have to find someone else for the clinic. That's all there is to it.'

'I obviously haven't made myself quite clear. It's yours to do whatever you like with. There can be no doubt about the terms of the will. It's not up to me or Mum or anyone else for that matter. It's your business. It's your wee bit of Scotland if you like,' he said smugly.

'But I'm on the other side of the globe. It's of no use to me.'

'Well . . . ' He seemed to be enjoying this. 'You could sell it and use the money . . . ' he plucked a blue flower from the grass at his side and gave it to me, ' . . . for other purposes.'

'I don't understand.'

'Jaya, are you thick? He's left you a bloody fortune!'

★ ★ ★

Tahir stared straight ahead at the old woman's face on the rocks. How he loved his country, the mountains, the people and the animals. But he was tired of fighting. Tired of a lifetime on the run. His gut told him he wouldn't be able to keep this up forever. He had had plenty of time to think of a way out but his thoughts always moved in circles. Petty victories, not getting him or his brothers anywhere. They needed one conclusive act, one that led to freedom, freedom for all his countrymen and the right to run their country as they saw fit. If only they had money, resources to fund their actions. Money bought weapons and they needed more weapons, good weapons to fight the final battle. He racked his brains. No one would take his heritage away from him, he swore. He reached for his binoculars to see if Ramed, who had gone down into the valley to replenish their supplies, was anywhere in sight yet. As he swept over the terrain he spotted two figures talking near the lake.

Tahir watched the woman through binoculars. She was bareheaded, a sure sign she thought she was unobserved. She turned and he focussed on her face. Shiva! It couldn't be . . . but there could be no doubt. He couldn't believe it. Jaya was alone with a man! She had taken some *sahib* to one of their childhood's most sacred places. The man was a westerner, from his build, from what he had on, from the way he behaved towards Jaya. They knew no boundaries, those colonial scum. They thought they could come over and take anything they wanted . . . even his sister! How did she know him? How could she stand there with this outsider, heads bent in intimate conversation and not die of shame? The man took her hand and Jaya did not pull away. The woman he no longer thought of as his sister had betrayed everything he, Tahir, stood for. The *sahib* would pay for this. Tahir thought long and hard and suddenly the solution was as tangible as the scene before him.

★　★　★

The trek downhill was easier but still took us two and a half hours to reach the car just as the sun was setting over the luminous Himalayan tips. A purple mist was rising from the Jhelum River whilst the Thajiwas Glacier was alight with the last golden rays. We were quiet as Alastair negotiated the hairpin bends with ease.

'This almost beats the Paris-Dakar run,' he said as we squeezed past a choking truck.

'Alastair, I can't come back,' I blurted out.

298

'Yes,' he sighed. 'We've established that fact by now. But I could organize the sale. It'll mean I have to fly to and fro a couple of times but I might manage to overcome my reluctance.' He smiled over at me just as something black and white appeared in front of us.

'Watch out!' I screamed.

He braked and a badger scampered into the bush. My heart thumped in my ears. He looked at me. 'Of course you'll have to be extra nice to me.'

'That's blackmail!' I exclaimed.

'I know!'

★　★　★

It felt so right for me to introduce Alastair to Avani and Madhav. My brother from my new life talking to people I knew from my childhood! I was pleased that Madhav was there because otherwise things would have been a little uncomfortable for Avani. We drank tea and Avani giggled, shy in the presence of this tall white stranger.

Madhav took us out on Wular Lake. Everything looked so different from out on the water. He threw out his nets as Alastair talked to him through me but soon the two men were laughing over something I certainly hadn't told them. Alastair was so damned charming, how could anyone not like him?

On the way back, Alastair sat next to me as our feet dangled over the side of the boat. 'All this water and the mountains. You have everything here apart from the actual sea,' he said. A fat fish jumped out of the water and plopped back in.

And you, I thought.

★   ★   ★

Next day I took him along to the hospital, even though I still had time off. I explained to the nurses that I was showing a *sahib* from Scotland around the place and they bowed to us respectfully.

'I've never seen you on duty as it were. You seem to be pretty important here,' he looked at me with raised eyebrows, 'in your element — much more confident than I've ever seen you before.'

Later we walked back through the streets at night. There was still debris left over from the riots, a burnt-out car, and the barricades had only been cleared to one side. I still felt a little nervous even though the curfew had been lifted but safe with him by my side. I wished he could always be with me, that I didn't have to go through my life by myself, that we wouldn't be separated by an ocean and who we were.

'This is such a contrast to today,' Alastair said as he surveyed the havoc. 'I don't think I've felt as alive as I do here. The poverty, the beauty, the peace and the violence. Such extremes separated by the bat of an eyelid.'

'It totally confounds me, too,' I said as we approached Alastair's hotel. 'I'll leave you here, then.'

'No, you won't. I'll walk you back to the boat. Nothing's going to happen to you while I'm around; not on my watch, it isn't.'

A couple of children were scrimmaging in the rubbish, and a baby who was tied onto one of the older children's backs looked at me with huge brown eyes, framed by black eyeliner.

'Have you got any nearer to finding Tahir?' he said as we walked along the banks of the lake. I could hear my pulse in my ears. Would he judge me for being a terrorist's sister?

'It's a long story,' I replied. 'D'you mind if I tell you about that another time?'

'Sure,' he replied. 'What's that over there?'

'The Nishat gardens.'

You can live in a town all your life and rarely go to the places people came from far away to see. I had last played here as a small child. The evening sun was dousing the canal-like waterways of the gardens in its golden light. In the distance the flanks of the Pir Panjal Range cradled the edge of Dal Lake. Behind us the Zarbarwan Mountains created the spectacular backdrop for the terraced landscape and its many fountains. Even at this time of the day, the gardens exploded with all the colours of the rainbow with the blossoms in full bloom and the air heavy with their scent.

'This is quite extraordinary,' exclaimed Alastair. 'I think I'm beginning to understand.'

'Understand what?'

'Why you came back. It's where you belong.'

He wanted to casually take my hand as we wandered past the flower beds but I pulled away. It was not the proper thing to go walking hand in hand in public, not with someone you were not promised to. Not even then. He smiled for by now he understood that we did things differently here in Kashmir. A couple overtook us, walking arm in arm, chatting gaily. How I wished we could change places with them. We walked past a mother carrying a baby whilst her husband chased a toddler. An older woman, perhaps her mother or mother-in-law, was walking serenely by her side. Common scenes, yet a world away from my life.

Out of the blue Alastair grabbed my hand and pulled me into a small enclosure of trees and bushes. He pulled me to him.

'Alastair!'

Before I could say much more he put his hand gently over my mouth. 'Jaya, I love you and that's all there is to it. I want to be able to hold your hand when I want and do this to you, too.' He bent his head and kissed me.

It wasn't wrong anymore, there was no one we were hurting, just Alastair and me in this garden of paradise. There were no prying eyes here. I kissed him back. I kissed him as I had always wanted to. I kissed him for an eternity.

He pulled away, fell down on one knee and pulled out a ring. 'The moment you left was like some electric shock that woke me. I didn't love Amanda. She was a good sport. We had great fun together but she wasn't you. Jaya, I've been an idiot. Will you marry me?'

★   ★   ★

Next morning we sat out on his hotel terrace with two glasses of champagne on the table.

'How do I know that you're serious about me? You might change your mind again and how are we going to make this work? I live here, I will never leave and you live . . . '

'Jaya, look at me. I've never been more serious about anything in my whole life. I can't live without you and the rest will have to solve itself. I don't know all the answers now. I only know that I love you.'

I recognized the truth of his words, for I too knew that I would never find anyone so precious in my entire life. The obstacles that stood between us simply melted in the face of our feelings for each other. Crickets chirped all around us as if applauding our happiness. He took my hand with the ring on it under the table. It didn't really matter as the people at the other tables on the terrace of his hotel were preoccupied but I was grateful to him that he was making every effort to behave properly even if the hotel served as an island for expats. He understood that I had reentered the old world of conventions and expectations the minute I landed in Jammu Airport almost a year ago. As independent as I was, there were still strict boundaries that I would never cross in India. We could only go public if we really had a future together. I wanted to be his wife but I also wasn't going to give everything up at the snap of his fingers.

'I had to see you. It was the only reason I came over. The lawyers could have taken care of the property.'

We got on the bikes supplied by the hotel

and cycled along the winding banks of the Jhelum past the old stone *ghats* and wooden shacks where women were washing their clothes in the river.

'Can't something be done for these people?' Alastair shouted into the wind.

'It's worse in the hills,' I replied.

Then the city melted away as we rode through yellow fields of mustard flowers and the poverty evaporated in the glorious sunshine. We didn't do much talking when we found a sheltered spot under an apple tree a little way off the beaten track. It was then that I told him about Tahir, about how disappointed I felt, how ashamed I was of being his sister, about how hopeless any thought of changing him was.

'Jaya, there's nothing you can do about him.'

'But I feel dreadful. Shouldn't I tell someone? Do something to stop the killing? I feel so terribly helpless.'

'You're doing enough. You're saving lives. You can't solve Kashmir's problems all by yourself. And they would find him no quicker. He's a man on the run. Somewhere up there. He hasn't exactly got an address you can give them, has he?'

I smiled. 'No, you're right but he's my brother.'

'Yes and as we've clearly established, I'm not. You don't need that here,' he said as he pulled off my scarf. 'No one's around for miles.' I shook my hair out and he kissed me before pushing me gently down on the warm grass.

★ ★ ★

The last couple of days before Alastair's flight back passed in a flash. Work was waiting for me, I knew, as the urge to drop everything and jump on that plane with him all but overpowered me. The magnetism between us had never been stronger. We said our goodbyes below deck. I knew I wouldn't be able to accompany him to the airport. I simply couldn't take another minute off. What would Marie say when she found out about us? Would she be happy? Or betrayed that I had snapped up her son?

'She'll be delighted. She loves you. You're family anyway.'

'That's the problem!'

'Look, stop worrying about it. Let's ring her up. There's a phone at the hotel.'

'Alastair, it's four o'clock in the morning at the Mains and I'd rather you told her personally. That way you can gauge her reaction better. I couldn't go through with it if she disapproved. I just couldn't do that to her.'

Alastair frowned. 'You'd be willing to throw all of this away?'

'I couldn't go against her wishes, not after all she's done for me. It's unthinkable to go against your family in Kashmir and Marie is family.'

'Don't be daft. She'll be over the moon and I've always been able to wind her around my finger. Just wait for me to have a little talk with her.'

I looked down at my ring, three diamonds which I knew I wouldn't be able to wear at work or anywhere else for that matter until things were truly official, until we had solved the practical and family problems that lay in our way, until we actually fixed the day. As if he read my mind, Alastair said, 'Let's set a date. Everyone should know!'

'As soon as you've talked to her, OK?' I stood on my toes and kissed him.

43

Tahir peered through his binoculars just as the Land Rover rounded the bend. It flashed shiny green in the sun, like a slap in his face. How could this man, this enemy afford to drive a brand new car when his people could barely scrape together the next meal? Lording it over them like the *sahibs* of the past. These people weren't satisfied with their own island, their own country which they could rule as they liked; no, these people couldn't leave Kashmir alone. They came back to witness the shambles they had left behind, convinced that they were invincible. They all thought they were better than him, showing off in the cars they drove. How dare they? Joining forces with India and Pakistan to keep his homeland in a stranglehold that drained its very lifeblood. The white pigs deserved everything that was coming to them.

Just a few seconds more. Now! He gave a sign. A tree smashed down in the path of the vehicle. The car came to a screeching halt. For a moment all was still. Then the door slowly opened and the tall man got out. Tahir took aim. He could depend on his skill as a marksman even in this situation. Ping! The front tyre deflated. The stranger dived to the ground. Then another bullet bored its way into the back tyre. Tahir sent a third bullet through the windscreen for good measure. The man started running. Tahir laughed. He could not escape. Tahir waved and his comrades swooped down on their prey.

Reuters: A British man has been kidnapped on the outskirts of Srinagar, in the much disputed Indian region of Kashmir. The man has been named as Mr Alastair Hamilton, aged thirty-six and his next of kin have been informed. The Home Office has issued a statement that it utterly condemns the targeting and use of British citizens as pawns in India's internal affairs. It will do everything possible to bring the terrorists to justice and find their victim. As yet a ransom note has not been received, but the Home Office is determined not to set a precedent by giving in to possible future demands.

44

Marie was gabbling something to me on the hospital phone. Whatever she was saying, it didn't make sense. She had never been in such a state, not even in Stuart's last days. I finally grasped what she was saying. Alastair, my Alastair. Not Alastair. No!!! I could feel myself falling apart. Tears running down my face. The blood drained from my head. I sat down, receiver still in my hand.

'I'm sorry. I'm so sorry, Marie.'

It was my fault. My fault that her son was now in the hands of . . . of whom? If he hadn't come to see me, he would be safe in Dumfries or sitting in front of a fire in the Mains. I uttered words of comfort that I did not even believe in myself and couldn't remember afterwards. Then I replaced the receiver and stared at it. He was here! Here in Kashmir. But he might as well have been on the moon.

I bowed out of the next operation, muttering something about being unwell. It was totally unacceptable; I was shirking my responsibility, to my patients, to the hospital and most of all to myself. But I only had one thought in my head. I had to help Alastair somehow. Nothing else mattered. I looked up at the Giants over the hospital gates. A wall of silence stared back at me. He could be anywhere.

Down at the police station the officer looked at me as if I were demented. 'I do not understand,' said the officer behind the counter, a burning *bidee* in hand. Thick cigarette smoke filled the air, biting my sore eyes. 'What do you have to do with the kidnapping of the foreigner? This is now a matter for the British and Indian authorities. An international affair! Leave the matter in our hands and go home to your husband.'

'I'm single,' I retorted. I had tried to make myself presentable, dried my tears but I wasn't me anymore. I was a purpose.

He raised his eyebrows and then as if to end the conversation, stubbed out the rest of his *bidee* and returned to the comic book open in front of him.

'You don't understand. Mr Hamilton was . . . is a dear friend of mine. He came here to visit me. He was on the way to the airport when it happened. His mother just rang me.'

He finally looked up. 'Please sit down. I shall see what is possible.'

He knocked and entered the door behind him, came out and told me to wait. He rolled himself another *bidee* and lit it. I watched him smoke another three before I was finally led through to the chief of police's office. My palms were sweaty and my hands trembled. I hadn't eaten or drunk anything for hours. I was beginning to feel as nauseous as if I had smoked a couple of cigarettes myself.

The police chief took his feet off the table in slow motion. He was sporting a turban and the most impressive moustache I had ever seen. There were huge patches of sweat under his arms and the buttons on the shirt looked as if they would fly off any moment as they strained over the bulge of his stomach.

'Good morning. Please take a seat. You are Miss . . . '

'Dr Jaya Vaidya. I work at the government hospital. I know Mr Hamilton well. We have to find him! You have to help him.'

There was a knock on the door and an officer came over and whispered something in his ear. The latter then turned on his heel and exited quickly.

'Many people want to talk to me today — the press, the British embassy.' He twirled the ends of his moustache. 'Now Miss Vaidya, err . . . I mean Dr Vaidya, how do you know the victim?'

'He's like a brother to me . . . no, he's even more.'

'How could a *sahib* be your brother? Do you have any real brothers? What do you mean more?'

I thought of the engagement ring languishing in the drawer back at *Grasmere*. I couldn't possibly tell him, then Marie would know. She would know it was my fault.

'He's a very dear friend. His family took me in and educated me when mine perished in the quake.'

'I see. Please accept my heartfelt condolences. I lost two cousins myself.'

The phone rang. He made a sign to me. I sat there, involuntarily listening to a conversation about the fate of two drug dealers in Karachi who hailed from Srinagar. The conversation dragged on and on. Alastair might be hurt; he might be . . . No! What was I thinking? Marie must be terrified. Was it better to be far away now or so near to him that it drove me mad? The chief slammed down the receiver.

'Idiots! I let them off with a warning only a month ago because I know their families very well. I am far too good-hearted. Now they are going to hang. Our Vale is a village which I know intimately. It makes me the best police chief ever! A son of our Vale, here to enforce law and order and not some foreigner!'

Was he against foreigners in general or was

he referring to the Indians? I couldn't imagine that he could be too open about his beliefs; he could have scarcely have got to his present position otherwise. Who cared? The only thing that mattered was Alastair.

'Officer.' I bowed my head in respect. 'Do you have any other news? I . . . Mrs Marie Hamilton, his mother, is desperate.'

He tapped his moustache, leaned over and almost whispered, 'We have had word from his abductors. His family will no doubt be informed by the British police soon.'

'What, what did they say?'

'The police?'

'No, the abductors!'

'That they have him, that he is alive.'

'Thank Shiva!' I fought back my tears. 'What do they want?'

'I'm afraid I cannot disclose anything more at the present moment. Now, Dr Vaidya, if you'll just leave me so that I can continue my investigations. I'm a very busy man. Give your contact details to the officer at reception and we'll let you know if there are any new developments.'

★ ★ ★

'I must board the next plane!' said Marie. She had been as electrified as me by the news

314

from the abductors and she listened intently to my detailed account of my visit to the police station. Despite my guilt, it was a great comfort to hear her voice, to hear someone else who cared about Alastair as much as I did.

I replied, 'No, wait. There's nothing that can be done here at the moment. Wait till you hear more from the British authorities. What their next move will be. Wait until we know a little more. Right now you can do more from where you are. I promise to phone you the minute I hear anything.'

'I suppose you're right. Look, I'll get my lawyer to send you power of attorney so that you can do more for me in India.'

'If you're sure . . . ' My guilt was growing by the moment. She trusted me totally and I still hadn't told her how I felt about Alastair, how he felt about me.

★   ★   ★

That evening I sat up on deck and held onto a loudly purring Shaila as if my own life depended on her. Tears fell on her dark fur and I suddenly had a horrific thought. What if Tahir was involved? No, I dismissed it as quickly as it came. There were all sorts of groups out there fighting for this cause or that. Hindus fighting Muslims, Muslims fighting Hindus, fighting India, Indians fighting Pakistan and even China. Such thoughts didn't help Alastair a damned bit. Fresh tears welled up. It was only a day since he had held me here. Twenty-four hours and his life hung over a dark precipice.

With power of attorney in India I could deal with the bureaucracy much faster. I flew to Delhi, getting on the very same plane that Alastair should have boarded only days ago. The taxi took me to a different Delhi, a Delhi of breezy wide boulevards, a Delhi of white imposing colonial villas; a city so different from the one I had known that I might never have been here before. The whole experience would have been fascinating, had I made it under any other circumstances.

After showing my British passport to the policeman at the entrance of the embassy, I was ushered into the majestic building with its wine-red carpets and magnificent interior. There was no forgetting who once ruled this country. I was shown directly into the office of the British High Commissioner, an honour I hadn't expected, presumably because the case had now made Fleet Street.

Sir Elder was a white-haired man in his sixties with a ruddy complexion and a walking stick, who, after shaking my hand, gestured towards the two seats in front of a window overlooking the most beautiful garden I had ever seen. A man, dressed all in white, was hanging precariously from the top of one of the coconut trees with a knife in his hands. Over the polished mahogany desk, a large picture of a young Queen Elizabeth gazed down upon us and a framed wedding photo of Prince Charles and Lady Diana took pride of place on the mantelpiece. Weddings were something other people did. The High Commissioner limped to his chair.

'What can we do for you, Dr Vaidya?'

'Sir Elder, I am most grateful for this reception today. As you know, I am here on behalf of Mrs Hamilton. She . . . we have heard that there has been some contact with the kidnappers.'

'Yes, although I am not at liberty to disclose all the details. I'm afraid Mr Hamilton has fallen into the hands of the Kashmir Leopards. Blood-thirsty terrorists who have been waging war against India and Pakistan for decades now — responsible for the attack on the army base up in the mountains eight years ago. I'm sure you've heard of the avalanche that buried hundreds of soldiers in its path. Tragic. Absolutely tragic!' He shook his head.

I wanted to put my hands over my ears.

'They're asking for a ransom which is quite out of the question, politically and financially.'

'How much?' I asked.

'Three million US dollars.'

'Three million!' I slumped back in my seat. Where could anyone get that much money from? 'We must find it!' I said. Surely that was clear.

'Dr Vaidya. Even if we had that kind of money at our disposal, we would never give in to terrorists. We cannot encourage this kind of thing and endanger the lives of thousands of British tourists and expats. There's too much at stake.'

A lump formed in my throat, my hands started to tremble. I wondered if there would be any point in getting down on my knees and begging. There was only one Alastair on this planet, I wanted to scream but instead a tiny voice escaped me.

'Sir Elder, we are talking about a man here, a British citizen, not an object. I beg you to consider all possibilities. This can't be the first time this has happened. What about the past? I'm sure you could find a way to save him.'

'Well . . . ' His breath hitched as if he were contemplating whether to give me an honest answer. 'We did have a similar case last

October but different in that it took place on the Bangladesh border. We didn't give in. I must emphasize that. However, we're not inhuman. No, we turned a blind eye once contact had been established. The family rustled up the money somehow. Sold their house, borrowed money from friends. That sort of thing. Should've listened to us, though.' His eyes roamed the room as if he were expecting the Queen to nod. 'Should've listened to those with experience. We don't get this far without knowing what we're doing, Dr Vaidya.'

He was worse than the chief of police. 'What exactly happened?' I asked.

He shifted in his seat and winced as he adjusted the position of his bad leg. 'Transfer of money went terribly wrong. They couldn't find the designated spot and the hostage was shot in the head. You might have heard about it in the press.'

My heart thumped in my ears for hate of this pompous old man and his stories.

'Dr Vaidya, I am not implying that this will happen in your dear friend's case. Just don't expect miracles. They rarely happen in this kind of an affair. But still . . . ' He stood up, signalling the end of the meeting. 'You have my word that the British Embassy will help you and Mrs Hamilton in every way possible.

We cannot, however, risk word of this getting into the press. If a ransom is paid for Mr Hamilton, it must be without our knowledge, do you understand?'

I shook his cold limp hand.

45

Alastair strained at the ropes that cut into his wrists. They wouldn't budge, not even in the slightest. Wriggling didn't help, either. He was in some sort of a cave but light spilled around the corner. Sitting on the cold bare ground with his feet tied together, too, the greatest problem was he badly needed to pee. He tried to attract the attention of the guard outside. Only he couldn't shout because a tight gag was in place. So he brought his feet crashing down on the floor again and again. A slight man with a headscarf that covered most of his face apart from his eyes came in.

'What do you want, *sahib*?' he said mockingly.

Thank God he could speak English, Alastair thought. He made some muffled noises, whereupon the man pulled the gag down. 'I need to go, if you know what I mean.'

The man took the gag, stretched it and tied it around Alastair's eyes. He untied his feet and led him outside where Alastair could feel the warmth of the sun. A few paces and blessed relief. The man immediately led him back inside, took off his blindfold and prodded him with his gun. 'Sit down!' The man then bound his feet together once more and tied these to a post for good measure.

'Who are you?' asked Alastair.

'Hold your tongue!' The man got up and headed towards the light but just before he turned the corner, he underwent a change of heart. 'The Kashmir Leopards. We will fight to the death and even in the next life to liberate the land of our fathers!'

'Why me?' The words burst out of Alastair.

'You are English. Have you ever thought about the devastation your empire left behind? Have you ever even thought about us? How we can never stand on our feet because India and Pakistan kick them from underneath us as soon as we try? How they sap our wealth and leave us to die? And then you come here on holiday,' he spat on the ground, 'like some English prince because you think you own us. Because you still think our country belongs to you!'

'Look, I'm actually Scottish. We have a bone or two to pick with the English ourselves. As for the holiday bit . . . '

'Scottish?' The man looked at him more closely. 'Most unfortunate.' He shrugged his shoulders. 'But it is as it is. We cannot change things now . . . '

'But . . . ' Alastair protested.

The man raised his hand to silence him. 'You will serve our purpose just as well.'

'What purpose?'

'Enough! You know too much already. But who knows, you may not live to tell the tale.' And he pulled the gag down firmly back in place.

★   ★   ★

Sleeping was best. He had been given a mat to lie on and a coarse, rough blanket that pricked and scratched his skin. When he slept, he dreamed of Jaya, of the touch of her soft skin, of the smell of her hair, how she always walked as if her feet weren't quite touching the ground. Of that stubborn, determined look in her eye when she had an idea and the warm laughter. Of the way she looked at him and how he had always known that she loved him. He dreamed of the sea and fresh Scottish drizzle in his face. Sometimes he saw himself writing. Would he ever finish the book he was working on now? He was halfway through his third novel, the first had been a success relatively. With his second book at the printers and the third on his desk back at Dumfries, happiness had been so tangible until he realized that it was

323

all worthless without Jaya.

★   ★   ★

Something ran across Alastair's face. He shook his head, opened his eyes to see a small creature lying on its back in front of his face. A scorpion flipped back over and glared at him, tail high in preparation for a strike. He couldn't scream. What happened if it stung him? Would he die from its venom or his face be paralyzed? Sweat ran down his forehead. He was sure it could smell his fear, draw it to him. He had never felt so helpless in his life. It turned and scrambled off into the dark. A shudder ran through him. What else was hiding in the depths of the cave, a rattlesnake or deadly spiders? There was no question of sleep now.

When the guards rose, they let him do his business and gave him something that was almost inedible, except that he was starving and grateful for the water. He drank and drank until they pulled the water bottle that tasted of animal hide away. Then the most amazing thing happened. They led him out of the cave and let him sit outside for a couple of hours. An indescribably wonderful feeling after the gloom of the cave. Not that he could see anything. His blindfold was still firmly in place but he breathed in the fresh warm air and savoured the sun on his skin. The smells were incredibly strong after the musty, damp aroma of inside: the scent of flowers, the fragrance of pine, better than any perfume he had ever smelt. He listened to them talking but could not understand a word. He could distinguish at least five different voices. Not good news. There would always be one of them watching him. He wanted to just stay there; he lay down and fell asleep after the trials of the night but all too soon they dragged him back in, the only comfort being that they undid the blindfold. Now, though, he couldn't relax as he was always on guard for creepy crawlies that were lying in wait for him.

He couldn't remember when he finally fell asleep that night. He had tried to stay awake by pinching himself or trying to recall the faces of all the people he had ever had anything to do with at work. He had shifted position and tried to stay sitting up but his back started to ache so he lay down in between. The next thing he knew they were prodding him with a rifle.

'Get up!' the slight man with the headscarf demanded.

He blindfolded him adeptly and Alastair found himself out in the cold night air. God, it was freezing out here at this time. For the first time he wanted to turn and go back in the cave and crawl back under his blanket. But they had other plans. They made him get on what felt like a donkey which was anything but easy in his sightlessness. Alastair had learnt to ride as a child but doing this sightless was frightening, especially as he knew he was up high somewhere in the mountains. But there was no point in protest. His stomach rumbled as the donkey plodded on. It took him all his wits to hang on and at one point he found himself slipping down. It was rough terrain; he could feel that in his behind, in every step the donkey took. And cold. He couldn't stop shivering.

When they undid his blindfold it took him a few seconds to see anything at all in the glare of the daylight. The basement room was a five-star hotel in comparison to the cave although there was only a bed, a bucket and nothing else. But the best thing was the narrow barred window at the far end above his head. He would be able to see something, perhaps attract someone's attention. The man pushed him on the bed and undid his hands as his comrade looked on, his gun trained on Alastair all the while.

'You behave or we shoot!' And then they left him to inspect his new cage.

He took the bucket, turned it over and placed it underneath the window. He could just about peer out but it wasn't the room with a view he had hoped for — just a couple of shrubs. He guessed he was somewhere up in the hills. He pulled on the bars, hung with all his weight on them until his hands had to let go. They were good, fast solid work not to be budged without tools. He was just about to kick the bucket over in frustration when he remembered the guard's last words. Instead he paced the room three times: five steps in one direction and four in the other. He threw himself on the bed and stared at the ceiling, once again alone. The thought of his mother made him feel terrible. Worrying herself to death all alone at the Mains. It was all too soon after the old man's death. And Jaya. A glow warmed his heart when he thought of her. He hoped that she had told Marie about the two of them. What they meant to each other. He didn't even have a picture of Jaya with him, to keep him going when it was possible to see anything by the light of the small window.

He was bloody scared. He knew what happened to hostages; how they had their ears cut off before they were finally decapitated. He mustn't annoy his captors, no matter what. He must try to engage them in conversation, make them see him as a person, not as a piece of booty. He was genuinely interested in their cause, in what drove them to live outside the law. What had turned them into such fanatics?

It wasn't much different to the cave. The long stretches of doing nothing. How long would this go on for? The disgusting remnants of food and the bitter-tasting water. He would have spat it out if he hadn't have been so thirsty. Worse still, he was never sure about when they would actually come. And then they just stopped coming. He was terrified that he would die of thirst because they had been captured. The last anyone saw of him. He shouted but no one answered, just a deathly silence. The door was solid. No chance, he knew there were two locks on the other side. It was so deadly quiet he could hear the blood in his head. In here he couldn't even hear the birds. He shouted until his voice was hoarse. Then he lay down on his back, put his arms over his eyes and wept for the first time since his father had died. Sleep was the only blessed relief down here.

After two and a half days they finally brought him something to eat, and he almost fell into their arms, had they not worn such a grim expression and told him to shut up immediately. The worst thing was they disappeared after only ten minutes. He could not stand the solitude a moment longer. He could feel himself starting to panic, so he sang songs, old Beatles hits, and then anything he could remember but the waiting continued. With no newspaper to read, no book to lose himself in, no photo of Jaya to stare at, he feared losing his mind.

46

This was pure torture. Alastair should've been on this plane, not me. Whilst I was dallying in Scotland, his life might be stamped out like some cockroach in their path. If only I could stay put, but there were no two ways about it. I had to speed up the sale of the clinic and it would be easier to talk to the lawyers myself. I couldn't wait to see Marie. Under any other circumstances it would have been the most joyous of reunions. I pulled my scarf tighter around my head as the rain and wind lashed me on the way into the terminal. Summer — when was it ever summer here?

'Jaya, thank God you're here!'

Marie threw her arms around me. Dark shadows under puffy red eyes told me that she hadn't slept for days. Usually immaculately dressed, she now wore a pullover much too big for her, probably one of Stuart's, and tattered jeans. Her beautiful hair, now almost completely grey, escaped from her bun in untidy wisps and she wasn't even wearing her pearl earrings. Bunny, the grey-muzzled cocker spaniel, stood close at her side and eyed me suspiciously.

It was unreal to be standing here in the living room at my beloved Mains, like stepping out of one film into another. I froze as the mist crept in over the sea and wrapped the house in its cold damp blanket. We drank tea brought by a shaken Aileen who, overjoyed to see me, mumbled something about the bairn's terrible situation.

'You're the only person I could stand to have around me in this situation.' Marie poured me another cup of tea as Bunny lay at her feet. 'I'm so grateful that you're selling the clinic. How would we meet their demands otherwise? It'll bring in almost the entire ransom; the rest can be topped up with my savings. I'll pay you back some day, Jaya. You know I will.'

'Don't be ridiculous, Marie! What would I do with a clinic here, anyway?'

Her gratitude made me feel uncomfortable. I wasn't doing it for her. I wasn't who she thought I was. I had to tell her what Alastair meant to me. That I'd do anything to get him back. I loved Alastair, always had. And she thought I was doing something that shouldn't be expected of me. She thought I was trying to repay her kindness.

'Marie, I feel terrible.'

'Of course you do. We both do.'

'No, it's something else. Alastair came to see me for a reason.'

'Yes, he wanted to tell you about the clinic.'

'He proposed to me. It's all my fault.'

Delight lit up her face. 'Don't be silly! Oh, Jaya, why didn't you tell me before? I should have guessed.' She took my hand. 'I'll be so happy when I see you two together!'

I nodded through my tears.

★   ★   ★

Outside the wind wailed and I felt strangely in tune with it. I wouldn't have wanted to be enjoying myself at the sea, not with Alastair always in my thoughts. I had to stay a week until the business was finalized. Time to keep Marie company. We could worry together which made the unbearable fractionally better. She told me about the visit from a man from the Foreign Office.

'The man had a very posh accent and I couldn't help wondering if anyone from Glasgow ever stood a chance.'

'Was he all by himself?'

'No, he brought two policemen with him. What on earth was I going to do to him? I ask you. We left them on the settee and went outside. He told me the kidnappers had very clear demands: the money in dollars and delivered to a location of their choosing by the end of the month. The thirty-first, that's right, isn't it?'

'Yes, that's what I heard, too,' I replied.

'Then he went on about how we mustn't give in to their murderous demands. Yes, that's what he called them: murderous demands and that there was absolutely no guarantee we'd ever see Alastair alive again!' Marie's voice trembled. 'He didn't want us to hold out any false hope. These men were terrorists who didn't want anyone alive to identify them.'

Such words were unbearable. 'What did you say to him?'

'My son kidnapped and I was meant to sit back and do nothing! How dare he stand there and tell me I would never see my son again. What the hell did he know about my Alastair anyway?'

I had never heard Marie talk like this before and the ghost of a smile touched my lips. We were united in our despair. Why did they have to take our Alastair? There must be hundreds, if not thousands of foreigners in Kashmir. No one should be telling us what was right or wrong.

'You know, I've learnt how to fall asleep in my bed with the empty space beside me, not to reach out for Stuart anymore in the middle of the night. It's been so tough but Alastair and you have made me want to live on. I can't lose him. No, I won't lose him. Not like Lily. I won't allow it.

''Mr Huntington,' I said. 'Huntington-Smythe,' he replied. 'Mr Huntington-Smythe. You are talking about my son and I shall move Heaven and Earth to get him back. Is that quite clear? Now please go back to London and tell the Foreign Office that I will listen to no more of your nonsense.''

★   ★   ★

Bunny wouldn't go out with me. She had come to Marie after a stay of over two years at the animal home and never strayed from her side. Yet even with Marie along outside, she would want to turn around pretty soon, only to collapse on the carpet and snore loudly. She made me miss Beauly all the more but occasionally I had to escape the situation and tread the old paths by myself. The ocean made me forget everything for a few moments.

We were overwhelmed by the sympathy and concern we encountered whenever we saw anyone. The villagers had even started a campaign to raise money. There had been a fête for Alastair's cause and regular collections in the local pub which amounted to a couple of thousand pounds. We were grateful for every penny and their actions gave us the feeling that we were not alone.

A doctor from Inverness expressed a keen interest in the clinic but we were as desperate as ever for word from the captors. We had heard nothing since I left Kashmir. What if they got impatient? All manner of things could make them act rashly even though we were well within the deadline. What if the police simply smoked them out? With their pride at stake, what chance was there of the police being cautious? What chance was there of Alastair leaving in one piece?

47

Alastair was given some candles and two books. One was the Koran and the other *Heidi*. The only two books they had in English.

'We are of many faiths united in one cause. I may be Hindu but my brothers have found this for you. We are tolerant of everything but oppression. You westerners know nothing! Nothing of anything that does not concern you. It will not hurt you to learn more.'

Alastair actually smiled at what would not have been his first choice in a book shop. But anything, absolutely anything was better than this endless whirlpool of dark thoughts that drained down towards his own death.

Could any of this have been avoided? If he had stood by his feelings all those months ago when the old man was dying? If he had told Jaya how he really felt about her? If he had been man enough to own up to Amanda in time? Would it have all turned out differently? He might have been able to persuade Jaya to stay; she loved Scotland almost as much as he did. She had cared about him even then. And they wouldn't all be in this damned mess. He wouldn't be staring death in the face. No, a voice piped up in his head. She always wanted to come back, he must know that. In his heart of hearts he knew it wouldn't have made a scrap of difference.

He looked down at his dirty clothes hanging from his body, his belt fastened as tight as he could so that his trousers would not fall down. He was beginning to resemble his tormentors — all beard and hair and before long his teeth would go rotten and fall out. His gums were already swollen and bleeding in places. There were times when he wished it would just be over, one way or the other. The endless hours of solitary confinement were unbearable except he had no choice. He picked up *Heidi* first. He swore his mother had read it to him as a child. What would a grown man want with a child's book? He opened the cover and there, neatly printed in a child's handwriting, was JAYA. He looked at the cover once more. It couldn't be — he remembered it lying beside his bed. It was as if Jaya were there in the room with him, as if she were telling him it would be all right. They would meet again. He traced the writing with his finger again and again until he finally kissed it.

48

We were one gigantic step closer to getting Alastair back alive. Word had reached us through a Kashmiri chef in London (we didn't dare question the contact) that the terrorists wanted to arrange a drop-off point. Marie and I hugged each other when we heard.

'It's OK. Everything will be fine, just fine,' I said as much for my sake as hers.

Marie nodded and pressed her lips together tightly. I ran upstairs to start packing. I would personally see this through. Fortunately we had seen the lawyers two days previously and arranged that Marie would have power of attorney. The sale was imminent and when it went through, she could then simply transfer the money to India. We couldn't take any risks. Alastair would come back to us and everything would turn out well. I was still packing when I heard the phone ring and rushed down the stairs to hear a broad Glaswegian voice say, 'I'm afraid the investor from Inverness has got cold feet. I'm sorry but the sale has fallen through.'

I sat down. How could life be this cruel? A

game of poisonous snakes and slippery ladders. Marie came in and stared at me wide-eyed when I told her.

'You've only got a sixth of the ransom in the bank. Where on earth will we get the rest?' I asked.

'Well, that's that. We'll have to put the Mains on the market.'

The Mains, not the Mains! But of course Marie was right. There were only ten days left.

⋆   ⋆   ⋆

I phoned Prof Lone.

'Dr Vaidya, this is a most irregular situation. We are having great difficulty filling in for you.'

'I am terribly sorry but I have to take indefinite leave.' It hurt so much to say this. 'I fully understand if you give this opportunity to someone else. Let me explain. The foreigner, you know, the one who was kidnapped. He's the son of the family I lived with in Scotland. I'm with them now. They're all the family I have left. I wouldn't be a doctor if not for them. I have to do everything I can to help them. I'm sorry but I must interrupt my training for the moment.'

'I shall discuss it with the board of

directors. You will be hearing from us presently.'

I replaced the receiver slowly. There didn't seem to be any space in my heart for any more sorrow.

★ ★ ★

Two days later, a professional footballer with his wife and baby walked into the living room. They deposited the carry cot on the rug whereupon Marie dragged Bunny out the door.

'It's luvly,' said the woman with white-blonde hair and bright red lips. How had she managed to squeeze into her polka dot dress?

'I can see us putting a bar in the corner, can't you, Val? And we could get rid of all those bushes and hedges outside so the lad can start kicking a ball about once he's walking.'

Marie's bright expression was in danger of cracking. 'My son loved football. There is land at the back of the house.'

'Would you like to see the upper floors? There are five bedrooms on the first floor alone,' I suggested.

'Ooh, we'll have to get busy then, won't we, Val?' He pinched his wife's bottom.

'Joe, honestly, you're such a lout. Can we

leave the little man with you?'

Marie, more than happy to bow out of the rest of the tour, sat down next to the sleeping baby, looking deflated.

49

'Where did you get this?' Alastair asked his captor. 'I think . . . I think I know its owner.'

The man grabbed the book from Alastair's hands.

'Please give it back!'

'Of course you know her. She was my sister.'

'Was? You . . . you're Tahir?'

'I am not the same person anymore.'

'What do you mean?'

'You can have many lives. Before the earthquake I was Tahir.'

Alastair tried to get his head around the man's reasoning. 'And who are you now?'

'Leader of the Kashmir Leopards!'

'I intend to marry your sister.'

The leader hit out with his rifle butt and sent Alastair flying against the wall. Alastair saw stars.

'She is no longer my sister. She has betrayed her country.' And with that the man who used to be Tahir opened the door and slammed it behind him. Alastair put his hand up to the back of his head which was warm and inflating with a nasty lump. Now even the book was gone. Was this a sign, too? Should he just forget about his life out there, resign himself to what inevitably lay before him? His thoughts whirled into a black hole of hopelessness. No one would ever find him. He would go mad here. He had to think of something else . . .

He touched the Koran. It was black with gold letters and he started reading: *In the name of God . . .*

★ ★ ★

The leader returned later that afternoon. 'You are reading one of our sacred books.'

'If I have to be here, I want to know why . . . I want to understand. Look, I'm not just some foreigner. If I have to be sacrificed, if I have to die for this, I want to understand. You owe me that much.' The leader eyed him suspiciously. The white pig was speaking like a man. The leader sat down at a safe distance from his captive with his gun across his legs. 'I must leave you alone for three days but we do not depart until nightfall.'

Alastair felt a wave of panic. He couldn't be left alone again. No food, no fresh water, the uncertainty that they would be caught and he would never be found. He was about to start begging when the leader waved his hand and said, 'Until then I will answer all your questions.'

* * *

Alastair swore loudly. He had drunk the last of the bitter water an hour before. His stomach was on fire, his head throbbed and the next stomach cramp was coming. He could feel it cutting him in two like an iron ring. He had never had the runs like this. He rushed for the bucket, sank onto his knees and vomited violently. He dragged himself back to the bed, sat down and waited for the next bout of cramps. He tried calling out but it was as futile as ever. There was no one out there. He was burning alive when the next cramp hit him. When he finally came out of its vice of iron he breathed deeply, like a woman in labour. That's what they did, wasn't it? It helped them. Fuck, it didn't do the slightest good. Someone had to come and help him. Now.

* * *

Tahir thought of all the things that could be done with the fortune. Ammunition, guns, horses, food for the winter and beyond. Money to keep the cause going for years to come. Not that they would need to. This would be the decisive victory, the one that would tip the scales and end all their struggles. He could feel it in his bones. Too many of his people had died for it to all come to nothing. There was no question about giving up now. Catching the foreigner had been a stroke of genius. Why hadn't they done it before? One life could bring so much reward. Perhaps they wouldn't even have to kill him. But he doubted it. They couldn't take any risks. They would get the loot in either case.

★　★　★

Pink mountains and shimmering golden deserts appeared before Alastair. His father turned up out of nowhere and handed him a drink. It was much better than water. He drank and drank and it made him feel strong and powerful. His father looked quite healthy now, in fact better than he ever remembered him. Alastair was indescribably happy to see him, happier than he had ever felt in his life before. His father beckoned for him to follow and they walked towards the mountains.

★　★　★

The leader wasn't a monster. The westerner had lost a lot of weight but that couldn't be helped. Now he knew what it was like to live like them. A surprise was in order. He would bring the man some fattening mutton. An old sheep slaughtered to celebrate the imminent conclusion of the affair. Why not let the foreigner have a taste of their success, even if he never made it back to Scotland? He would not have anyone say that he had not treated his hostage well — given the circumstances. He waited until cover of darkness before he approached the building. You could never know even though he was pretty sure that they had covered their tracks.

It was a full moon and the leader left the door open.

'Keep watch,' he said to Abdul, his second in command, as he pulled his rifle up and entered the room. It stank like a stable in here. Fresh air would do the man good. No candle burned even though they had left enough to see the Scot through. Ah. He must be sleeping. Silver light fell in a long oblong across the floor and onto the bed.

'Wake up, *sahib*. Wake up, I said.' No reaction. He turned to Abdul. 'Stand in the doorway. The white pig is playing a trick on us.' One more step and he prodded the man. Nothing. He leant forward to catch the shallowest of breaths. A feeling of panic rose in his own breast. But his thoughts immediately cleared. This made things easier. There would be no killing involved. They would simply take him where no one would ever find him.

And it wouldn't change a thing.

50

The footballer hadn't taken the Mains. Instead a family of six from Ireland arrived.

'Jesus, this is perfect, Mary, isn't it?'

'Damien, don't say Jesus in front of the lady, will you? I can see us moving in tomorrow. It's just like Kerry.'

'I want the room in the tower, Mammy!' exclaimed the little boy who had just come running down the stairs.

They had cash in hand. The sale could be finalized and the money transferred within three or four days. It was faint comfort that the house would resound with children's voices and I could see that Marie actually liked the new family. They were enchanted by the property, especially the grounds and soon Marie was making comments like: 'It's for the best anyway. It's far too big for me now that I'm alone. What would I have done with it when I grew old?'

Later, I saw her through the sitting room window wandering around the garden, lingering at every one of her beloved arrangements in a way that belied her words. Take Marie away from that garden and you'd be ripping out its very heart. Under normal circumstances inconceivable. But life had taken the strangest of turns when Alastair disappeared. There could be no Mains as we knew it without him.

The drop-off time was in just over a week.

★ ★ ★

I stepped back out onto the runway and looked up at the Giants. Everything seemed so lush and green after Scotland and the flowers were bursting with colour. In a single week the season had shunted headlong into summer. The air was full of the scent, the sun burned my face. It was so wrong. How could the landscape be this beautiful when Alastair was suffering? I swear I could tangibly feel his presence out there somewhere. Could Alastair see this? Feel the sunshine on his face? I found myself making plans for his return. We would get married as soon as possible and I would go with him wherever he wanted. Of course there wouldn't be the Mains to return to but that didn't matter. Nothing mattered as long as we were together.

My heart bled for Marie. Her waiting must have been even worse than mine. At least I was near him. I hoped that selling the Mains didn't completely destroy her. All would be well; I just knew it, once we had Alastair back.

Money was all that stood between Alastair and his safe return. I prayed before I fell asleep that the sale of the Mains had gone smoothly. I rang Marie from the phone at the post office in Srinagar the minute it opened in the morning. It must have been the middle of the night but I had to know.

'Sorry, Marie, I couldn't wait another moment. Have you got the money?'

'Don't worry. I couldn't sleep anyway. The clinic. There's someone . . . '

The line cracked loudly.

'I can't hear you very well, Marie!'

'The clinic has been sold. The money's on its way!'

'Yes but how . . . ?'

The line went dead.

⋆　⋆　⋆

Two days left. Two days until the kidnappers got what they wanted. Two days until I would see Alastair. The touch of him, his wavy hair, his muscular frame, the sound of his voice. Time crept past almost at a standstill. I wanted Alastair. I had never wanted anyone or anything this badly in my life. I couldn't think about anything else, not the hospital, nor the future. I had to take life one moment at a time. On the other hand there were only two days to make sure everything went like clockwork. The bank, the money, how I would get there.

Nothing was as it had been before. I couldn't settle down in this tense situation but on top of that there was absolutely no sign of Shaila. I called and called for her but no welcoming meow echoed across the water. No soft coat of fur pressed against my legs as I prepared something in the kitchen that I could hardly eat anyway. She had simply vanished even though the kind family had taken over the job of feeding her whilst I was gone. Their little boy told me that Shaila had turned up on the first day only to sniff the food and turn away in disdain. I felt so terribly alone with my last ally gone.

The morning after I arrived, a police officer turned up at the boat. I was still in bed due to jet lag but called for him to wait a few minutes. What could he possibly want? When I appeared on deck he handed me a note.

Dr Vaidya. You are kindly invited to attend a meeting with the chief of police at your earliest convenience.

Invited, I knew what that meant. I was expected immediately. Was this bad news? My hand started to tremble as it clutched the note. Did they know something about the handover? We had been so careful. Everything had been done in the utmost secrecy. Nothing had been leaked to the press; we had not talked to anyone but the Home Office. I dressed as quickly as I could and made my way to the police station.

'Dr Vaidya, please take a seat.'

The chief of police looked at me and twisted the ends of his moustache which he could have tied together at the back of his head. 'We are very happy to see you again. We have been in very close contact with the British Embassy.'

I wanted to hit him. How dare he endanger the deal in any way!

'You need not fear. We will accompany you to the drop-off location. Just to make sure you are not in any danger, I assure you we will stay a safe distance away.'

It took every remnant of my self-control not to shout back at him.

'Sir.' I bowed my head. 'I would prefer to do this by myself. Any number of things could go wrong if there is even the slightest sign of police presence. It is an absolute condition of the other side.'

'Out of the question. May I respectfully remind you that you are a woman, Dr Vaidya and as I have recently discovered, also a British citizen. Can you imagine what the press and the British Embassy would say if a single hair on your head were harmed?'

'In that case I refuse to give you any more information regarding further developments!' I regretted it the moment I said it. Why had I risen to the bait?

'Come now, Dr Vaidya. It is no use keeping any details from us. The British Embassy are keeping us fully informed . . . '

'I suppose you're right,' I replied. 'If you promise to keep well away . . . '

I knew that whatever I did, I must not let anyone know. Not even Marie because they might get it out of her somehow. From now on, I was completely and utterly on my own.

★ ★ ★

I had to disappear. I couldn't put Alastair at risk. But where to? I walked towards Dal market at midday, not that it would be open but there would still be a few tradesmen on the banks. I looked back. That was strange. A boy appeared to be following me at a short distance. I was sure I had seen him before playing outside the police station. Unsure whether I was imagining things, I stopped to chat to the melon man on the corner. Out of the corner of my eye I could see the very same boy loitering at the crossroads. I walked on quickly and turned a corner. He was nowhere to be seen and so, convinced that I had shaken him off, I reached the waterside. No chance, there he was, his eyes fixed on me. I would have to find a way to leave the boat without being seen. I didn't need to take much, just the money.

Next day I picked up the money from the bank and stayed in the boat for the rest of the time. Later that evening I put out some food for Shaila in the vague hope that she might return whilst I was on my mission, then under cover of dark I crept out of the boat. Just as I stepped onto the bank, I noticed two bright yellow eyes watching me.

'Shaila!' I picked her up, and pressed her tightly to me. She was thin but otherwise in good health. 'Wait for me,' I whispered as I put her down and crept past a policeman who had fallen asleep in the car across the road.

★   ★   ★

'What on earth happened to you? You look exhausted!' exclaimed Avani when she saw me. I mentioned some problem with the authorities but didn't go into details. 'Jaya. No! We have never been in any trouble with the police. Why, they might take Madhav away. You know what the law is like here. Never on your side. At the very least they might take his fishing permit away from him. Then what will we do?'

Her swollen belly was what defined her now. I wished I were visiting her under other circumstances. How could I endanger her and her beautiful family? Yet all I could think of was Alastair.

'It's more of a misunderstanding,' I lied as my bag of money burned in my hand. 'Let me stay just until nightfall. Until it's all cleared up. That's all I'm asking.'

She put her head to one side and sighed. 'You know my home is your home.'

I explained to Avani that I had to meet someone and couldn't be seen. I was grateful that she didn't ask me any questions but instead she lent me some of her clothes. Much less conspicuous, much duller and simpler. It seemed as if we had been transported back in time; if it hadn't been so serious, I might even have enjoyed this dressing up. The hours crawled past. I couldn't get in touch with Marie anymore. Her situation must be even worse than mine. At least I was doing something. I had arranged for a driver to come and pick me up once night had come.

Avani cooked but I couldn't touch a thing. One of her daughters came and sat down next to me and I watched Madhav checking his fishing nets in the evening light. Such peace in the midst of despair. Soon the cards would be dealt and I would have to live with whatever the gods decided.

51

Houses and villages came and went with earthquakes but I knew the lie of the land here like Alastair's face. I could have found the drop-off point even without a map. We wouldn't be able to drive much further. I fingered my bag the whole while, checking if the money really was there.

The road became no more than a dry bumpy track. If the driver was wondering what on earth I was doing up here he certainly wasn't showing it, but instead gave the impression that driving a woman around in the mountains at this time of the night was his regular run. The track petered out and it was time to walk. I got out of the car and looked around. There were lights far down in the valley but nothing up here. Apart from a few clouds, the mountains glowed silvery blue in the light of the bloated moon.

'Please switch off the engine and wait two hours. I have something I must do.' I opened my bag and handed the astounded driver a wad of notes. 'You will get as much when I am back. If I don't return, drive back to my friend's house and give her this.'

It was a letter for Avani.

He nodded solemnly. I had instructed Avani to inform the police, Alastair's last hope. The driver lit a *bidee*. I looked at him and the car one last time and imagined Alastair in it with me before the sun rose over the Nun Kun.

I could clearly see my breath in the moonlight as I pulled my coat closer around me, my precious bag in one hand. I took my bearings from the mountains in front of me and the glacier at their peak. I was aiming for the dip between the rocks on the lip of a ravine. The path was precarious but I had a torch and good shoes. Nothing was too difficult if this led to Alastair.

Soon, all I could see of the car was the thin beam of its headlights far behind me. They lit up my path but not for long. When I next looked back the driver must have switched them off. I listened intently for any sounds that I was being followed. Nothing. My senses welcomed the stillness of the night as something I had grown up with. This was how it should be. I walked on and on into the night.

A mad squawking. A bird shot out across the valley and my heart beat like a machine gun. I listened again for anything but all was once again serenely quiet. I shone the torch on my watch. Twenty minutes. It wasn't far now. I knew I mustn't be late, whatever happened. A few minutes could cost Alastair his life.

★ ★ ★

The leader's feet trod the familiar path. A good choice. Higher up might have been better but he was not quite as at home there as here was where he had raced Garuda as a child. He knew every nook and cranny; the escape routes and the ridges from which there could be no return. He thought back to where he had left the man. It wasn't his fault. They had done everything they could for him. A doctor would have been out of the question. Better to shoot him perhaps. The leader's father had helped the rebels whenever he could but then his father had helped everyone. Pa had been stupid not to take sides from the very start. He didn't want to think about him. This would have been too complicated for his father to understand. They wouldn't find the Scotsman anyway. No one would find him. Not there.

He squinted and went down on his haunches. He reached for his binoculars. The silhouette of a tiny figure on the ridge. He scanned the surroundings. Nothing else moved. One person, no others. Just as he had stipulated. Still, he undid the catch on the trigger and ran his hand along the barrel; he could depend on it like an extension of his arm. One wrong move and he would not hesitate.

★ ★ ★

I stopped to catch my breath. I could afford the break; it would only be a matter of minutes now. I hoped I would recognize the designated point — three boulders around a shallow pit. Something rustled in the undergrowth to my right and my heart skipped a beat. Don't be so jumpy, I told myself. There were bound to be animals hiding up here. It was getting darker, as clouds slipped across the moon and I was having difficulty seeing. The stones. I must be near them now. I was reluctant to attract attention with my torch. The moon flicked on through a gap in the clouds and there they were, exactly where I remembered.

I placed the bag carefully under the twigs in the hole, stood up again and looked around. Nothing. What if? No, I mustn't wait. They had been clear about that. I should go back over the ridge and there would be a sign. Then they would set Alastair free. There was no point in deliberating, no point in harbouring the slightest doubt. Either they kept their side of the bargain or ... I suddenly felt very scared out there. I wished it was over. I couldn't bear it to last a minute longer. Alastair, I pleaded silently, give me a sign that you're still alive. Let me know where you are. Silence drummed in my ears. There was nothing for it but to turn and leave.

I picked my way back, all certainty taken from me. I was leaving Alastair to his fate. I couldn't stay there. Somehow I had always believed that I would return with him but now it dawned on me that they might set him free anywhere, or not at all. Had I come from the left or the right track? I slipped on a smooth rock underfoot and knocked my ankle. I wished the taxi driver would switch on his headlights.

A shot shattered the silence. The sign? Then another shot. That wasn't what I expected. They had the money. Alastair should be free. What were they telling me? Flashes and a round of machine gun! Shouting. The police? The army? I could see the beams of torches. Were they out of their minds?

'Stop, stop!' I shouted.

They were killing Alastair with every shot they fired. They were worse than his captors. I ran back as fast as I could, stumbling across the rocks. It took an eternity to get anywhere near them.

'Stop!' I screamed. A beam hit my face. More shouting and then I was lit up by the light of four or five torches. I put my hands up.

'The doctor!' someone shouted.

'We have the rebel!' A man lay crumpled on the ground next to the three rocks. Two policemen had their guns and torches trained on him. I recognized the chief of police behind them.

'What have you done?' I screamed. 'Let me look at him.' They didn't want to let me near him. 'You heard! I'm a doctor.'

A low murmuring and then the chief of police nodded. The man lay lifeless. No one would be able to find Alastair now. I crouched down. The man's clothes were soaked in warm blood. I felt for a pulse. He was still alive! There was no point in trying to move him. I tilted his face towards me and he opened his eyes. A bolt of lightning hit me. I would recognize those eyes anywhere.

'Tahir!' He looked at me. 'Tahir, it's me, Jaya.'

His beautiful blue eyes widened and he tried to say something but blood only seeped from his mouth.

'Tahir, I'm with you now. Listen to me, it doesn't matter what happened. But the man, the man is Alastair Hamilton. He's the son of Pa's friends. You have to tell me where he is.' More blood streamed from his mouth. 'Tahir, you owe this to Pa!'

Tears mingled with blood as he lifted his hand, pointed straight at the old woman's face in the rocks and took his last breath.

⋆ ⋆ ⋆

I couldn't stay to grieve for my brother. This time the police didn't argue. They drove me to the rock face. As soon as their jeep stopped, I grabbed my black bag and jumped out. Alastair could only be in the cave at the end of the track.

'Alastair!' I called as loud as I could, torch in hand. Bats fluttered past my head as I ducked into the cave. 'Alastair! It's me. Where are you?'

All I could see were the dark walls of the cave and a few rocks at the back. A repulsive smell filled the cold night air. Flanked by two policemen with guns in hand, I ventured towards the back and spotted what seemed to be a scruffy pile of rugs. I crouched down. It was a body! My heart shattered into a thousand pieces.

'Alastair,' I whispered.

I lifted an impossibly scraggy arm. It wasn't stiff; I put my face near his mouth and felt the faintest breath. My hands were trembling as they never did when I treated anyone else, not even Stuart. It was all I could do to open my bag. I found a syringe and felt for his vein underneath the sagging flesh. I knew now why I had survived the earthquake, why I had become a doctor. If I got him alive to hospital, we might stand a chance . . .

52

I must have nodded off to the beeps of the intensive care unit when I felt a hand on my shoulder.

'Dr Vaidya, you must go home and sleep.'

'No!' It had been two days since we had arrived, two days of agony, two days of vigilance. Alastair had not regained consciousness but lay there, pale and unnaturally thin. I stood up and gently wiped his brow and checked his fluid intake. He was still in danger.

Marie had touched down in Delhi earlier in the morning and was on the last leg of the journey in a small propeller aircraft at that very moment. I had organized a car to pick her up and bring her straight to the hospital. What would she say when she saw him like this? But of course she had to be here. For . . . for her son's last days. A tear dropped down on Alastair and I cursed myself for losing my grip. What he needed now was help, not me going to pieces. I was a doctor, wasn't I?

I walked over to the window and looked at the Giants in the distance. What was the point of me being here? What had Tahir died for and why had he done this to Alastair? Had any of this helped my fellow Kashmiris? I shook my head. There was no sense, not a single morsel of good in the whole affair.

'*Heidi* . . . '

I whipped around. His eyes were open. That familiar amber speckled with gold.

'Alastair!'

I ran over and took his hand. He mustered a weak smile.

'You wrote your name in *Heidi* . . . '

My tears of joy flowed freely.

Epilogue

Sonamarg, 1989

The ancient chenar tree spread welcome shade over the long queue of people. It was unusually hot with the wind blowing up over the mountains from the Thar Desert. Mothers with children stood in line with the sick and the elderly, whilst others sat on benches beside the prefabricated blocks, patiently waiting their turn. I had been working all morning. Dr Bhatt and Dr Dhar were sick with the same virus that had caused severe dehydration in the two-year-old boy I had admitted for overnight observation.

The compound resembled an army camp with its three treatment rooms in the front block, each identically equipped for the doctors who worked there. The second block contained two small wards, one for men and one for women. A third housed what passed for an intensive care unit. In the background were the staff quarters and supplies. All of them were rudimentary but would serve their purpose until the skeleton of a larger building could finally be completed. It

367

looked as if the September deadline would be met, give or take a couple of weeks, which could be decisive if winter descended early on the valley. Our biggest problem, though, was financial. Costs were already fifty per cent over budget and I racked my brains about how to raise the difference.

I sat behind my desk with a fan whirling above my head when the next patient, a heavily pregnant woman, waddled into the room, dragging behind her a girl with a short neck and tongue lolling from her mouth. She must have been about four or five. You didn't see many girls with Down's syndrome around here. I offered the child a sweet which she snatched before disappearing behind the folds of her mother's *kameez*.

'What's her name?'

The woman looked at me with her good eye; the other shimmered grey-white like Mandeep's once had and was probably the consequence of the same easily treatable condition. I couldn't remember seeing anyone with the same affliction in Norwich.

'Hazirah.'

'A beautiful name.'

The girl squinted at the drawer where I kept my stash of sweets. I gave her another and she seemed happy to watch as her mother lay down and let me feel her swollen belly.

'How old are you?'

She put up both hands twice. Then dithered, and put up three more fingers. How was she to know?

'When was your last period?'

Nine fingers shot up. Her bulge told me that her baby had already dropped. An arm, the back, the bottom: it had already turned, ready for the imminent birth. I listened through the small trumpet for the beat of the foetal heart. Fast and regular. Everything seemed fine. The mother caught my free hand and pressed it tightly to her face.

'It is a boy this time, isn't it?'

It was the only reason why women like her came to me. I was suddenly grateful that we hadn't acquired the ultrasound scanner on my wish list.

'You have every chance of having a healthy child this time.'

She looked away, uninterested in any further information. Her smile had faded and I noticed deep shadows under her eyes. It would mean everything to her to have a son, especially after her special little girl. Yet, even if I knew the answer, I would not be complicit in a culture where female infanticide was rife.

'Go to the nurse with this prescription for iron tablets to make your boy . . . or girl strong.'

The woman adjusted her sari and left the room, her little girl waving at me behind her. I smiled. I had made a little friend.

★ ★ ★

That evening, with the outpatients finally seen to, I checked that all was quiet on the wards. Then I walked around the complex. Although it was still part building site, the sign at the entrance to the complex proudly proclaimed:

THE HAMILTON-VAIDYA CLINIC

Where would we find the money to keep it up for generations to come? I was stumped. We had come too far to stop now. Marie was full of ideas; she might come up with something. Perhaps a fundraising tour, as soon as I could get away. Or we might strike lucky with a grant from the Indian government for projects in conflict zones. There were too many trouble-torn regions in India.

I looked in on intensive. I was incredibly tired after operating in the middle of the night on a man still fighting for his life. A bullet in his shoulder and the first signs of sepsis. Someone must have brought him, dumped him at the entrance to the

370

compound and fired the shot that woke us. What would we do with him if he actually survived? Hand him over or let him go? Too much to think about now. We never turned anyone away. Our application for money would be thrown out and our clinic burnt to the ground if they knew who we were harbouring.

The responsibility of the clinic weighed heavily on my shoulders. There was the everyday red tape to deal with and the issues of security that the military loved to play up. I spent far too much time on administration, keeping everything going. I did have some help though, volunteers who subsisted on board and lodging. Jiji was invaluable, a set fixture of the office who cheered everyone up with his upbeat nature. He had made the clinic his home and I couldn't imagine the place without him.

Today was what this was all about. The people I had seen. The rest was unimportant.

I took a deep breath and sat down on a bench. It had cooled off as it always did in the evenings and I was glad of my shawl. Shadows played on the mountain slopes and the rocks were already forming the old lady's face. She would smile down at me tonight, just like she had when I was a child.

From behind the staff quarters a figure

appeared. Alastair was walking towards me, his chestnut wavy hair shining in the red evening sun. On his shoulders, a toddler with the same colour curls waving at me. I got up to meet them.

Acknowledgements

I would like to thank my writer friends: Cheryl Lim, Vicky Whitfield, Ruth Watkins, Liesel Schwarz, Susan Bergen, Katherine Hetzel, Louise Walters, Jody Klaire, Mandy Berriman and John Taylor, whom I met along the way. Special thanks to Joachim Boldt from Jena University, who has been most supportive of my writing. Then, there were my selfless first editors: Howard Atkinson and Andrew Liston.

Jim Crace, Maggie Gee, Emma Darwin, Martyn Bedford, Manda Scott and Debi Alper have all been inspiring teachers both through their writing and their workshops, especially the ones I attended at the Arvon Foundation.

I would also like to thank Team Ireland: Katarina Runske, who let me stay at her amazing writers' retreat at Grove House in Schull, Cork, just when I needed it most, and Mary Walden and Frankie Ross for helping me with my short stories. Last of all, I feel incredibly lucky to have found my agent Jane Conway-Gordon, who grew up in India and immediately appreciated this book.

Other titles published by Ulverscroft:

SEE HOW SMALL

Scott Blackwood

One late autumn evening in a Texas town, two strangers walk into an ice cream shop shortly before closing time. They bind up Zadie, Elizabeth and Meredith, the three teenage girls who are working behind the counter, set fire to the shop, and disappear . . . As the community attempts to rebuild their lives in the aftermath — from Kate, the mother of Zadie and Elizabeth, to Rosa, a reporter covering the murders for the *Chronicle*; from Jack, the firefighter who found the corpses, to Michael, the arsonists' getaway driver — all the while, the girls' spirits watch from above . . .

THE SNOW QUEEN

Michael Cunningham

Barrett Meeks is walking through Central Park when he is inspired to look up at the sky. There, he sees a pale, translucent light that seems to regard him in a distinctly Godlike way. Barrett doesn't believe in visions — or in God, for that matter — but can't deny what he's seen. Meanwhile, his older brother Tyler is trying — and failing — to write a song for Beth, his seriously ill fiancée. As Barrett turns to religion, Tyler becomes convinced that only drugs can release his creative powers, and Beth tries to face mortality with as much courage as she can summon . . .

NOTHING ON EARTH

Conor O'Callaghan

A frightened girl bangs on a door. A man answers. From the moment he invites her in his world will never be the same again. She tells him about her family, and their strange life in the show home of an abandoned housing estate: the long, blistering days spent sunbathing; the airless nights filled with inexplicable noises; the words that appear on the windows, written in dust. Where is her family now? Is she telling the truth? And can the man be trusted?

FAMILY LIFE

Akhil Sharma

For eight-year-old Ajay and his older brother Birju, life in Delhi during the late 1970s follows a comfortable, predictable routine: bathing on the roof, queuing for milk, playing cricket in the street. But everything changes when their father finds a job in America — a land of carpets and elevators, swimsuits and hot water on tap. Life is exciting for the two brothers as they adjust to prosperity, girls, and 24-hour TV — until one hot, sultry day when everything falls apart . . .